The Reapers MC,

Reaper Restrained

Book One

Harley Raige

Copyright © 2023 Harley Raige
All rights reserved.

No part of this book may be reproduced or transmitted in any form, or by any electronic or mechanical means, including photocopying, recording, or by any information storage and retrieval systems, without written permission from the author, except for the use of brief quotations in a book review.
For permissions, contact: harleyraige@gmail.com

This is a work of fiction. Names, characters, organisations, and incidents are either products of the author's slightly deranged, mildly twisted imagination or used fictitiously. Any resemblance to actual persons, living or dead, is purely coincidental.
Edited by www.fiverr.com/immygrace

For updates on my upcoming releases, please follow me on
www.tiktok.com/@harleyraige

www.instagram.com/harleyraige

www.facebook.com/harleyraige
Join our group at
www.facebook.com/groups/the.rebels.of.raige

Become a Rebel of Raige and join the Rebellion!

Authors Note

The author is British. This story does contain British spellings and phrases. This book also contains possible triggers, including but not limited to murder, rape, and kidnapping. It also contains explicit sexual situations, strong violence, taboo subjects, a shit tonne of offensive language
and mature topics, some dark content,
plus, F/M and M/M.
18+

Dedication

Sunshine,
I couldn't have done this without your support.
Love you infinity.
This ones for you!

Contents:

Reaper Restrained	
Authors Note	
Dedication	
Contents:	
Daniel	1
Ray	8
Pa Cade	49
Jer	58
Ray	65
Jer	69
Scar	72
Ray	76
Priest	107
Ray	111
Scar	148
Dice	152
Scar	157
Ray	166
Scar	169
Ares	180
Ray	183
Scar	190
Demi	195
Bran	202
Ray	208
Blade	223
Ray	227
Dice	229
Ray	238

Dice	246
Tank	270
Viking	279
Ray	291
Dozer	294
Ray	301
Scar	319
Ares	326
Scar	333
Acknowledgements	346
Books by Harley Raige	347

Daniel

The latched window creaks gently in the mild breeze, just like it has done for the last forty-five minutes. With an eerier creak than before, it swings open slightly. My eyes dart to it. A slim, tall, hooded figure peers inside. They push the window open the rest of the way and climb silently into my room, turning and shutting the window and curtains behind them.

From my position on the bed, I can see a glint from the lamp sparkling on their blue-grey eyes, staring out at me from beneath the hood.

"You're early. Did everything go okay?" I whisper as a finger raises, pressing to their lips, gesturing for my silence. They give a single nod in reply.

I blow out a silent breath, one I didn't realise I was holding. They step further into the room towards me, gently removing the book from my grasp and closing it.

They smell like petrol and smoke and a faint hint of something ... woodsy. They place the book face down on the bedside table, removing the cigarette I'm smoking, shaking their head at me and stubbing it out in the ashtray.

The hooded figure whispers, "Are you ready?"

I take a deep, shaky breath and nod in reply. I knew my time was almost up. I had arranged this myself—my death, that is—down to the very last detail. I knew precisely when the Grim Reaper was coming for me, which is more than most people get the luxury of.

I wanted to go out on my terms, so I made a deal with the Dark Angel. The most beautiful and darkest of angels, my sunshine in the darkness, I trust them without a shadow of a doubt. The Reaper is here to collect, having delivered three of the worst souls to the Underworld with hopefully horrifyingly bloody deaths over the last hour.

I will surrender my soul in return for all the gory details of how the Reaper has taken them out. Did it hurt? Did they realise what was happening? Did they beg? Did they know who was bringing about their demise and why?

Slipping into the bathroom, I hear them rummaging around. They step back out a few minutes later, smelling less like smoke and fuel, and more like something citrusy, still with the woodsy smell clinging to them. They walk over to the chest of drawers, and with their back to me, they press stop on the cassette player. They remove the tape and slide it into their backpack, replacing it with the one at the side and pressing play. They walk over to the window and drop the backpack outside onto the patio before closing the window again.

The music gently fills the room. With their back to me, In a hopeful hushed tone, the hooded figure whispers, "Are you sure about this? It's not too late to change your mind. We don't have to do this."

I smile at their back. I reply, "You're not going soft on me now, are you, Reaper?" My voice has a slightly playful tone that neither of us expects.

Slowly turning and lowering their hood, they let out a sigh, followed by a sorrowful smile. "Never." They give a nod which I return. "It's showtime! Game faces on."

I take another deep breath and nod. I close my eyes to gather my thoughts and feelings. This is it. This is the end. I always thought I'd go out in a blaze of glory in a foreign country, taking on insurgents, making a difference—not like this. Not to fucking cancer.

It took my wife, and now it's come for me, well fuck you. I'm going out my fucking way. I'm not waiting for it to take me. This is what I want, what I need. I take another deep breath and let out a deep sigh. I open my eyes, finding Ray's gaze. I focus on my daughter's face, the most precious thing in the world. She's beautiful, just like her mother had been. She's five foot ten, long, poker-straight dirty blonde hair, and blue-grey eyes that appear to change colour depending on her state of mind.

They range from the brightest blue to a stormy grey, almost swirling like a violent vortex. Sweet and kind to dangerous, when they appear to be grey approach with caution. She's got a smile that lights up a room, and her laugh is infectious. She's got a heart of gold and a fierce need to protect those around her.

She's stunningly beautiful with an edge. She swears worse than any sailor and has an aversion to anything remotely feminine. She's a total heathen. She plays by her own rules and is tatted and pierced. Her nose and lip piercings glint in the light from the lamp as she rolls her tongue piercing between her teeth.

I smile, and she returns it genuinely. She's breathtaking. I take her all in, memorising every feature. She has a pale dusting of freckles on the bridge of her nose, fading under her eyes to her cheeks. She really is the most intelligent, caring and beautiful creature.

I'm so proud of the powerful woman she's become, and it's time for her to carve her own way in this world, to follow her own destiny.

"Let's do this," I cough out.

Squeezing my hand, she nods and heads for the door leading into the rest of the house.

"Maureen, it's time," Ray says to the nurse who is waiting in the kitchen. She's an older lady, maybe only in her late fifties, but she looks much older. She has tiny round glasses perched on the end of her nose, and her kind, warm brown eyes peer over them, her wisdom shining through. She has short dark curly hair with a dusting of grey throughout, looking all salt and pepper-like. She's a short five-foot-three, a stout woman with kind, soft features.

They're all congregating around the kitchen: Maureen, my daughter's best friend Scarlett, her sister-from-another-mister, also known as Scar; Scarlett's dad David Harrington—or Pops as he is affectionately known—and three of my brothers, she calls them her Pas: Cade, John (JJ) and Steven.

Following her back to my room, Maureen places her hand on her shoulder and asks us if we are sure. I tell them both I'm ready, and I nod to her. She places her medical bag on the bed, draws the liquid into the syringe, and leaves it on the bed.

"I'm just going to the bathroom to wash my hands." She nods in the direction of the syringe, and the corner of my mouth turns up slightly, a semi-sad smile in acknowledgement of what I need to make my daughter do. Maureen steps out of the room.

Ray takes the syringe, gazing into my eyes without speaking. Is this what I want? Am I sure? She doesn't think she can do this. She can't live without me. How is she even supposed to do this? How can she survive without me? I place her hand in mine to steady my nerves and nod, closing my eyes and leaning back against the headboard.

She injects me, sliding the empty syringe into her boot. She walks over to the drawers and gets the envelope of cash we have stashed in there. She slips it into Maureen's bag as she comes out of the bathroom and grabs her things to leave the room.

Stopping at the door, she says, "It will be a little while, so I will send the others in to say goodbye, but say what you need to say. It won't be as long as you think. I'll be in the kitchen when you need me."

"Thank you, Maureen."

She exits the bedroom. Scar and Pops come in to say their goodbyes first. While they take their turn with me, Ray leaves. She needs a minute to herself. She steps out of the room with Maureen. Scar's eyes are glassy with unshed tears. She's trying so desperately to hang on, trying to be strong for Ray, but that girl is the epitome of strength. She's got this.

Scar and David have been our close family friends for nearly nine years now. Those girls went through a traumatic event that no one should have had to live through, bonding their souls together for eternity. David saved Ray, and for that, we are all eternally grateful. Bringing them into our lives and our family was inevitable.

"Hey, princess, she's gonna be okay, you know?" I say in reassurance as she sits on the bed, taking my hand in hers.

"I know, Pops, I just wish…"

"Hey, I know, but as long as she's got you, you know she'll be fine, and so will you." I kiss her hand and squeeze it in my own "Take care of each other for me, yeah?" Nodding, she leans forward and hugs me before rising from the bed.

"Love you!" she chokes out as she leaves the room.

Smiling down at me, David nods. "I will keep an eye on them. You know I love her like she's my own. I can't thank you enough for this extraordinary family you've let us be a part of."

"That I do. David, you're a good man, and although I wouldn't wish the way you came into our lives on either of them, I'm so glad you did. We'll always be family."

He smiles at me, and a single tear rolls down his cheek. He squeezes my shoulder and leaves the room. Three of my brothers enter next: Cade, Steven, and JJ. Cade pulls out his phone, video calling Bernie, our other brother, who picks up immediately.

"Is it done, Brother?" Bernie asks.

"It is." I smile at them all.

"Fuck, man, this is insane." JJ shakes his head. "I can't believe this is happening. This shouldn't be happening!"

"I know, Brother, but it is, and we don't have long, so I need to ask this of you—"

Cade interrupts me. "Fuck that, Dan. You don't need to ask us. She's our daughter. We will look after and love her until our hearts stop beating."

"And even after that." Steven smiles at me.

"I love you all. You've been my family for as long as I care to remember. I'm so glad to have you all, don't let her drown, though. Force her to flourish, push her and challenge her, don't let her suffocate, and try and get her to stop being so restrictive. She needs to free her inner self."

"Don't worry. We've got her." JJ hugs me, stepping back.

"I'm sorry I'm not there, Dan." Bernie grimaces through the screen of Cade's phone.

"You couldn't be. It would've been obvious something was up. I'll see you in the next life, Brother."

"You can count on it. Save me a seat next to you, okay?" Bernie smiles, and I nod in return.

"See you all in the next life, my brothers. Be good to each other in what's left of this one." After hugging me, they all leave. I take a deep breath and close my eyes for a second to compose myself as Ray walks back into the room.

Ray

I step back into the room, leaving just me and Dad.

Patting the bed beside him, he says, "Hey, kiddo!"

"Hey, Dad."

"Okay, spill." He grins at me. I laugh humourlessly and sit on the bed, scooping his hand in mine and clutching it tightly. I lift it to my lips, kissing the back of his knuckles.

"I love you, Kiddo."

"Love you more, Dad."

"Love you most."

"Love you infinity." I take a breath and give him what he wants.

As I describe everything to him, his eyes light up like he's seeing it himself in person, almost like a movie. It was like he lived every word, like he had carried out every single act. He cups my cheek, and I hold his hand there for the longest time. We gaze into each other's eyes, wanting to say a million things but knowing none of it will make a damned bit of difference.

"I'm so proud of you, Ray. I'm going to be fine. I will finally be back with your mother. I could never love another after her. Our love was all-consuming, forged in Heaven itself. I will finally get the missing part of my heart back. One day you'll find a love as strong as steel, someone who will love you unconditionally, all of you. You'll never have to be half again. Remember what you promised me!"

I nod. Dad wants me to get away for a while somewhere new to recharge myself. I've grown up here, but now there's just so much pain.

I don't know how I will cope being here without him. It would be too hard to stay. Everywhere reminds me of him, smells of him, too many reminders of what I'm losing. First, my mum when I was four, then my twin brother when we were nineteen. Although my brother and I were never close—he hated me, loathed me even—he was still family. My dad was the only blood relative I had left.

Although blood doesn't mean anything. I've always been closer to Bran, Dane and Scar than my actual blood brother.

I understand I'm different from other girls, but I can only embrace my light where we live in Northern England. My darkness has to be restricted and kept in check at all times. I'm scared that she will appear, and I won't be able to control her.

I'm growing weary of keeping her caged, hidden, chained. My dad wants me to embrace her, embrace the dark, too worried that if I don't, she will take over and destroy me, and I won't be able to live a full life.

That I will end up going off the rails and end up dead, or worse, in prison.

"I promise I will, Dad. I will see you on the other side. Hug Mum for me, and don't let her go till I find you both again."

His breaths start shallowing, and his breathing stutters from trying to talk too much, and he slowly drifts off to sleep. I'm not sure how long I sit there just staring at him, taking in all his features, memorising every single one, down to his straight warm chocolate brown hair, normally shaved short at the sides but longer and floppy on the top to his dusting of stubble, normally clean-shaven. He thought the stubble made him look cool. It made him look so much younger than his fifty-six years.

He's so handsome, slightly taller than me at five foot eleven, and when he smiles, he has a dimple on his right cheek. Although his eyes are closed, he has the most beautiful blue eyes, always twinkling with passion and excitement and, more often than not, mischief. I don't look anything like my dad, but my sarcastic personality is all him.

I run my fingers over his brow, over the military tattoos on his right bicep, watching his chest slowly rising and falling, gently slowing to almost shallow gasps. Tears roll down my cheeks before he finally passes away.

I wipe my face and take a deep breath. Steadying myself, I lean in and kiss him on the cheek. I make him a promise there and then that I will make a fresh start and be one hundred percent myself. Fuck holding back, fuck living on the edge. She will be released, and what will be will be. I'm not holding back any longer. I'm going to be who I was meant to be all along.

Stepping away from him for that last time, taking a breath and then another before I dive into action. We have a plan, and I'm going to carry it out to the letter, just as I'd promised.

Two days later, the door swings open as I'm in the kitchen making coffee.

"Where's my baby girl?" Ma Marie rushes into the house. Pa Steven has been to fetch them from the airport. "Ray? Where you at?"

"In here, Ma."

She barrels into the kitchen. "Sweet child. I've missed you." She sweeps me up into a hug and then sobs in my arms. "I'm so sorry, baby girl. We should have been here with you."

I smile at her and hug her back. "Coffee?"

She nods as she slumps into the chair. They've come from the States. My Pa Bernie, Ma Marie, and their sons Bran and Dane, we've been brought up as siblings. As far as I'm concerned, they're my brothers, and I'm their sister. Very confusing to those on the outside. To me, though, they're my family. Pa Bernie strides into the room with Dane and Bran close behind him.

Sweeping me into a hug, "Fuck, Squirt!" He lifts me off the floor and spins me around. As he puts me down, my brothers grab me, squeezing from either side.

Tucking a stray strand of hair behind my ear, then cupping my cheek, Bran looks down at me, searching my face, taking in every single detail. "You good?"

I smile back at him. I bury my face in his shoulder. He smells like home; they both do. They both have a woodsy undertone, while Bran smells like a dense forest in the summer. Dane smells like a winter forest around the sea. He rubs circles on my back while we hug each other. I've missed them so much. They're here for Dad's funeral, and I know I won't get through this without them all.

Pa Cade breaks through my thoughts as he comes in with their bags, followed by the rest of my pas. "Debrief, five minutes," he says almost robotically. I nod in Bran and Dane's arms.

"We should've been here. We should've done this together," Bran whispers into my hair as he kisses the top of my head.

"It wouldn't have worked. It would have been too suspicious, you all already being here. It had to be this way." I frown at him.

"We're coming with you," Dane says, staring over my head at Bran, cocking a brow at him, questioning if he's going to argue with that. Dane's the youngest at twenty-one. There are only two months between me and Bran and eighteen months between me and Dane. I'm the oldest, well Bas was. There were nineteen minutes between us. Now I'm nearly twenty-three.

We really do look like siblings. They both have dirty blonde hair, the same as me. Bran has grey-blue eyes like his mum, while Dane has hazel eyes like his dad. Bran and Ma Marie's eyes are similar to mine, but mine are mostly blue dependent on my mood. Bran is built more like his dad, only a couple of inches shorter at six foot to his dad's six foot two, while Dane has a slimmer swimmer's body at five foot eleven. Looks-wise, there isn't much between us.

"Office!" Pa Cade barks down the stairs. All the pas have already headed up there.

I smile over at Ma Marie, reaching over to squeeze her hand. "We won't be long."

I head down to the office with Bran and Dane flanking me. Stepping inside, Pa Cade is sitting in the chair behind the desk. Pa Bernie and Pa Steven stand to his left, and Pa JJ stands to his right. They're standing at ease, feet apart, hands behind their backs.

I wince as I walk in. It smells like him in here, like Dad. I expect to see him standing in here next to Pa JJ.

Walking to the front, before the desk, I stand at ease, and Bran and Dane stand slightly behind me on either side, assuming the position, too; this isn't our first rodeo. We're military brats through and through, even though they had all "officially" left by the time we were born. It's just how we were raised.

"When you're ready," Pa Cade says while grasping his hands together on the desk in front of him. We aren't always like this, but when important things need to be shared, we call for a "debrief." That way, we know to come into this room with the facts. Emotions are left at the door. These debriefs are for truths and facts only. We deal with them all together, as a family.

"Thursday afternoon, we— "

"*We?*" Cade interrupts.

Taking a breath before starting over, I say, "Thursday afternoon at twelve hundred hours, myself, Scarlett Harrington and David Harrington went to fetch Daniel Reins from the hospital as per his request and orders. Upon arriving back here, I situated him in his downstairs bedroom, the one looking out over the patio leading to the Adventure Centre.

"Daniel Reins had arranged for a palliative care nurse Maureen Smythe to meet us here. She arrived an hour after we did, around fourteen hundred hours. Maureen Smythe made sure Daniel Reins was comfortable and relaxed over the next few hours. Myself, Scarlett Harrington, David Harrington"—I nod to each of my pas in turn as I speak their names—"Cade King, John James, Steven Morris, and Maureen Smythe spent time alone or in groups with Daniel Reins.

"At approximately twenty-two hundred hours, Daniel Reins asked if I could read to him for a while so he could relax. Everyone else left the room. As the door closed, I passed him a book and his cigarettes, pressing play on the cassette player, which had a pre-recorded C120 tape of me reading the book in his hands so my voice could be heard. The tape was me reading with him, asking questions every now and then throughout. The cassette would play for one hour.

"I grabbed my pre-packed backpack containing matches, a lighter, the gun in case of an emergency, although I didn't plan on using it and four bottles of petrol from the bathroom. I climbed out of the bedroom window, leaving it on the latch behind me. I had strapped my thigh holster over my jeans containing two blades, and I had a blade on each side of each boot, totalling a further four, six blades total. I ran towards the shed, staying low and in the shadows to retrieve the motocross bike from it. I ran to the driveway and jumped on the bike, letting momentum carry me to the road.

"Upon reaching the road, I pulled the clutch and slipped it into second, releasing it. I bumped the bike and crossed the road into the forest. Heading directly for the squat house, I had carried out recon on the three in question over the last four weeks: Edward Lee, James Lewis and Timothy Spent. They were due to be at the squat house cutting and packing their speed shipment all night. Upon reaching a half mile from the squat house, I abandoned the bike and went in on foot. Edward Lee and Timothy Spent were in the living room. I didn't have eyes on James Lewis, but the bathroom light was on upstairs. I had broken into the house previously, making mental notes of every room, where things were kept, and the weapons they had and where they were.

"Making my way to the back door, I checked it, and it was unlocked. I retreated further to the back of the property and chose to shimmy up the soil pipe. I was wearing gloves, so I didn't see a problem. I climbed to the second floor, the bathroom window was open, and I could hear James Lewis in there whistling. I could hear pages flicking on what sounded like a magazine or newspaper. Glancing through the window, he was on the toilet right underneath.

"Stepping gently onto the window frame, bracing myself, I slid a blade from my boot, silently leaning the top half of my body in through the window, leaning down and grabbing his mouth to stop him from alerting the others at the same time as plunging the blade into his carotid artery, removing it and sinking it in again, keeping hold of his mouth till he stopped thrashing and was dead. I slid back out of the window and down the soil pipe entering through the back door. Upon reaching the living room, Edward Lee was there alone, snoring slightly, his head tilted back and resting on the back of the sofa. I could hear Timothy Spent down in the cellar. I crept over to Edward Lee, grabbing him from behind over the mouth and plunging the same blade into his neck simultaneously.

"He thrashed for a few seconds but passed quickly enough. I pulled a threadbare blanket from the armchair and tossed it over him to hide him for the time being, then commenced to stomp on the floor multiple times as loud as I could before flattening my back against the wall at the side of the door down to the cellar. As predicted, Timothy Spent came charging out of the cellar, where I jumped him from behind, stabbing his carotid from either side with the same blade I had used on the other two, plus another I had retrieved from my boot while I waited.

"He spun around to face me, and I jumped back, avoiding the blood spray, while he grabbed his neck, but it was too late. The look on his face said he recognised me, though, so I smiled at him as he dropped to the floor.

"Heading upstairs, I doused James Lewis with some of the petrol, leaving a trail down the stairs to Timothy Spent and Edward Lee, dousing them both, then leaving a trail down the cellar to the drugs.

"Setting fire to Edward Lee, the flames licked over the sofa and along the floor, then down to the cellar and upstairs to the bathroom. I headed out the back door and into the trees waiting approximately eight minutes till the house was fully ablaze.

"I decided rather than drag their deaths out to kill them cleanly and efficiently, taking no chances and less time than needed to complete the task and return back here.

"I headed back to retrieve the bike, making my way back here. I stashed the bike back in the shed and climbed back through the window. I spoke to Dad, Daniel Reins, briefly before entering the bathroom. I changed into an identical set of clothes, sealing my dirty clothing in the backpack and heading back into the bedroom.

"I collected the tape, sliding it into my backpack before replacing it with a music cassette. Heading to the window, I dropped the backpack onto the patio, closing the window and curtains afterwards.

"I called Maureen Smythe back into the room and told her we were ready, I carried out Daniel's wishes, and Maureen left the room."

I take a deep breath before I say the next bit, as I'm trying to hold it together, and the last fucking thing I need is to fall apart in front of these men I love so fiercely. I know they could never see me as weak, but still.

"After Daniel passed, Maureen called the time of death and arranged for the coroner, and they collected the… " Shit. I have to hold myself to stop my voice from breaking. I can feel myself about to lose it, and I can't let that happen. "...the body. Once that was done, I burnt everything, disposing of the ashes from the burn bin throughout the Adventure Centre. Then, I cleaned everything leaving the cleaner clothes and boots in the bathroom wash basket in case they were needed later.

"There has been an article in the local papers, a story on the local news and radio about the local squat house being torched and three bodies being found but no formal identification yet, and Detectives Dumb and Dumber haven't been near." Letting out the breath I've been holding, I add, "Yet." Then I nod at my pas and give them a grimace of a smile.

"Proud of you, Sunshine!" Pa Cade rises from behind the desk with his dirty blonde hair artfully dishevelled, and a layer of stubble coating his strong jaw. With his lopsided grin and sparkling blue eyes, he reaches over the desk with his fist. I lean forward and bump it, and as he stretches his arm out, his shirt sleeves ride up, revealing the tattoos that cover most of his body.

With brightly coloured sugar skulls, Day of the Dead designs, beautiful women and flowers, he is a work of art. I went to the tattooist with him growing up and even got my tattoos done there. Pa Cade was not happy about that. Well, he wasn't happy about catching me fucking the tattooist, but that's a different story!

Pa Cade is just as big as Pa Bernie, about six foot two and built like a brick shit house. All muscles and bad intentions, we always to say.

Pa Bernie comes around the desk and sweeps me into a bear hug. He drops me back to my feet. Pa

JJ roughs up my hair, and Pa Steven kisses me on the head.

"Right, now I'm fucking starving. Let's go order pizza," Pa Cade says. Typical guys, all business and no emotions. They all push past us and out of the room. Bran and Dane both rest their hands on my shoulder.

"K.F.D," Dane whispers and I reach up and hug him, and Bran hugs us from behind.

"Why don't you come back with us to the States, hang out a bit? You know that little issue we're having? It would be good to have you there for backup, and we miss you. Might do you good to get away from here for a while."

"You sound just like Dad. He made me promise to go somewhere for a break. I'll think about it. I'll speak to the pas and see what they think." I promise.

"If you fuckwits don't hurry up, I'm putting fucking anchovies and jalapeños on yours!" Pa Cade bellows upstairs.

"Fucking knobhead!" I laugh.

"I fucking heard that, shit bag!"

We head downstairs to order decent pizza before we end up with the shit that Pa Cade would order just to spite me for the knobhead comment.

There's a knock at the door. Dad has been gone for three days, ten hours and fifteen minutes. I open it to see Detective Jones and Detective Johnson.

"Arseholes… I mean, gentlemen." I nod, smiling while crossing my arms across my chest and resting my hip against the door frame. "Come to pay your respects?"

"Respects?" Johnson snarls. He's an arsehole of the finest order. He has an attitude problem, especially regarding me and my family.

Johnson's a short man, maybe five foot six. I use this term exceptionally loosely. He has fiery red hair scraped back with gel and emerald green eyes with gold flecks. He's slightly overweight but not massively. His moustache is a few shades darker than his hair and wiry, with big bushy eyebrows and pale milky white skin, almost opaque. He smells like a lime that has been arse-fucked by ten-day-old fag smoke coated in BO.

"Yeah, respects. That's why you're here, right?"

Johnson and Jones share a look as Jones says, "Not sure what you mean, Miss Reins. We're here to ask you about your whereabouts between 9 p.m. and midnight on Thursday evening?"

"Whereabouts?" I breathe out a huff. "I was here. My dad passed away that night. I was with him from when we bought him home from the hospital earlier that day."

"Well, isn't that convenient, Miss Reins," Johnson says while Jones gives him a death glare.

"Convenient?" Stepping forward out of the door, I fold my arms across my chest tighter clenching my fists under them, straightening my back. "Hardly!" I spit, and Johnson smirks, knowing he's touched a nerve, but lets out a breath as his cheeks flush ever so slightly.

I always manage to rile him up and have done since I was in my early teens. He likes to try and push me but always ends up backing down, frustrated.

"We're sorry for your loss. We didn't realise he'd been ill. Would you mind coming down to the station to give a statement? Is there anyone who can corroborate your story?" Jones replies.

Jones is slightly taller than Johnson but shorter than my five foot ten, maybe five foot eight. They are both in their late forties. Johnson has silver hair, making him look far older than he is. That could be my doing, though, which makes me internally smile. He's a stocky guy but still fit for his age with pale blue eyes. He always takes more pride in his appearance than Johnson. He's just a little more put together, suit is just a little more expensive, a little less creased and fits a little better, and he smells better, too, like some designer fragrance—all cedar and spicy with a hint of sea salt.

He's definitely the more professional of the two of them and less easy to rile than Johnson, but he can also hold his frustration, whereas Johnson's a bomb waiting to go off. I carry matches at all times just because I like to fuck with them.

"The palliative care nurse Maureen Smythe, who was here about an hour after we got home till the time of his passing in the early hours. Also, Scarlett Harrington and her dad, and three of my pas," I snarl at them both. Fuckers!

"Mr Harrington, as in David Harrington? Your lawyer?" Johnson says with a look that insinuates that this all sounds mighty convenient.

"You mean our close family friend? Yes, he was here all night too. What is this actually about?"

"We will discuss that with you down at the station," Jones replies.

"I'll give them a call and ask them all to meet me there if you like. I can be there in around an hour."

I step back and slam the door. I'm fed up with these guys' bullshit. They've hounded me since I came onto their radar when I was around fifteen. Resting my forehead on the door and reaching into my pocket for the phone, I call Scar.

I pull up at the police station. Sitting back on my Ducati, I switch off the engine and lean back as I remove my helmet. I'm twenty minutes late. I'm never late usually, but they made my blood boil, fucking dickwads. I made myself late on purpose by taking the scenic route to get here, needing to blow off some steam before I lost my shit.

Pops and Scar are standing in the foyer, and Pa JJ and Pa Steven are sitting in the seats lined against the wall. Scar is pacing the foyer, and Pops is at the counter talking to the clerk. I can see them through the glass front of the building.

I thought about sitting on my bike and having a fag, making them wait longer, but as I don't smoke and never have, I slide off, locking my helmet to my bike. Hearing another bike come close, I glance up to see Pa Cade pull in at the side of me. Getting off his bike, he sticks out his hand, clenching his fist, and I fist-bump him. Without saying a word, he winks at me, and we head inside.

My pas and Scar are taken into separate rooms while I wait in the foyer. Pops goes in with Scar while they all give their statements. When Scar comes out, they request I enter the room.

After questioning where I was on the night in question, they asked when I'd last seen the three douchebags who had tried to kill me and had managed to kill my brother.

"The trial," I reply,

"You've not seen them since then?" Jones asks.

"Nope," I sing out, popping my 'P' obnoxiously, smirking as the sound makes Johnson's shoulders bunch.

"You didn't see them on the night in question?" Jones asks.

"Nope," I reply, again popping my 'P' and grinning internally at the look on douche one and douche two's faces. Fucking priceless!

"You haven't seen them in the last, what … three years? Even though they live in the same area?" Johnson pushes.

"Nope."

"Did you kill them?" Jones gets out before I jump up from my chair with a gasp.

Thinking to myself, no, *I* didn't kill them, *she* did, I spit out, "Are you trying to tell me they're dead? Is that why I'm here? You think I killed them? Are you fucking shitting me right now? You're unfuckingbelievable." Pops places his hand on my shoulder, and I instantly rein it in, sitting back in my chair before I lose my shit even more.

23

Pops stands up and asks, "Are we done here, gentlemen? My client has no further comment at this time." I smirk, shaking my head at Jones and Johnson, and my look says it all, fucking amateurs. Knobheads!

They have been trying to pin shit on me for years, but I was always too slick. They could never find any evidence as to whether I was there or not or if I had killed them or not. If they had found anything, I would have been arrested already, and there was nothing left of the house. Just the charred remains of the building and three smoking corpses.

Any evidence I had was taken with me, and that has been destroyed as well. There is nothing to tie me to them other than said issue three years earlier, hardly enough to hang a case on, and with so many alibis in my favour having me in that room hearing me read to my dad for an hour while they were all in the kitchen, good luck finding anything to link me to it other than their weak arse hunches. They always suspected me but could never prove shit, and they aren't gonna prove shit this time either.

I slowly rise from my seat. "Is there anything else you need, gentleman? As soon as my dad's funeral is over and he's been cremated, I'm going to stay with Pa Bernie in the States for a while."

"How long will you be gone?" Jones asks.

"Six months, maybe longer, who knows?" I shrug.

Johnson grins, sneering, "Don't rush back, Sunshine! We won't be missing you!" He points his fat finger in my direction. "Hopefully you'll stay there, and you won't be our problem anymore!"

I lean across the table, winking at him and letting my smile fill my face. "Come on, Johnson. You know you'd miss me too much. I mean, if it wasn't for you running around trying to pin shit on me for the last, what, nearly ten years, your arse would be fat as fuck from all the sitting around eating chips!" I bark a laugh as we leave the room, turning and blowing a kiss over my shoulder.

Johnson mutters under his breath, slamming his fist into the table. "Little fucker. Good riddance!"

"*¡Hasta luego,* motherfuckers!" I fire back over my shoulder, and we stroll into the parking lot. My pas have already given their statements and left. Pops stops me as I get on my bike.

Pops is a tall, slender guy, slightly taller than me, in his mid to late fifties, with light blonde hair styled like a Lego man, not a hair out of place. He has piercing blue eyes like Scar. Right now, they're twinkling at my mischievousness, with his perfect, dazzling white teeth, sharp suit and shoes in which I can see my face. He always smells so good, I can't quite put my finger on it, but he smells … classy. Expensive.

He carries a leather briefcase in his hand. I often wonder if he carries it to look the part of a lawyer. Maybe he has a sandwich and this week's *Big Busty Blondes* magazine in there. Who knows?

He smiles at me and asks, "You know I love you, right?"

"Yeah, of course! What's going on, Pops?"

He laughs. "Nothing, just letting you know, that's all. And also, just saying, you don't have to try to rile them up every time you have an interaction with them."

"Yeah, I know, but I'm just so good at it, and it's kinda fun."

Then he smirks again. "Yeah, yeah! Are you coming over for dinner tomorrow? We can finalise everything for the trip."

My pas think it's a great idea for me to get away for a bit, and when I told Scar, she refused to let me go without her. My sister-from-another-mister has serious FOMO issues.

She's recently finished university and is now a fully qualified criminal lawyer like her dad. She has spent a lot of time away from me over the last five or six years and vowed not to leave my side longer than to sleep ever again. Her dad also thinks it would be good for her to have a six-month break with me before starting at his law firm.

"Sure, sounds good. Love ya, Pops. See ya tomorrow." I ride off, two-finger saluting to Scar as I leave laughing. She shakes her head at me and flips me off!

God, I love that girl. She is my ride-or-die, my bestie, my sister-from-another-mister. I can't wait to head off on this trip together. Hopefully, it will be life-changing or some shit like that.

It's the morning of the funeral. We've waited three weeks for today to finally come. It's rained constantly for the last week, miserable, grey, foggy rain, basically mirroring my mood, almost as if I'd conjured it myself, my own personal rain cloud of misery and devastation. When I woke up this morning, it was sunny with a slight breeze in the air. I could see the leaves on the trees dancing. I can still smell the rain in the air, but it's bright with clear skies for now. I can hear the ravens in the forest cawing and the rustle of the leaves as the trees sway gently.

I shower in a daze and head downstairs in my sweats. The funeral isn't for a few hours, so I don't need to get dressed just yet. Everyone is gathered in the kitchen as I walk in.

Pa Steven grabs me and just hugs me. He isn't as tall as the rest of my pas at five foot eleven. He has darker, dirty blonde hair than the rest of us, with warm chocolate brown eyes. His hair is shaggy on top with a wave to it, short on the sides. He's slimmer, too; more lean muscle than brick shit house muscle like Pa Bernie and Pa Cade. He smells like the outdoors; they all do. Like trees and lakes and fresh-cut grass.

We used to joke that the only two of them who didn't look like they could be my dad were my dad and Pa JJ. Pa JJ is six foot with dark chocolate brown hair buzzed all over. He has a designer stubble beard, neat and trimmed with hazel eyes, the gold and the green flecks in them making them look metallic or even cat-like. He's not as thick-set as Pa Bernie and Pa Cade, who are both fucking monsters. He's slightly bigger than Pa Steven, but they are all stacked and maintain their physiques even after leaving the military years ago. Their day-to-day jobs still keep them in peak physical fitness.

There were definitely times when Pa Cade, Pa Bernie and Pa Steven questioned my paternity growing up. I mean, they all knew they didn't sleep with my mum, but the similarities looks-wise are undeniably close, and personality? Fuck, I was like them all. There was definitely that nature over nurture question answered in a nutshell. If I favoured one of them, though, it was Pa Cade. He has rubbed off on me more than we would have liked.

They have all been such a massive part of my upbringing that it was inevitable I was going to share their stronger traits, and it's why no one ever questioned Bran and Dane being my brothers. There are only two months between me and Bran, and everyone thought me and him were the twins, not me and Bas. Bas had the same hair and eyes as my dad, but we both looked like our mum. I think that's why he hated me so much. I always reminded him he lost her, well, we both did, but my brother was a twat, so there's that.

We are all individuals but also so similar, cut from the same cloth, you might say. Even Ma Marie looked like she was my mum, but I don't remember my real mum. I have a few pictures of us from when we were younger, but since she died when I was four, I have no physical memory of her at all.

As I walk into the kitchen, Ma is plating up pancakes, not the American kind but the ones we love to have on Shrove Tuesday, more like a thicker crepe. I always have freshly squeezed orange juice and sugar on mine. Bran opts for Nutella, while Dane has orange juice and Nutella. He's a wrong-un, that one!

After eating together, we go over the plan for the day, and I head upstairs to get ready.

"Can I come in?" Ma Marie knocks at the door to my room.

"Sure." I turn and smile at her. She walks over to hug me and pulls me into her. She smells like a summer day and wildflowers. Her scent always reminds me of the meadow we used to play in as kids. It was covered in wildflowers and was on the hill, so there was always a slight breeze. That's what I think of when Ma Marie hugs me, of a happy childhood, running free barefoot, rolling down the hills, and laughing till we couldn't breathe.

"It's okay to not be okay, you know. It's okay to cry. I know you tough it out like the guys do, but if you need a break, a time-out, I'm here!"

"Thanks, Ma. I know. It just still doesn't feel real yet. I still expect him to walk in. I can still smell him in his room and his office, all over the house. The patio chair where he used to sit to smoke still smells like him and fags. It's like he hasn't really gone yet." I give her a sad smile and shrug one shoulder. "When it hits me, I *will* let you know, okay?"

Kissing my head, she turns and leaves. Ma is shorter than me, about five foot seven. She has shoulder-length dirty blonde wavy hair with highlights in it, and she has a fuller figure, curves for days.

I envy her and Scar. I would love a womanly figure, but it wasn't meant to be. Maybe if I stopped working out so much, but then I can't see that happening. It's my addiction, my therapy, somewhere to focus my energy, *her* energy. I'm so competitive, too. I need to be the fastest, the strongest, and the funniest. I think growing up with so many strong men in my life. I just wanted to be like them, only better.

Dressing in my black blouse, tucking it into my black trousers, and slipping on my Mary Janes, tying my hair in a braid over my shoulder, I apply a little tinted gloss to my lips but don't bother with any other make-up. I'm not sure I'm gonna make it through the day without crying, so I don't want to tempt fate and potentially end up with panda eyes.

My pas, Bran, and Dane carry the coffin, and Ma and I walk behind it. Scar and Pops are already inside. The service passes by in a haze until it comes to my part. I have a reading Dad had written and wanted me to share. Clearing my throat as I step up to the podium, I grip the wood tight like it's the only thing in the world holding me up right now, and I don't want to let go in case that's true. I let out a shaky breath, straightening out my black blouse and black trousers. Standing tall, I clear my throat again.

"I Will Never Be Truly Gone,' By Daniel Reins.

You will feel I have disappeared, but our souls are still bound. From now until eternity, our lives have been entwined, but in death, I will always be around.

You will see me in their smiles, in the twinkle of their eyes, the smirk of their lips, the trace of tears as you cry, In the laughter of your children, in the caw of the raven. When you feel at a loss, I'll be your foundation.

I will always be there, closer than you believe. Never forget my lessons; that's where I still live.

I will stay with you forever, always at your side. Remember us together, always with burning pride.

Remember me always. I won't truly be gone. I am always in your heart. You are never alone."

I step back from the podium, take a deep breath, and I retake my seat. Pa Cade's arm slides around me as he squeezes my shoulder, and Pa Bernie grips my knee. I don't look at either of them. I know I'll break if I do, so I rest my hands on my lap and stare straight ahead, concentrating on breathing and breathing alone. I will get through this. I just can't break. Not today, not here. Maybe not ever.

Dad's being cremated, and we are going to scatter some of his ashes at the Adventure Centre. We aren't the only ones here, to our surprise. We don't have many friends, we keep to ourselves, but we have regulars at the Adventure Centre, and they've come to the funeral to pay their respects. It's nice to see how well-liked Dad was.

After it's all over, the family, Scar, and Pops head back to the house. We're having a wake of sorts for him with a bonfire near the lake where we can all sit around and tell stories and drink. It will be a perfect send-off. He would have loved it.

We have assembled a bonfire of sorts out of old crates, and we carry blankets and camping chairs up to the side of the lake. It's beautiful here, one of my favourite places on the property. One of Dad's, too.

We've spent so many hours up here canoeing, camping, making rafts and racing across the lake.

We light the fire and sit around it, huddled under the blankets we brought up here. We all brought a bottle of our choosing. My dad loved tequila, and I think that's where my love of it comes from. Me, Scar,

Dane, Bran and Bernie all have tequila, Cade and Steven have whiskey, JJ and Pops have vodka, and Ma has her white wine, as, apparently, she isn't a heathen like the rest of us!

"Remember that time when Dad told us that the tooth fairy had got lost trying to find the house, so we had to go look for her? We looked for hours and didn't find her, but when we got back, there was a quid under the pillow, so we assumed she managed to find her way eventually, that she was just late."

Cade laughs. "Shit, yeah! When you woke up, she hadn't been. We had all forgotten, so we sent you on a wild goose chase while JJ went into town to get some cash."

"Yeah, when I got into town, I tried to take money out of the cash point, but it would only let me get a twenty-pound note, so I then had to find a shop open to buy something to get the change. There was no way I was giving you twenty quid for a tooth, as we would then have to do that for all four of you, and that's a shit lot of teeth!" JJ grins.

"Remember that year we had the raft race across the lake? We were in four teams, and Marie and Daniel were in charge, and Dane slipped and knocked his tooth out, and it fell into the lake. Then he panicked, thinking the tooth fairy would never pay him, only to find a quid on the bank of the lake the next morning!" Steven chuckles. "The shit we did to make you kids happy!"

"Remember that dance you had when you left primary school before going to secondary school? You would have been what… eleven? Your dad thought it would be better if you and Bran went separately with dates, so he paid some kids at the school to ask you to go, and you both turned them down as you said they were gross and went with each other anyway!

"Cost your dad twenty quid each to bribe those kids to have the courage to ask you two out! Ray made that little boy cry when she turned him down!" Bernie laughs.

"Hey, no fair! He was a total wuss, and he used to sit and eat his bogeys in class. Dude was gross!" I spit out.

"Yeah, and the girl you made ask me was just as bad. She used to fart into her hands, clap them together, then open her hands under your nose and shout cupcake. I mean, what the actual fuck? Come on. We could do so much better than that!" Bran shakes his head.

"We tried to bribe everyone in your year. They were the only ones who even dared ask you guys out. You had a… reputation, let's say. The Reaper and her Shadows, they used to call you behind your backs. They were all terrified of the three of you. Bas was the only one who had other friends, and he fuelled the rumours, making them ten times worse. You guys were scary little motherfuckers. Ray, you were worse with your aversion to colour and anything remotely girly!" Cade grins at us.

"Still is!" Dane leans over and fist-bumps us both.

"I can vouch for that." Scar grins at us.

The guys slide into stories of my dad during their military missions and how they became friends, saving each other's arses on more than a dozen occasions.

They reminisce about building the Adventure Centre and the loss of Sebastian. He would have been here with us but died before they opened the Adventure Centre. They still hunt for his kid that disappeared in the States.

Ma told us how she tried to help me become girly and said I fought her tooth and nail and didn't even want my hair brushed. She tried taking me to ballet and spa days, doing my hair and make-up, flower-arranging and shit like that, but I always preferred rolling around in the mud with my brothers, shooting and riding dirt bikes. She did manage to convince me to go into gymnastics, which I was really good at. Parkour, too, and macramé. Well, that's how it started. It ended in shibari, which I have ulterior motives for. What can I say? I lIke tying shit up. It's highly effective in the "family business" and possibly in the bedroom. I haven't found a willing participant—yet!

"You were feral, totally barefoot and bonkers. You'd run around with twigs in your hair and mud on your faces. I've never seen three children happier. Bath times were always a challenge. One summer, you refused to bathe, saying you would wash in the lake. That lasted three and a half weeks before we had to intervene and scrub you all clean. I mean, the smell was horrific!" Marie was shaking her head.

"That was our *Stig of the Dump* phase!" Bran laughs. God, I loved that book when we read it at school and then found the tv series.

"It was Bran who thought that phase was a great idea!" I laugh out, pointing my tequila at him.

"You didn't argue. You all thought it was brilliant," Pa Cade barked out, laughing. "God, that smell lingered for weeks after, too. I could still fucking taste it, and they fought us like wild cats when we tried to get them in the shower. Hades, give me Iraq and Afghanistan any day over you three!"

"Pa." I gasp. "You know you wouldn't change us for the world. We're the best things that ever happened to you all!"

There's a pause for a few seconds before everyone except me, Bran, and Dane burst out into fits of hysterics.

Once the laughter dies down and he can breathe again, JJ adds, "Oh, you're serious?"

"Motherfuckers!" Dane spits out.

They descend into fits of hysteria again.

"Wankers." I shake my head, cursing them all. We're right, and they know it. They'd be bored and lost without us. All our pas loved us and thought of us as their own. We really were lucky to have them, but I was not telling them that. Fucking bellends!

Pa Bernie and the gang head home a couple of days after the funeral. I'm a bit twitchy. I need to blow off some steam. Scar is helping her dad today, and the pas are clearing some junk out. I think they're just trying to keep busy.

Grabbing my helmet, I text the family group chat. That way, everyone knows where we are.

Ray: Taking the bike out.
Cade: K.

JJ: Will you be back for dinner?
Ray: Not sure.
JJ: Ride safe.
Steven: xx

I have no idea where I'm going till I pull into the car park behind the shop and curse myself. "What the fuck am I doing here?" Shaking my head, I get off the bike and take off my helmet, securing it to my bike.

I shove through the door of the shop. It has been maybe ten months to a year since I've been here. It looks and smells the same.

"Be there in a minute!" the familiar gruff voice sounds from the back before he steps out of the back room, then freezes staring directly at me, mouth open, breath held.

"Hey, Jer." I raise my hand in a slight wave, suddenly feeling rather nervous. What the fuck am I thinking? Pa Cade is gonna skin me alive.

"Ray?" A whisper of my name on his lips before he strides forward, collecting himself. The shock turns to almost anger and maybe betrayal. Yeah, things did not end well. As I hold my breath, I'm transported back to being nineteen again.

***

Then...

I've been coming to the tattooist with Pa Cade for years. The two tattooists here know me well. Jeremy Bird, also known as Jer or Birdy, and Liam St

John. They own the shop together. They started it in their early twenties. Pa Cade has been coming here since they opened. I must have been about six that first time.

Jer was twenty-four back then. He's about five foot eleven. He has dark wavy hair and dark eyes. He's covered in tattoos and is muscular. He always had a smile for me and a lollipop if I had been a good girl and sat patiently while Pa Cade got tatted by Liam.

After losing my brother, Pa Cade brought me for my first tattoo. I wanted so much done that I came on my own the next sitting. Over the months, I got both my right arm and left leg done and a full back piece.

Jer and I have talked a lot, and he's a kinda nice guy. We have definitely become friends, he's asked me out for a drink, and while I like him, I'm not sure dating is gonna be for me anymore. My last few relationships have gone to shit quickly. Guys love the badass bitch I am till they have me, then immediately want me to submit, which isn't happening. I'm never gonna be submissive. They think that's what I need, to hand over control. Nope, definitely not what I need.

I had told Jer about my past relationships. It wasn't really a long conversion, that one. I told him how I'd never let a man touch me like that again. It was easy to talk to him while he was tattooing me. It was almost like therapy for me. I don't want to get with a guy who tries to dominate me. It isn't happening. Jer seemed to understand and asked me what I wanted. I told him just a fuck every now and then, with no strings and certainly no unwanted contact.

After pondering over that while, he finishes up tattooing me. He asks if I'll consider a proposal. He's older now, about thirty-seven. His muscle has long gone, and his hands are large but soft and gentle, but he's still in shape-ish, just a little softer than the years previously and still not bad looking for an older dude.

"What are you proposing, Jer?" I ask, curious, and honestly, I have liked the attention I get from him. He makes me feel… comfortable. Maybe it's because I've known him for so long.

"What do you want, Ray? Sexually, I mean? What do you need?"

I thought on it for a time. "I want a guy to do what I want when I want. I want him to only touch me when and where I say, and I want to be in control at all times, on my terms." I can feel her purring. *She* wants all the above; if he can give us that, *she'd* be happy. I'd be happy.

"But you let me touch you now, while I'm tattooing you."

"That's different, there's nothing sexual in it, and I trust you. I know you. It's just different."

"What if I said I could give you that? I would give you whatever you wanted, Ray. You're beautiful, you know that, right?"

"Jer—"

"Don't decide now," he cuts me off. "Think about it. I can be that for you. I can give you what you want. You deserve that. I've always thought the world of you."

"Jer—"

"Don't, Ray. Don't say it now. If you want it, just call and book an appointment for a… consultation. Okay if not…" He shrugged. "No harm done. There are a few bits I'd like to add some more detail to. We could just work on that. Now, let's get you wrapped up."

As I climb off the table, he wraps my back. I cock my head, inspecting him. He's a nice guy. Maybe he's just what I need…

I can feel her trying to push to the surface. "No feelings. No pressure. No touching unless I say. What I say when I say it."

He nods. "Whatever, however. It's your call."

"Okay."

"Okay? Ray, you sure?"

"Yeah, Jer. I'm sure. When can you book me in for a… consultation?"

"Wait here. I'll go check."

He comes back a few minutes later, shoving the door closed and reaching for the lock. "How about now? I've got an hour free." Staying with his hand on the lock, he turns to me. "Only if you want to. Your rules."

I nod. *She* likes the idea of this. If I can satisfy *her* hunger, I can be less on edge, wondering if she's gonna rise to the surface to wreak havoc at any given moment. "Deal." I step towards him. "Do you have any condoms?"

Swallowing, he nods and goes to the filing cabinet, grabbing a box out and dropping it on his chair.

"On the table, Jer. On your back, cock out, condom on," I speak clearly and firmly.

As he removes his jeans and lies down on the table, he looks a little nervous, which only fuels my inner confidence. I take my jeans off as he rolls the condom over his already hard dick. He isn't massive, but he is well-proportioned. His pubic hair is dark and neatly trimmed, and he has a nice dick, as far as dicks go.

"Ready?" I ask as I climb up over him. There's just enough room on his tattoo table for my legs on either side of him.

"You sure about this, Ray?" His voice is not as confident anymore.

"I'm sure. Arms above your head. Grip the top of the table and keep them there. No kissing. No touching, okay?"

He nods. I reach between us and grab his dick, and he moans as I pump it a couple of times. I'm not massively experienced, but something about the look on Jer's face makes me feel so… powerful.

I press him to my slick entrance. I'm surprised by how wet I am. Yeah, he's still a good-looking guy—kind of—but it's more how he's making me feel like I'm totally in control. I slide him through my lips a couple of times, causing him to groan, and his eyes roll closed. He bites down on his lip.

I plunge him into me, impaled by his dick, and he gasps as I lift and slam onto him again, bottoming out. He stretches me in all the right ways.

"Jesus, Ray," he gasps out, eyes rolling into the back of his head. A flush rises up his cheeks. I start to rock back and forward across him, rubbing my clit into him, grinding myself down onto him. His hand comes off the table and grabs for my hip.

"Don't!" I spit at him.

"Shit, Ray, stop a minute." He slides his arm back up to the top of the table.

"You gonna come, Jer?"

"Yeah, Ray, if you don't stop, I'm gonna blow my load in about five seconds."

"Race ya," I challenge as I rub myself into him again, and his back arches off the table. I grind into him over and over again, his breath stuttering. I can feel his thighs tense beneath me, and I throw my head back as I slide my hand up his T-shirt to his throat. As my hand hits the flesh of his neck, I squeeze and push him down.

"Ray… Shit, Ray… " he pants out as my orgasm hits, and I fuck him harder than I ever have anyone before.

Flashes of white ping around my eyes as my breaths come in ragged. I bite down on my lip, drawing blood, the coppery metallic taste making my lip twitch into a feral smirk as I try to rub Jer through the table while we both come. His fingers are gripping the table that tight I'll be surprised if he doesn't get cramp. I ease my grip off his neck, slowly allowing him to breathe again.

With his eyes still glazed over, he gasps for breath, still gripping tight to the top of the table. He smiles up at me. "Jesus fuck, Ray, what the fuck just happened!"

"I'm pretty sure you just became my new fuck buddy, Jer." I wink at him. "I'll call you to set up another appointment soon for a… consultation." I grin at him, pulling my jeans back on and grabbing my stuff. He's still hanging onto the table, panting and flushed. I flick the lock on the door.

"You okay, Jer?" He just nods, grinning at me like a fucking idiot. "Mum's the word, Jer. Our little secret. okay?" He nods again, panting, as I stroll out of the room and out to my bike.

"Ray!" he snaps it this time, bringing me back to the now. "What the fuck are you doing here?"

"Jer, I… I… I need a consultation."

"A consultation? Are you fucking kidding me right now? After what happened last time and then nothing? I've not seen you for ten months, Ray. No contact, no explanation, no nothing. I thought we had something. I called, I texted, and I even showed up at your house, but you ignored and blocked me … don't deny it. Two fucking years, Ray. We were together for two fucking years. I fucking loved you, Ray, and you just left and never looked back. I didn't mean fuck all to you, did I?"

He crosses his arms over his chest and glares at me. I can see the hurt in his eyes. We'd said no feelings—well, I'd said no feelings—but I knew Jer had feelings for me. If I think back, I knew he had when he offered what he did.

We were together without actually being a couple for just over two years. For me, he was a fuck buddy who did what I wanted when I wanted. I had no attachment to him other than he gave me what I wanted. Don't get me wrong, I enjoyed every minute of it all. He was a good lay when I wanted it. He let me take it how I wanted it, and it worked for me.

He would often ask me out on a date, but I would back off, and he would apologise and make out he was just testing to make sure I was still on track, still taking our rules seriously, but deep down, I knew he had fallen in love with me. I just chose to ignore it because it suited me, and now here I am, rubbing salt in old wounds, picking at scabs, and ripping off Band-Aids. And from the look on his face ripping hearts out and stomping all over them while I'm at it.

"You've got nothing to say? Getting over you is the hardest thing. I'm still fucking trying, for God's sake. And you fucking waltz in here like it was yesterday, and shit didn't go fucking sideways. Are you serious right now?"

"I'm sorry, Jer, I should go."

"Ray." The gasp leaves his lips as he grabs for my arm, the anger fading to hurt, then panic, as I flinch away from him. "Shit, sorry. Ray, it's just you were gone and… " He trails off, looking down at the pen on the counter.

I storm out of the shop and throw myself on my bike, tearing off out of the car park. As I look back, Jer's standing in the doorway of the shop, looking like he's seen a ghost, gripping the door frame as if that is the only thing keeping him upright. Well, fuck. Maybe it is.

As I'm pulling off on the bike, I hear him shout after me, "Fuck, Ray, I still love you! Come back!"

Needless to say, I don't. I ride straight out of the car park and don't look back. Again.

As I storm back into the house, I slam the door.

"What the fuck, Squirt?" Pa Cade spits out from the kitchen. "Fuck's up with you?"

"Nothing. I'm going to my room." I stomp upstairs and throw myself on my bed, pulling the pillow over my head and screaming into it.

The last time I saw Jer, I'd gone for a "consultation." Every time we fucked, he booked a full-hour slot. We were always done in between ten minutes to twenty-five minutes at most. He would then add more and more detail to my tattoos. That's why they're as detailed as they are. Thoughts of the last time I saw him fill my mind.

***

Then…

Walking into the tattoo parlour, I'm greeted by Liam. "Hey Ray, another consultation? Do you have any room left?"

"There's always room to squeeze a little something in, Liam." I laugh out.

Jer's door swings open. "Hey Ray, come on back!" His grin widens as I walk towards him.

Strutting back there, I slide into the room, sliding out of my jeans as I walk through the door.

"Shit, Ray, let me shut the door first." As I walk past, I grab him by the front of his shirt, and he kicks the door shut behind him. "So, what do you fancy today?"

"Fuck me from behind," I say as I kick my jeans off. "Condom."

He's already walking over to the filing cabinet and grabbing a couple of condoms. He knows me by now and knows what I want. I lean over the table, arse in the air. It isn't very often we do it this way, but every now and then, I just want to be bent over and railed into oblivion, but I still don't let him touch me properly. He's allowed one hand on my back to steady himself, and that's it. But today, I want something a little different.

"Jer... fuck me in the arse, hard."

"Ray... I'm... I... erm, Ray?"

"Slide in steady, Jer, then once you're settled, I want you to fuck me like your life depends on it. You can hold my hips, but that's it. You hear me, Jer ... that's it!"

Releasing a shaky breath, he asks, "Ray? You sure?"

"Jer, just fucking do it!"

He removes his jeans and slides in behind me. Sliding the condom on, he lines his tip up to my throbbing pussy and pushes in, slowly coating himself. Thrusting a couple of times, he groans and stutters out a breath before pulling out and then realigning with my arse, pushing in gently. I grit my teeth as I push past the burning sensation, controlling my breaths, making sure I stay relaxed and don't tense up. He gasps as he pushes in inch by painfully tight inch, slowly sinking till we can't fit a sheet of paper between us. Once he's fully inside, he pauses a second, taking a deep breath. He backs off a bit, pushing forward gently again. I look over my shoulder at him. His eyes are scrunched tight, and he's trying to breath steady but failing. I make the most of the pause, taking a breath myself. I'm so tight, so fucking full, it feels delicious now the burn has died away.

"Give me a sec, Ray. You're so tight… fuck… I'm… I need a sec, okay?"

Nodding, I glance back over the table.

He reaches up and gently places one hand on either side of my hips, and I grimace. He must feel me tense as he lifts his hands in defence.

"It's fine, Jer. Just do it, okay?"

He reaches up again, grabbing a firmer grip this time as he backs off and slams into me, groaning as he bottoms out, taking a breath and pausing. He pulls out and thrusts again, and I groan. "Harder, Jer."

He thrusts in again, but this time, he pulls straight back out instead of waiting before pounding in again.

"Shit," he mutters under his breath.

I reach down, sliding my hand over my stomach and into my soaked lips. I start rubbing my clit with one hand. Resting on my elbow, I slide my other hand under my T-shirt, pinching my nipple and groping my tit through my bra.

My head's thrown back, the heat rising through me. His thrusts are coming thick and fast now, and he's found his rhythm, slamming into me over and over again while I rub furiously. My orgasm is building, and I'm starting to feel the dizziness flashing behind my eyes. I rub harder, gasping.

"Shit, Jer, don't fucking stop," I manage to pant.

He thrusts into me again and again, the sound of skin slapping filling the air, and my breath stutters. I can feel his thighs tensing and shaking, the spots dancing in front of my eyes. I'm so, so close.

"Like that, Jer, fuck me just like that!"

And then the door opens. My head flings around. I gasp and look straight at Pa Cade and Liam.

"Shit." I freeze.

Unfortunately, Jer's in the zone and hasn't even noticed as I freeze. I must tense and grip tighter on him.

He gasps out, "Fuck, Ray, your arse is so tight!" as he thrusts into me again and again. He's hanging on for dear life, head thrown back, eyes closed as he stutters, tenses and comes with a groan, "Fuck yeah." He holds me so he's buried as far in me as he can get, opening his eyes and panting before seeing my gaze on the door.

Pa strides across the room in two strides, and as Jer's gaze clashes with his, his eyes go wide, letting out a gasp. Still with his dick inside me, hanging onto my hips, his grip tightens. Pa reaches him and punches Jer straight in the face. "Get your filthy pedo fucking hands off. My. Daughter!" he roars, and Jer falls sideways onto the floor as Pa Cade grabs the neck of his T-shirt, pulling him up only to punch him back down again and again.

Grabbing his shoulder and trying to pull him back, I shout, "Pa! Please stop, Pa, enough!" He pulls back, rising to his full height and glaring between us both.

"Put your fucking clothes on, Ray! Now!" he bellows at me, looking for my jeans. I scramble to grab them. Liam's still in the doorway, mouth open, knuckles white where he's gripping the door frame, face pale. He's clearly in shock, too, frozen, looking at the carnage in the room.

Jer lays on the floor with blood all over his face, his nose broken, a fat lip, and at least one black eye, dick out still in the come-filled condom. He's definitely limp now. He rolls onto his side, groaning, reaching a hand up towards me. "Ray." He gasps.

Pa storms out of the room as I pull on my jeans and slip my boots back on. "Pa, wait! Pa! Fuck!" I run out the door after him and don't look back.

Pa Cade

Then...

Liam calls to say he has a cancellation. I'm always down for filling in little gaps I have in my artwork, and I'm not busy, so I head straight over.

"Hey, Cade, how's it going?" Liam asks as I walk in. "Ray's here with Birdy having another consultation. Seriously she must be as covered as you now. I would love to see the work. They've seriously been putting the hours in!"

"Shall we have a sneak peek while I'm here? I'm sure they won't mind!"

Striding past him, I head to Birdy's room. As I open the door, I'm speaking to Liam behind me, and the sheer look of horror on his face as I fling the door open, my eyes shoot around, and the look in her eyes bores into me.

I lose my fucking shit, that fucking animal, that fucking paedophile, fucking asshole, absolute total wanker, fucking dead man!

Balls deep in my daughter's ass, my fucking daughter! She gasps as I walk in, and that fucking dead man just keeps pounding and pounding, saying how tight she is before groaning his release. Then it all goes red, hazy, silent. The world stops turning; my heart stops beating, my breaths stop coming, my mouth goes dry, my eyes glaze over, and my skin feels like I'm burning up from the inside. Rage. Pure unadulterated rage washes over me.

Then, everything slots back. The world speeds up, my heart hammers in my chest, and my breathing comes rapidly and sharply as I gasp for breath. I've been in war zones. I've killed people with my bare hands, watching life leave their eyes. I've tortured people, removing body parts, limbs, stripping and tearing at flesh to find information, and nothing has turned my stomach like this moment. This single solitary moment breaks something inside me. I tremble, my breaths stutter, and I can't breathe. My fists clench automatically. His gaze meets mine, followed by the shock of realisation, and then two strides. I can kill that daughter fucker.

As I stride in, she knows she's fucked—literally and figuratively. The kids called us uncles until Ray's mum died, and that's what we were, their fun uncles. After her mum, her dad struggled to cope with four-year-old twins. Bas was a handful and rebelled against everything, and Bernie and Marie had Bran, four, and Dane, three, by then, so we stepped up. The titles of Pa kicked in and stuck. We brought them all up as our own, and we treated them all the same, all four of them, even though she got under our skin more being the only girl. We were all their dads, so when I lose my shit, I know she knows she's made a grave mistake. She tries to soothe the beast in me, trying to quieten my rage. She knows that she has right royally fucked me off and let it loose.

Fuck, seeing her like that. Jesus, what was she thinking? What were they playing at? Why was the fucking door unlocked? What the fuck made them think this was a great place to fuck?

I'm not sure what happens as I stride into that room. The rage is too much, and the haze fills my vision. The next thing I know, I'm climbing into the truck.

"My bike?" she says as she climbs in too.

"Fuck your fucking bike, Ray!"

"Pa," she whispers out to me.

"Don't fucking 'Pa' me, Ray, seriously! What the fuck?" I growl, looking over at her. She shoots me a look. "You can put 'her' the fuck away too! How fucking long has he been fucking you?" I can sense the shift coming in her. If she comes out to play, this is going to end real fucking bad.

I have taken on insurgents, terrorists, rapists, and murderers, but she makes the hairs on the back of my neck stand to attention. None of us knows what she is truly capable of. Ray keeps her locked down tight most of the time, but now right this second, she's starting to show— brimming, boiled, fighting to erupt.

The set of her jaw, the blank expression that falls across her stunningly beautiful face, like all the fun and emotion has been syphoned out of her as the darkness creeps in, suffocating the light out of every cell. Then we know we should be wary. Shit is about to get real.

I mean, she shot Bernie when she was seven and stabbed Steven when she was six, and she wasn't even angry then, just curious. That was a time before they were separate, before she held her tight and caged deep down, a time when they co-existed so seamlessly. We may have said she wouldn't do it, which may have thrown fuel on that tiny spark that was always there before.

We soon learnt red rag and bull came to mind with her. Never tell her she couldn't do something or wouldn't do anything, as I swear to Hades she would do it just to prove you wrong, and prove she could.

She crosses her arms over her chest. She's pissed now, her defiance rolling off her in waves; she's battling to keep her quiet. "I've been fucking him for over two fucking years, Pa! I'm fucking twenty-one. I'm not some kid. I wasn't even a virgin when I started fucking him."

"Do you fucking love him? How long did he groom you for? Did he touch you when you were little? Did he—"

"Wow! Fuck no! No, he didn't touch me, and he didn't groom me. He asked me to go for a drink when he'd done my tattoos. I said no, but I was up for being fuck buddies, and that's all it is, all it ever was. It was just fucking, Pa. That's all. Just fucking."

I drag my phone out of my pocket, slamming on the brakes and pulling over at the side of the road. I scroll my fingers on the touch screen repeatedly before slamming it to my ear. "I need an appointment … my daughter… morning-after pill, full workup, contraceptive implant… ASAP… name? Reins, Sunshine Reins… yep, see you then."

"Are you fucking serious right now?" she spits.

"Fucking deadly, Ray. Do. Not. Test. Me!"

She sulks, flipping back into her chair. To her credit, she locks her down tight, and for that, I'm thankful.

We arrive back at the house, and we walk inside. "Debrief!" I bellow. "Fucking office, now!"

Stalking into the office, I stare at the chair before going to the cabinet and grabbing a whisky, throwing back the amber liquid till I feel it burn all the way down my throat, cracking my neck and my knuckles.

I throw myself into the chair. I have called the debrief, so I'm in charge. Everyone walks into the room. "Get Bernie on the phone! Now!"

Bernie and the family moved back to the States a few years previously, but we still run this family together. Nothing happens without us all knowing and all deciding the outcome, and if Reaper is gonna make a show, we'll need all hands on deck!

As Bernie answers, "Hey guys! You good?" and is put on speaker, Ray storms into the room, centre of the desk and stands at ease. Smart girl.

"Debrief, Bernie," is all I get out.

"What's going on?" Daniel asks.

"Fucking her, that's what!" I gesture wildly in Ray's direction as I glance up. She is now standing there, hip popped, arms folded across her chest.

"I can't fucking do this now!" I spit. "I'm gonna rip his motherfucking head off!" I stand to leave.

Reaper laughs out, "Oh no, Pa, we're doing this. Right. The. Fuck. Now!" She slams her hands on the desk before me and stares into my soul. Yep, Ray is long gone, and left in her wake is this unpredictable, unshakeable scary-ass motherfucker. My daughter has officially left the building.

"Erm… guys… what the fuck?" Bernie questions, picking up the phone and flicking him onto video call so he can see her. "Oh," is all he says.

I can see the fucking shift glaring into her eyes, but when we are like this, we clash, and I can't help myself, just like she can't. It's like a fucking car crash. You can't help but slow down and stare at it as you pass.

"Who the fuck do you think you're talking to?" I glare at her. This is not going to end well if we start. See, me and Ray are the same. She gets that from me, she got all our worst flaws, and at the height of her anger, they will turn them back on us in an argument.

I'm confrontational and feisty, fiery and quick to fight. Bernie is aggressive as fuck and vicious. JJ has a fucking frustrating answer for everything. His brain works so quickly. Steven can be really spiteful and remembers details of fights ten years ago just to throw back at you in the heat of the moment. Daniel, he's leary, always right, and so God damned sarcastic.

Put all that together into the beautiful daughter with every one of us wrapped around her finger, who we all see as an angel. The only problem is she's an angel playing with a fucking hand grenade. We're all just waiting for her to flip and rip the pin out.

Most of the time, she's sweet and caring and a pleasure. But then she will let her run free, let Reaper loose, turning all our wrath back upon us or any unsuspecting motherfucker who has underestimated her.

She's enough to make a grown man piss himself with a single look, holding that grenade till we all explode in a ball of fiery 'no fucks to give.'

"Fuck's sake, Ray, rein her in." I pinch the bridge of my nose again.

"This fucker"—she leans over the desk, jabbing her fingers at me—"barges his way into the room where I'm fucking a guy, then proceeds to beat the shit out of him and leaves him on the floor bleeding with his fucking dick out!"

"Fuck, Ray, I do not need that visual again. I'm gonna barf, and I will have to bleach my fucking eyeballs to get rid of it!"

"She's twenty-one," JJ interjects, trying to reason between us. "I don't like it, but I mean… we knew it was gonna happen sooner or later."

"Are you fucking shitting me, JJ? I mean, seriously, this dude had her bent over, fucking her in the ass!"

"Cade, I know that can't have been the best image, but she is twenty-one, mate! We can't hold onto her forever! She's not a little girl anymore," Daniel says. "She's a grown woman!"

"Birdy!" That's all I can get out; all I need to say. I should have led with that fucker!

"Birdy?" Bernie questions at the same time.

"Birdy?" JJ repeats.

"Fucking Birdy!" I spit.

"Jeremy Bird? The fat old guy at the tattooist?" Daniel asks.

I nod. "Apparently, they've been 'fucking' for two years! Two fucking years, Dan!"

"Ray?" Dan gasps at her. "Is this true?" When she doesn't reply and glances away, he asks again, "I fucking asked you a question, Ray! Is. This. Fucking. True?" Daniel's the least one likely to lose his shit. He's the calmer, more reasonable one out of all of us, but Birdy… I should have started with that sick fuck.

She nods once at him, staring back at me with a murderous glare, and that's it. We all just end up screaming and shouting about whether to kill the son of a bitch or torture the motherfucker first. It should have been funny. We are all highly trained, patient to a fault in the line of battle, unfazeable, unshakeable, calm as fuck, but fuck, if the kids don't throw all those years of training out the door, lighting it on fire as they go, leaving us in a burning shitstorm of chaos.

"Stop! Fucking stop, all of you! You're gonna leave Jer alone, and I will too. He's done nothing wrong. He helped me. It was like therapy or something. After everything that went on with Bas, he was there for me. He was my friend!"

"Fuck, Ray, he's old enough to be your dad!" Steven gestures between us all, and I sag back into the chair, scrubbing a hand down my face.

"He's not that fucking old!" she barks. "Look, just leave him alone, okay, and I won't go back. I won't get in touch. I'll just walk away. Just promise me you'll leave him alone?"

"You'll go to the clinic tomorrow?" I ask.

"Clinic?" JJ questions.

"Booked her in, full workup, the morning-after pill, contraceptive implant, the works!" I state.

"Sounds sensible," Daniel adds.

"Fucking fine, I will go do that bullshit, but fucking me in the arse isn't gonna get me pregnant. Just saying, but we were always careful!"

"Just stop fucking talking, Ray. I can't focus on all that again. Just leave it. Be ready for 9 a.m."

I stand up from the chair and stalk out of the room to my bedroom, slamming the door behind me. Fucking kids will be the death of me, well, that particular one, that's for sure. She gets under my skin far worse than the boys, and the worst thing is, honestly, she fucking could be mine, the way she looks and her attitude.

She's enough like me to make me almost certain she's mine. Whether someone's screwing with me for all the shit things I've done, I'm not sure. If she turned up on my doorstep now and said I'm your daughter, Cade, I wouldn't question it, and there'd be no reason for a DNA test which just freaks me the fuck out if I think about it too much. The apple definitely won't have fallen far from the tree.

Jer

Then...

I roll onto my side groaning, reaching a hand up towards her. "Ray." I gasp.

Cade storms out of the room as she's pulling on her jeans, and slipping her boots back on. "Pa, wait! Pa! Fuck!" She runs out the door after him and never looks back.

Liam's stood in the doorway. "Shit, what the fuck, Birdy?" He runs over to me, grabbing my hand to help me up. I slump over the table, breathing heavily.

"Fuck." I gasp. "I need to go after her." I stagger forward, still woozy and disoriented. Cade punches like a fucking freight train. I'm gasping for breath. I think my nose is broken.

"No!" Liam spits. " You need to sort yourself out, Birdy. For fuck's sake, put your dick away and clean yourself up. You're going nowhere near that girl!" he spits the last word at me. "What the fuck were you thinking?"

"I love her!" I breathe out. "I fucking love her, Liam!" He closes his eyes and shakes his head as he closes the door.

I lean on the table and try to make sense of what has just happened. I blink as tears roll down my face. I'm not sure if I'm crying at the pain in my face or the pain in my chest, but both hurt, and I'm not sure what I'm going to do.

Pulling on my jeans, I tuck myself away and head into the bathroom, sliding my jeans back down and sinking onto the toilet. I slide the condom off, wrap it up, and throw it in the bin, resting my elbows on my knees with my head in my hands.

I try to breathe and process what the fuck I will do without her. I grab my phone but can't quite bring myself to message her. Standing up and tucking myself away again, I step in front of the mirror.

"Fuck." Shit, I look like a mess. My nose is definitely broken. I can't breathe through it. It's spread across my face at an unnatural angle, there's blood coating my mouth, lips and chin, dripping onto my shirt, there's a small cut in my eyebrow above my left eye, and it's bleeding over my swollen and blackening eye, my left cheek is swollen too, and I hope my cheekbone isn't fractured, but with the intensity of the punches Cade dealt, I'm lucky I'm not dead.

I think he could have killed me. Hanging my head and closing my eyes, more tears stream down my face. Fuck, how can you fall in love so deeply with someone and then have them ripped away? I need to speak to her, but I can't do it like this. I grab some tissue, wet it under the tap and try to clean myself up best I can.

Grabbing my nose, I try to reposition it, but tears stream from my eyes, making it difficult to see. I'm in agony, fuck. I wipe my face again as best I can and head out the door.

Walking into the reception area, Liam's standing at the counter. "Hey, Liam, can you take me to the hospital? I think I need to have something done with my nose." I sound all nasally. There's definitely something out of alignment.

"Fuck, Birdy, you look like shit. Come on!" Locking up, we head out to Liam's car. "You wanna talk about it?"

"Fuck, man, what do I say?" I shrug at him.

"Dude, how long has it been going on?"

Muttering under my breath, I say, "Two years."

"Fucking hell, Birdy, two years? All that time? What the fuck? She's a kid!"

"Trust me, man, she's anything but a kid. You've no idea!"

"Mate, she's been coming in since she was what, five or six? Jesus, you used to give her lollipops if she was a good girl. That's fucking sick, man, seriously. What the fuck were you playing at? Is this some weird fucked up pedo shit, cos trust me, man, if it is, we're done. I'm fucking serious. I'm not having my name and my business associated with that shit, I'm telling you now!"

Pinching at the bridge of my nose, "Shit, motherfucker." My eyes stream again. "Trust me, mate, it's nothing like that. We just became friends when I started the tats, and when we were nearly finished, I asked her out. She turned me down but said she just wanted to fuck. Come on, man, you've seen her. She's a total fucking smoke show, and she's funny and smart, and… fuck. I fell for her, okay? I'm fucked, and I'm totally in love with her. I wanna marry her. I wanna spend the rest of my life with her. She just needs time to see it."

"Jesus, mate, have you ever been on a date, fucked her anywhere other than that back room? Done anything an actual fucking couple would do? Seriously, man. She didn't even look at you when she left. You were bleeding, Cade fucking pummelled you, and she strode out of there and never looked back."

"She loves me too, Liam. I know it, she just doesn't know how to show it yet, but she's coming around. She let me hold her hips today. I mean, she's finally starting to let us get closer."

"What the fuck do you mean she let you hold her hips?"

"She doesn't like to be touched, kissed or anything, she just fucks, and then I add more detail to her tats, but she's letting me get closer. She's letting me in. She's falling for me, too. I can feel it!"

Shaking his head and rubbing his hand down his face, he says, "Jeremy, we're friends and have been for years. You've been fucking this kid for two years, and you've never even kissed her. You've barely touched her. That's fucked up. Can you not see that? I don't wanna sound like a cunt, man, but she doesn't love you. You're a fuck at best, and you need to stay the hell away from her, or Cade won't hold back next time."

We don't talk the rest of the way, and as we pull up at the hospital, I jump out of the car. "I'll get myself back. Thanks, Liam."

"Sure, man. Just leave her be, okay?"

Slamming the door, I walk into A&E.

After registering and taking a seat to join the hour-long wait, I grab my phone.

Jer: Ray, can you call me, please? I need to know you're okay.
Read 17.36

Missed call Jer

Jer: Ray, please let me know you're okay!
Read 18.16

Missed call Jer

Jer: Ray, I'm at the hospital. I need you to know I'm sorry, and I love you, and we can work this out, okay? Just call me. X
Read 20.55

Missed call Jer

Jer: Babe, please. They're keeping me in. I've had to have my nose reset. We love each other. You just need to admit it to yourself, and then we can be together. You can move in with me. Just call me. xx
Read 22.28

Missed call Jer

Jer: Babe, please just answer me. I can see you're reading these messages. X

Read 23.48

Missed call Jer
Missed call Jer

Jer: Just fucking answer me. I'm going mental here. I can come get you in the morning. I will get your stuff, just move in with me. xxx
Read 00.24

Missed call Jer
Missed call Jer

Jer: If you ever loved me, just call.
Read 01.05

Jer: You never loved me, did you?
Read 02.25

Jer: Did you even give a shit about me?
Read 03.36

Missed call Jer
Missed call Jer

Jer: Fuck you, Ray! Call me now. I'm not fucking kidding.
Read 03.48

Jer: You fucking bitch, Ray! I love you, and you don't give a flying fuck. We're done. Over. I don't give a shit. I fucking hate you. CALL ME NOW!
Read 03.52

Missed call Jer

Jer: Babe, please. I didn't mean it. I love you. I'm sorry. Please just call me. I'm dying here.

Voicemail

Jer: Ray, please!

Voicemail
Voicemail

Jer: Have you blocked me? Seriously? Ray?

All the messages except the last two were green and had delivery reports. The last two were blue, with no reports at all. Every call had rung till it went to voicemail. The last three just went straight to voicemail. I can't believe she would just block me, no explanation, no nothing, not even a "hope you're okay."
Shit, she really doesn't give a shit. I was just a fuck to her. How the fuck could she do this to me? For two years of my life, I was planning a future with her. I was picturing marriage, kids, and growing old together. I thought she just needed time, and then she'd come around. I thought she would realise I'm the love of her life like she's mine, and now I just feel foolish, empty and… alone.

Ray

Then...

"Get your snarky arse down here now. We're leaving in two fucking minutes!" Pa Cade yells up the stairs.

Fuck, he's like a dog with a fucking bone. I stayed in my room all night, and at around four this morning, I finally blocked Jer. He had been texting and calling non-stop. I'd read everything, which seemed to piss him off even more as I never replied. Liam ended up taking him to the hospital. I never wanted to hurt him, but in fairness, I told him straight what we were, and he's a grown-arse man, for fuck's sake. But also, this is my pa. I won't go against him. I know he will bury Jer if I push, and while I enjoy fucking Jer, it was nothing more than that. I don't get excited about seeing him. I don't get butterflies or any other girly shit I hear about in sappy romance. He submitted to me, did what I wanted, was reasonably good at what he did and made me come when I needed a release.

I will miss what we had. It worked for me, it really did, but my family is everything. If Pa Cade asks me to chop my own arm off, I will only ask which one. I would for any of them. Fuck my life. Where am I gonna get what I had with Jer now?

"I'm fucking coming. I swear to fucking Hades." I shake my head as I grab my bag. "Motherfucker!"

"I can fucking hear you, ya know?"

"I know! That's the fucking point, arsehole. I wasn't trying to be quiet!"

"Thirty fucking seconds, dickhead!"

"Wanker!" I spit back.

Pa Cade and I are on the same side of the same coin. To literally coin a phrase, we're too similar, and when we clash, which isn't often, everyone else makes themselves scarce. It normally goes on until we're both exhausted and can't remember why we are fighting in the first place.

I asked my dad if Pa Cade was my real dad on more than one occasion. I look the most like him, and our attitudes stink, but Dad thought it was funny. Apparently, the others thought the same. He thought I was his, a punishment for the kind of life he'd led. They all normally fucked off well out of the way when we started. Well, that's what normally happened. That's what I thought until I reached the bottom step. They're all there.

"Fuck's sake!" I mutter. I know I'm in trouble if they are all on Pa Cade's side. I raise my hands in defence, attitude dropped. I can win against one or maybe even two of them, but all five of them united, even though Pa Bernie isn't here with the four of them shoulder to shoulder, he might as well have been. I'm right royally fucking in the wrong, and I know it.

"I'm sorry, okay? It wasn't personal... I just... he was just... look, fuck it. I don't regret it, but I understand. I've blocked him, and I will find a new tattooist, okay? Come on, let's head out, or we will be late!"

Pa Cade scrubs a hand down his face as he sighs and walks over to me, scooping me into his arms. "I'm sorry too, Squirt! I fucking love you, you know that, don't you?"

Leaning up and kissing him on the cheek, I say, "Love you too, Pa!" I rest my head on his chest. I can feel him smile against my hair.

"Come on!"

I raise my head to look at him, giving him my best puss in boots eyes. "Can we go for ice cream after? Please, Pa?" I hear the sniggers from the others and boot steps as they retreat. They know I've turned the tables now.

"What are you, fucking twelve? Fuck's sake, Squirt! Fine, come on!"

Grinning, I follow him out the door. After the appointment, which was shit, we went for ice cream. I order us the unicorn sundae. It's the most obnoxious sundae they have. It comes with rainbow ice cream, sprinkles, squirty cream, a flake, a cherry on top and candy floss.

"So you wanna talk about it?
"Nope!"
"You sure, Pa?
"Yup!"
"That's it done then!"

"Yup."
"Okay!"
"Okay."
"Fine."
"Yep, fine!"
"Good talk!"
"Twat!"

And that was it sorted. Fucking men bury their heads in the sand and pretend they haven't just seen a guy nearly old enough to be their daughter's dad railing said daughter up the arse over a tattoo table while she rubs one out, then beat him half to death while he still has his dick hanging out, condom on, full of come, all while said guy's co-worker stands and watches. Fun times!

"Pa."
"Nope!"
"You don't know what I was gonna say."
"Still nope!"
"Pa."
"What, Ray?"
"While we're out, can we go to the gun club?"

"Fuck." He scrubs a hand down his face, clearly still uncomfortable about what he's seen and thinking I'm gonna bring it back up. Nope, definitely not. "Sure, Squirt, let's go, but I've got shit to do!"

I burst out laughing at that. They only ever did shit at the Adventure Centre, I mean, I'm sure they have relationships, but they never introduced us to anyone that I remember. He was just trying to avoid an awkward time with me, but tough tits, suck it up, buttercup. You're spending the day with me now, and I'm making the most of every damned second.

Jer

Then...

I must have fallen asleep at about 5 a.m.

They discharged me at 10 a.m. I grab a taxi and go straight to Ray's house. I don't give a shit. I'm gonna get my girl.

Pulling up at the house, I ask the taxi to wait. As I get out of the taxi, the front door swings open, and three guys walk onto the porch. They must be her dads. I don't know much about them, but they are intimidating as they stand there, their arms crossed across their chests shoulder to shoulder, T-shirts straining across their biceps. They're clearly all still in shape; me, not so much. They are all around my height, one a little taller. I suddenly don't feel so confident, but I push my shoulders back and take a few steps forward. "I'm here to get Ray."

One of them look's like Ray, the other two not so much, but then Ray looks like Cade the most, so fuck knows who's her actual dad.

One with brown hair steps forward. "To get Ray? You really think she's going anywhere with you? Are you shitting me right now?"

"Look, I don't want any trouble. We love each other. She's gonna move in with me. I'm here to get her stuff," I speak with conviction, and I keep my eyes on all three of them.

The taller one, the one with a dark shaved head and dark stubble, steps forward, barking a laugh at me and shaking his head. "Don't kid yourself, fucker! She doesn't give a shit about you. You were a fuck, no more. She wants nothing more to do with you. You're a fucking pervert. You stay away from our daughter, or what my brother did to you will pale in comparison to what the rest of us will do!"

I raise my hands in submission. "Look, I don't want any trouble. I just want my girlfriend, okay?"

The other steps past the other two, down the steps, now a few feet away from me. I swallow hard, taking a deep breath.

"Please, just let me talk to her."

He steps forward again, so he's right in front of me, his voice low and growly. "I want you to listen real close, Birdy. I'm gonna say this once, and then you're gonna turn around and fuck right off! You were nothing, you are nothing, you will never be anything. She blocked you because you were a fuck, and that's all. She's fucking shopping with Cade, for fuck's sake. She hasn't even bothered to check you're okay, and she blocked you because you're a whiny, weak, fucking excuse for a man who took advantage of a very young girl. I suggest you leave or even the police won't find your body! Do. I. Make. Myself. Clear?"

The other two step forward, and I involuntarily step back two steps.

"If you think I took advantage, you don't know her at all!" I say, trying to keep my voice even, but I waver as I swallow. I'm not sure I'm gonna make it out of here without an ambulance.

The blonde one spits at me, "If you think Ray has any feelings for you, clearly you're the one who doesn't know her. I suggest you leave while you can still walk and don't require a fucking feeding tube!"

I take another step back and then another as I bump into the door of the taxi, eyeing them all. I take a deep breath and am just about to speak when the taller one steps forward.

"I would think very hard before I said anything else if I were you, because the next words to come out of your mouth will be your fucking last!"

I fumble behind me for the door handle and swing the door open, sliding into the back of the taxi without taking my eyes off any of them. "Drive!" I yell to the taxi driver, who pulls off and speeds down the driveway.

My breathing is heavy, and I'm struggling to focus on the fact that I'm lucky to be alive. They have this unhinged look about them, and it wasn't how they said the words, although that was intimidating enough, the conviction of what they said made me believe they were capable of far worse things than I could think of.

I need to stay away now, but I don't know if I can. I will just give her some space. She will come back. I have to hope she will, anyway. I don't know if I can live without her, but pushing her dads is a sure-fire way to find out if I will live at all.

Scar

The plane comes to a halt on the tarmac. The pilot turns off the seatbelt sign. This is it; we've made it. We've waited six weeks to finally get here, and she's had to go six weeks without him, six long weeks alone. I tried to stop her from shutting me out, but she needed space. Six weeks to try and decide what the fuck she was doing with her life.

Her whole life has been the family business, the Adventure Centre and whatever else comes under that umbrella. I know some of what they do, and I know what I don't know, I'm probably better off not knowing. Ray never lies to me—ever! But there are things she can't tell me, and that makes me nervous. I know they have companies here, and she could slide in and help run things. Even though she never went to uni, she's so intelligent. With the knack she has with people and her knowledge from the businesses she helps her dads run, she's seriously a force to be reckoned with.

Where does that leave me, though, if she finds her place here? What do I do then? I'm not sure I can live without her. I'm the first to admit I love her and probably have an unnatural, obsessive bond with her. Our relationship was forged in the fires of hell, and she's the reason it didn't burn me alive. She's the reason I'm here, alive and thriving. Will things still be the same if she's meant to be here and I go home alone? Will I leave my heart here forever, forever broken? I don't think she still has any clue what she wants, and I'm terrified.

I know she cut all contact with Jer a good ten months before her dad died, and I know he'd been there for her while I was at uni the last few years. I know she'd slipped and gone to see him after the funeral, and it just dredged up all that guilt again, and she'd ran.

But the time without that release that he gave her had been strained, to say the least, and after her dad passing and her ending up back there after ten months, just seeing him again, she knew it had to be left in the past. He wasn't Mr Right. He was only ever Mr Right Then And There.

I tried to help her through it all, tried to make things make sense so she could process things and let her have what she needed. She only felt a mild tinge of guilt for not feeling anything at all for Jer. Two years together fucking, and she walked away like nothing had ever happened between them. But that was Ray all over. If she said there were no feelings involved, she wouldn't get feelings. She's that black and white. She never loved him, never even kissed him.

She told me a lot of stuff that went down with them, and it was honestly fucked up. Not for Ray. It gave her exactly what she wanted and needed, but to never get close to someone… I hope she finds that one day. That epic love where you can't breathe without the other one. Ray's my epic love. Not like that, well, not anymore. She once was, but now it's more, so much more. It's like she crawled inside me, burrowed her way in and set up in my soul. Our love is more than epic. There's no single word to ever describe it.

We sit chatting while we wait for most people to leave. We only have hand luggage as we are just gonna buy what we need here.

As we leave the plane and reach the tarmac, Ray's dragging her small suitcase, and I have on my backpack. I jump on her back, and in the most obnoxious, overly posh British accent, I point over her shoulder and shout, "To the Winnebago, peasant!" She drops me on my arse. "Motherfucking cockwomble!" I grumble at her picking myself up and rubbing my arse cheek.

"Oi, knobhead, stop dicking about and get this vacay started. I swear to Hades himself, I will smack your arse if you don't get a move on!" she bellows at me

I throw my arm around her shoulder, leaning into her ear. "I will swear to whoever the fuck you want me to if it means I will get a spanking!" Turning to look at her, I waggle my eyebrows, kiss her cheek, and grin. I know we have a weird relationship. Not many people get it, but she's everything to me.

She shakes her head, breathing out a laugh. "You'll be the death of me, Scar. I can see it now. And they think I'm the fucking crazy one!" I actually have to agree that most people think she's batshit crazy, think she's bipolar or schizophrenic, maybe a sociopath, or at least a psychopath. Truth is, she's the sanest person I know. All her multiple personalities have that in common.

Ray

After we got through the airport and collected the RV—motorhome, Winnefuckingbago, whatever the hell she called it, I'm going with van—we were on the road.

We stopped at Walmart and stocked up with the essentials like tequila, snacks, clothes, tequila, shoes, underwear, tequila… You name it, we bought it.

Scar looks fucking phenomenal with her cute sun dresses and sandals. She looks like a sexy teacher.

Scar's five foot nine, long natural blonde hair the colour of endless summer days running through corn fields, the bluest eyes like the sea in some tropical country. She's curvy in all the right places. She has a body to die for and oozes sex appeal. She's always the most effortlessly beautiful woman in any room. She has naturally plump pink lips with perfectly straight white teeth and a smile that could make the pope blush and possibly murder his own congregation. Celibacy would be right out the window.

She's just over a year older than me, and we can pass for sisters easily.

Then there's me, with my long sleeve T-shirts in different variations of greys and blacks. Sometimes they have skulls on them, sometimes a funny slogan or swear word, jeans, sometimes ripped, sometimes not, and combat boots. We're really an odd pairing.

Stopping at Dicks Sporting Goods for some camping shit, we were onto our first destination. We aren't supposed to be arriving for another two days. Well, that's what we told Pa Bernie when they left. They left a couple of days after the funeral and headed home to wait for us to join them.

He is working today at one of his gun shows. He runs our security firm over here as well as being a partner in the Adventure Centre back home, but he also buys and sells guns, knives and general bad-arse shit and paraphernalia at gun shows, so we are heading over there to surprise the shit out of him.

We pull up into the parking lot of the show. I grab a wad of cash from our stash and stuff it in my bra, heading out of the van and locking it up.

Scar looks at me, tutting. "Seriously? No handbag? Just stuffing cash in your bra? You could make more of an effort to look a bit… feminine. It wouldn't kill you. You look like if GI Jane and Bear Grylls had a fucking kid!"

I scrunch up my face, looking deep into her eyes. "You're saying that like it's supposed to be a bad thing? Is that not actually an accurate depiction of me in general?" I waft my arms wildly in a gesture of my whole self. I shrug, then burst out laughing.

"Knob off, dick face," she retorts, sending us both into fits of laughter again. I mean, if you don't insult each other on the daily, are you even really sisters at all? I've known this girl for nearly nine years, and she's still trying to get me in a fucking dress. It ain't happening, sweetheart, not on my watch. This bitch will be dead before that happens. Mark my words.

I spot Pa B's stand up ahead and wait for an opening.

Scar rolls her eyes at me. "You're still pulling this shit on him? You're gonna put his fucking back out one of these days!"

I turn and look at her. "It's our thing." Shrugging, I take off running full pelt, screaming, "Incoming!" at the top of my lungs.

His face drops, his eyes darting around frantically, searching every face in the crowd till he meets mine. As he meets my stare, his grin is enough to light up the universe. I jump up onto the table he's using and leap at him from the top, throwing my legs and arms around him and throwing him off balance.

Managing to steady himself by taking a few steps back with me still clinging on for dear life, he leans his face back, looking straight into my eyes. "Fuck's sake, Squirt. One of these days, you're gonna take us both out!"

Laughing, he gives me the biggest squeeze. I peel my legs from around him, dropping them to the floor.

"Nah, old man! You'll always catch me, you promised me when I was five that you would always catch me when I fall, and you've never not caught me since."

Laughing again, he smirks and drops my feet the last couple of inches to the floor. I'm not small by any means, but Pa B is well over six feet, built like a brick shit house. He's solid muscle, and for a guy who's in his fifties, he could still pass for late thirties, at least.

He was with the Navy SEALs when he met my dad, who was in the SAS. They were in their twenties, did a joint special op with their teams, and became like brothers. There's my dad, Pa John (JJ) and Pa Steven who were all SAS. Pa Bernie and Pa Cade, who were Navy SEALs with Pa Sebastian, who died just before I was born. I never met him. They became inseparable.

They all retired in their mid-thirties when Mum and Dad decided to have us. Dad talked them into moving to the UK to start up a business together before we arrived, which they did. Growing up, it was like having five dads.

We are still running the business, which has thrived and grown into something amazing, leaving us all really comfortable. With Bernie and Cade being from the US, we also have businesses here that we all travel back and forth to run. We spent a lot of our teen years at "summer camp" over here, and when Pa Bernie and the family finally moved back to the States, they all put more into our legal ventures and not so legal ventures over here. Pa Bernie now classes himself as a silent partner in the Adventure Centre, and now Dad is gone, I am too. We're all equal in all the businesses.

My pas want me to live my own life now as my whole life has been the business like theirs has, but with Dad not there, my heart is just not in it anymore.

When my mum died, Pa Bernie promised to always catch me when I fell, and I didn't believe him, so he said I had to test him, and test him I did. Only I've never stopped, although as I got older, he would make me scream, "Incoming!" to give him the heads up.

I peel myself off him, and Scarlett gives a small wave from the other side of the table.

"Hey, Uncle Bernie."

"Hey, princess."

"Hey! How come she always gets princess, and I get pissing Squirt? I'm an inch fucking taller than her too! Fuck's sake!"

Both shake their heads at me while I'm grinning like a Cheshire cat.

Pointing at me and shaking his head, he says, "Firstly, princess, you are definitely not! You're a fucking animal, Squirt, always have been. And secondly, Scar is a princess, and you damn well know it!"

It's my turn to shake my head, pouting as Scar looks at me and blobs her tongue out.

"Fucking shitheads!"

They both burst out laughing.

Pa Bernie rounds the table to give her a hug, then ruffles up the top of my head with his knuckles messing my hair up where it was scraped into a high ponytail.

"Nice hair, Squirt. You could pass for sisters even more so now."

"She made me colour it for the trip. It's okay, I suppose." I shrug my shoulders. Scar had taken me to her hairdressers before we left. Naturally, I was a dirty blonde, and she had made me have highlights, so my colour was nearer to her natural colour. I wasn't totally mad at it. "Anyway, did you manage to get me my toys?" I rush out excitedly, my hands held out in front of me, clasping and unclasping my hands together in a grabbing motion like a kid at Christmas, eyes all sparkling with mischief.

Barking out a laugh, Pa B grabs me and pulls me in for another hug. "I fucking missed you, Squirt, you raging psycho!" I beam up at him with a massive smile on my face.

"I saw you a few weeks ago. Is that a yes? Say it's a yes. It's definitely a yeah, right?" I bounce on the balls of my feet.

"It's a hell fucking yes. Now piss off and let me get some work done. Bran is around here somewhere. Go find him and terrorise him for a few hours, then you can come back and help me pack up. You gonna come stay with us for a bit?"

"Yeah, definitely. Can't wait to see everyone again. I've missed you guys, too."

"Don't cause any trouble, okay? I've got everything you asked for, so I'll catch ya later."

We head away from the stall, and I grin at Scar.

"Fuck me, Ray. What are you planning?"

"Nothing! Just can't wait to see what else is here. Let's go get Mumma some more toys!" Then, waggling my eyebrows at her as she shakes her head, grinning, I throw my arm around her. "Let's go buy shit I don't need but desperately want!"

We wander around, and I know Scar isn't interested in this shit, but she oohs and ahs at everything. I'm almost coming in my pants while she feigns interest. She spends more time biting down on her lip checking guys out, she thinks I don't notice, but I notice everything.

Arriving back near the stall, I give my bags to Scar as I see my brother, Bran. He's a younger version of Pa Bernie. They work together in the security/firearms business, with a similar build, only a couple of inches shorter at six feet. He, too, has dirty blonde hair and his mum's grey-blue eyes. He's more tanned than the others and covered in tattoos on both sleeves, chest and full back.

He's drop-dead gorgeous, apparently, if you like that kind of thing, but he's my brother, so he's totally gross. He's Pa Bernie's eldest. He's the same age as me. There's a couple of months between us, we're more like twins than me and my actual brother, even though technically we aren't related at all, but we're really close. I sneak up behind him and lick along the back of his neck, then run off as he spins on his heels, hearing me laugh as I run away.

"Ah, shit's going down!" he yells as he bolts after me. We spent time together while he was over for Dad's funeral, but I haven't seen him properly in a little while. We FaceTime all the time, and even though we saw each other a few weeks ago for the funeral, it wasn't the same. I mean, fuck, you can't lick someone on FaceTime or at a funeral. Apparently, it's frowned upon!

He really has filled out over the last few years. I squeal as he gives chase.

"Fuck's sake, you two. Grow up. This shit ain't gonna pack itself!"

"I can help, Uncle Bernie. Where do you want me?"

"Thanks, Scar. Look at them twats though running round like bloody idiots!" Running a hand down his face and shaking his head at our antics, he looks at Scar and all the bags. "Fuck's sake, what's she bought now? She's only been here five bloody minutes, and I've already aged five pissing years!"

I can hear Scar laughing as I pause to see what they're saying. Distracted by my curiosity, I'm thrown to the floor with a thud. The wind is knocked out of me, and Bran pins my shoulders down, licking up my whole face. "Fucking minger!" I snarl at him.

"Ha! Got ya back, knobhead. Missed ya twat face."

Laughing and wriggling trying to get out from under him without really trying, I say, "Missed you too, twat waffle." We both start rolling around and punching each other playfully in the ribs.

"Will you two pack it the fuck in and get up? You're showing me up. I don't want people thinking my family are hooligans that can't fight for shit!"

"That's our cue to cut the crap for a minute." I get up and reach down, pulling Bran to his feet. We hug each other, Bran tosses his arm around my shoulders, and we wander back to the stall.

After packing up and showing off my crossbow and rainbow-bladed throwing knife set, among other goodies, including two different sets of knuckle dusters, one set looks like rings with a big gem on the middle one, with a skull on one of the smaller ones, we pack up and go back to the van, heading to Pa B's house to surprise the rest of the family.

Arriving at Pa B's, it's just as amazing as the pictures. They moved here after he lost his mum not that long ago, so I've not seen this place in person, but it's gorgeous.

As we walk into the massive open-plan area, there's a clatter from the kitchen and an almighty shrill scream. We all freeze as Ma comes careering out of the kitchen, through the living room space, almost knocking Scar and me off our feet.

She crashes into us, hugging us both as hard as she can and jumping up and down, squealing.

"You're early... You made it ... You're here ... I can't believe it ... I've missed you both so much!" She peppers us with kisses in between comments, causing us both to giggle like teenagers as we hug her back.

"Oh hey, Bernie, love of my life, father of my gorgeous children, did you have a good day at the show? Why yes, dear, thanks for fucking asking. I had a fab day. Oh, I missed you so much too, blah, blah, fucking blah!" Bernie grumbles as he walks through the kitchen.

We all look between ourselves and burst out laughing, chasing after Pa Bernie and peppering him with kisses all over his face, asking about his fabulous day.

"Argh, get off me, the lot of you. Bloody heathens you are, all of you! Ray, this is your fault. You're a bad influence on this whole family; they don't normally act like twats!"

"Bernie!" Ma gasps. "Language. I swear, I will wash your potty mouth out one of these days." As tough as Bernie is, we all knew she would.

After our Bernie dogpile comes to an end, we make dinner and gather around the outdoor dining area. My other brother, Dane, has joined us. He's the quieter one in the family, but that isn't really hard considering the rest of us. Dane is like a boy version of me. Our personalities are so similar. He's funnier, whereas Bran is more serious. Sometimes it's like we're the same person. With Dane and me, the fun only escalates. He's ever so slightly taller than me, and at twenty-one, still has a year left at school. He's studying some computer shit I don't fully understand. He's a fucking genius when it comes to stuff like that.

He's sitting with Scar while the rest of us dick around, jibing at each other and generally causing Mayhem.

"God, how long are you two staying? You're so loud, Ray. Dad, tell her!"

"Sorry, not sorry, Daney boy." I mock, "I've not seen you all properly in forever, I've got shit to make up for, and you know you love me, really!" I blow him a kiss. It's only been weeks since the funeral, and before that, it was a few months at most. He eye rolls at me, the slightest twitch from the corner of his mouth as I pull faces at him across the table. It's all for show with us, the banter, the jibing, the fighting. We love each other more than life itself, we would do anything for each other, but the world didn't need to know that.

"Fine, but my girlfriend's coming over tomorrow, and I swear down, if you embarrass me, I will garrotte you in your sleep."

Dane is the youngest, so we were all protective of him, and also quite horrible at times as we love to wind him up. I love him and would do anything for him but not embarrass him. I don't think I'm capable of such a thing!

Laughing at him, I say, "Girlfriend, huh? So what's it worth to you for me not to embarrass you? It's a big sister's right, after all! Hmm… Let me think… I might tell her about that one time with the pigeon… or what about that time in the tree… Or how about that thing you did when you were five at Christmas time!"

Dane has his head in his hands, elbows on the table, shaking his head. "Hades, kill me now. Make it quick, I beg. I'll never ask for anything again!" Clasping his hands together and praying to the Underworld.

"You do realise if Hades was actually watching and decided to do as you begged, he would only send Reaper!" Bran winks as he reminds him.

Looking over towards where I was, then frowning when I'm not there, I peek my head over his shoulder, lick his face and say, "Request denied, motherfucker!" Then, I run.

Dane freezes for a split second as if he forgot what it was like for us all to be together, then bolts after me, laughing.

I run and cannonball right into the middle of the pool, fully clothed, boots and all. Dane's right behind me, whooping as he hits the water. We both come up laughing as I jump on him and shove his head back under. God, I missed my brother so much; we were thick as thieves growing up, and we still are.

"What is with all the face licking? I still don't get it after all these years. You're all gross, the lot of you," Scar says.

Then there's a scream as Bran runs around the table, licks her face, then runs towards the pool. "Cannonball!"

After nearly a week at Pa and Ma's, they've tried to convince me to stay. I promise I will check out the local areas. I want to see what jobs are around for someone like me. I can slide into the family business with the others, no problem. We have been actively involved growing up, so it won't be an issue. I just want to see if there's something I can have, something that could be just mine. We've worked together for so long. Maybe a change would be as good as a rest.

We head out on our way. The plan is to head over to the local coastal town of Castle Cove, about twenty miles from where Pa lives in Heighton, to check out the area. I'd promised all my pas I would really take the idea seriously of seeing if I could find somewhere out here where I want to start over. I know I'm only half-heartedly promising as I can't leave my pas. I know it would be great to be nearer my brothers, but I don't think I can leave home. I'm missing them already.

Fuck knows what I want, though. The thought both thrills and terrifies me all at the same time. After checking out the town and the beach, which is quiet and small, there are a couple of shops, a few places to eat, and a club, but it isn't a touristy place. There's a small bistro-type restaurant and a bakery, so it's quite chilled. We both like it and would probably visit again, but I can't see myself staying somewhere like this permanently. It's just too quiet for me. I would stand out like a sore thumb, and there's nothing for me to do other than be a waitress or bartender or possibly a bouncer at best, and for me, that isn't gonna cut it.

We decide to head up the coast a bit to set up camp. Along the coastal road about fifteen miles from Castle Cove, there's what's almost like a truck stop with a diner at one end of the massive parking lot and a bar at the other. Perfect.

We pull in, park up along the back between the diner and bar, and grab a shower. We head to the diner to grab some food before planning on heading to the bar later to get semi-wasted.

A couple of cars are outside the diner as we walk across the parking lot and head inside. The diner has a 1950s vibe. The door opens into the centre with two red and white booths in the window on each side, seating around four people each. The diner's clean but a little tired if you look closely. There are tall stools seated along the bar.

The waitress, who looks around our age, possibly a couple of years younger at most, shouts to take a seat wherever we like and she will be with us shortly. Grabbing a booth near the window in the corner, we grab the wipe-clean, dog-eared menus and decide what to have. A few minutes later, the waitress comes over, all bubbly and personable.

"Hey guys, I'm Demi. I'll be your waitress for today. Do you know what you'd like to order, or do you need a minute?"

"Nah, we're good. I know what I want," Scar says as Demi gasps and looks up from her pad, staring backwards and forwards between us as we are on opposite sides of the booth.

Cocking a brow at her, I ask, "You good?"

"Yeah, sorry, I love your accents! It was the accents that threw me. I'm not used to it around here. Are you guys... British? Such a dreamy accent. So very... *Game of Thrones*."

We laugh at the fact that we are from Northern England, so we tend to have that 'northern twang' rather than the southern, east-end accent that many people associate with England. We place our orders, and Demi goes to the hatch and then comes back over to us. We are the only people left here now.

"Erm, I'm going on break now, so George the cook will bring your food out when it's ready." She hovers for a sec, and I look at Scar, then back at Demi.

"Do you wanna hang out here? You could give us some info on the area if you don't have anywhere you need to be," Scar says to her.

She looks down at her shoes, then over to me through her long dark lashes, not quite lifting her head, shifting nervously and fidgeting her fingers in her apron. "You sure you don't mind? ... I would really like that."

"Sure," I say, shifting over a bit and tapping the seat beside me so she knows she's welcome. She grabs a coffee from the counter and slides in at my side. I give her one of my winning smiles, and she relaxes a little.

We chat while we wait for our food to come, and then when it does, we both share with Demi. Even though she says she doesn't want anything, she still has a few fries, onion rings and another cup of coffee.

Her thirty-minute break turns into an hour, but George, the cook and owner, an older gentleman, maybe mid to late sixties with dark, rich, chocolate skin and a wide nose across his face, even joins us for a coffee of his own before heading back to the kitchen.

George tells Demi she can finish up if she likes, as there's no one around. He's gonna close up early. We invite Demi over to the bar, but she says her boyfriend's gonna pick her up. We decide to wait with her till he gets here, and we continue chatting outside in the parking lot.

Demi has texted him to say she's finishing early, but she hasn't got a reply. She calls a couple of times, but nothing. "You guys can go to the bar. I will be fine. He should be here soon, anyway. It's now nearly the normal time he should come get me."

"Nah, we're not leaving you on—"

I was cut off by her phone ringing.

"It's him," she mouths. "Hey, how long will you be…? What do you mean you're not coming… seriously…? Are you kidding me right now…? Ben, what the hell! …Argh!"

Next thing, she's in tears. I don't know what has gone on, but she doesn't sound happy.

Scar sweeps her up into her arms, rubbing her back. "Hey, you okay?"

Through snot and sniffles, she pulls back, wiping her face, smudging her mascara and glancing at us both. "Yeah, sorry, it's fine, he's… he's not coming. I'm just gonna call a cab. You guys go. I'm good."

"Fuck that. You're coming with us!" I bark out at her. I grab her hand and drag her across the parking lot to the van. Scar is right behind her, almost pushing her along. I'm sure if there were anyone around, it would look like we're kidnapping her.

Once we get to the van, Scar and Demi sit at the table, and I grab the tequila and pour us all a massive shot. Technically it's more like four, but I think Demi needs it. She explains that Ben had told her he had packed his bags while she was at work and up and left with the girl he'd been fucking for the past six months. They are moving out of state.

"Shit! That's fucked up," Scar says as she sips at her tequila.

"You're telling me… we were saving up to get engaged… we had been together three years. What the hell am I supposed to do now…? And why is she grinning like that?"

Scar glances at me and back at Demi. "Ah, shit, this is gonna get messy." Scar's already shaking her head.

I stand up, grab Demi and drag her towards the bathroom. "You're a bit shorter than me, but my stuff should fit near enough. I will grab you some clothes while you grab a shower. You've got fifteen minutes, and you're coming to the bar with us to get shit-faced! In ya go!"

I shove her into the bathroom, then grab shit out of the room at the back where me and Scar sleep. I grab her some clothes and toss them in the bathroom.

I grab some extra bedding to make up the sofa for Demi. Scar's right. This is gonna get messy. Bring it on.

Twenty mins later, we are heading over to the bar, already on our way to a buzz from my heavy-handed shots in the van. We stalk into the bar as the whole place seems to be drop-dead quiet. You could hear a pin drop. All the glasses stop clinking, and the voices stop altogether. The only noise is the jukebox, and even the pool table falls silent. There are about ten guys in here, and they are all drooling. I wink at the girls, stride up to the bar, and order a round of tequila. The girls freeze for a few seconds before following me in.

"Jesus, I feel like a piece of meat … I don't feel safe. Maybe we should get out of here," Demi says.

Scar grins a sadistic grin, gesturing around the bar. "Take a look around. Find the scariest motherfucker in here."

"Seriously, not this shit again, Scar!" I shake my head at her. Just the look on her face. She loves this fucking bit.

Demi pauses, really taking in every single guy in the place, even the two guys behind the bar tilting her head to the pool table and giving the tiniest nod, then physically shuddering. "Him, that big guy, the one with all the tattoos and the shaved head, full beard and scar running across his temple, the one literally snarling at us with half his teeth missing."

Scar assesses him, leaning into Demi's ear. "Yep, he's a scary son of a bitch, but he's not the scariest motherfucker in here."

Raising a brow, Demi looks around, confused as if she's missed a guy. Barking out a laugh, Scar leans in again. "Take another look because, sweetheart, I can tell you the scariest motherfucker in this place is the crazy bitch sitting with us. Don't panic, babe, because while she's here, we've as good as got ourselves a demon bodyguard. Even hell rejected her as she was too 'fucked' up, and no one and nothing will trouble us while she's here!" Fucking hell, she even does the air quotes too.

Swinging around on my bar stool, I give Scar my sweet, innocent face and mutter, "Well, I think I may be slightly offended. I don't know what you mean. I take offence to the crazy bitch part and the demon part, and I'm almost certain there were a few more insults in there! Wounded, totally fucking wounded, you're a total douche canoe, Scar, do you know that?"

"Firstly, fuck off, then, erm… fuck off some more, and then… you can fuck right off cos that fake arse, sweet innocent bullshit might have Demi convinced, but me? I fucking see you, Ray! … I fucking see all of you!"

Jabbing me in the chest with her finger, I gasp, shooting my hand to where she's poking me. Then we both stare at each other, glaring daggers. Poor Demi holds her breath like it's almost stuck in the back of her throat, with her mouth open catching flies, wondering if we were gonna kick the shit out of each other. Then we both burst into fits of laughter. Demi wooshes out the breath she was holding.

"Seriously, you two are insane!" Poor Demi's face. Then we all start laughing again.

"Another round, my good man, make 'em doubles!" I stand up and neck my drink. I head over to the pool table, and the so-called "scary guy" eyes me as I grab a cue. "You guys done here? Me and my girls fancy a game. If I give you twenty dollars, you can go grab yourself a drink or two. What do ya say, fellas?"

"Sure, sugar tits, we were done anyway," the so-called "scary guy's" friend says, snatching the twenty out of my hand and heading to the bar. The scary dude slaps my arse as he passes me, and Scar gasps, a look of sheer panic on her face.

I shake my head at her, smirking. "It's fine. Don't panIc. I'm good."

Demi gives us both a look but doesn't say anything. Grabbing herself a cue and setting up, we drank and played for a couple of hours. I get a bit fidgety. Tequila makes me like that, fidgety and horny. Fuck's sake, why the fuck do I drink it so much? But it's my favourite drink. I think of Jer in times like this, and then the slight tinge of guilt hits.

Scar notices and laughs.

"What's up?" Demi looks confused.

Scar leans in, winking at me. "When Ray starts to get drunk-ish on tequila, not all the time, but when she's not had a 'release' in a while, she gets all squirmy and horny. Look, I've been there and done that, but now you're here, so it looks like you're gonna have to take one for the team!"

She cocks her head to the side in a questioning way. "Take one for the team?"

I'm sipping my tequila now, trying to hide my grin.

Scar continues fucking with Demi. "Yeah. Take one for the team. You know!" Scar raises her two middle fingers to her mouth, shoving her tongue between them and flicking it around, nodding and winking at her. "You know one for the team?"

Demi's face flushes the brightest shade of red, and the pulse in her neck quickens and starts trying to break out through the skin. "Oh… Wait, what…? Erm… no… nope… not me… nope, can't be me… I'm not gay. I don't do that, nope, nope… just… nope."

That's it. I literally spit the tequila out as I laugh that hard. Scar's literally crying, tears streaming down her face. I'm holding my side as I gasp and try to catch my breath.

Next thing, Demi punches us both in the arms. "You are terrible people! Totally the worst kind of people… You're playing with me again, aren't you, for God's sake?" She starts laughing too. "You're both going to hell!"

"Firstly, I tried. They won't let me in. Apparently, I'm too much for even them but don't worry, Demi, you don't have to eat me out if you don't want to… unless you do want to, that is!" I wink at her.

"Bite me," she says.

"Ooh, now there's an offer I can't refuse! Come here, you!" I chase her around the pool table.

I wake up the next morning with a mouth like Gandhi's flip-flop. This bit is no fun, but thinking back to the night before, we had a right laugh, and poor Demi had been on an emotional rollercoaster. Dragging myself out of bed, I head to the shower to scrub my tongue and try and get the feeling of something dying in my mouth out of it.

After showering and brushing my teeth twenty times, slight exaggeration but not by much, I head to the kitchen area. I start cooking bacon sandwiches, setting the table and laying out three shots of tequila, the hair of the dog and all that!

"Ray, have I told you how much I fucking love you?" Scar whisper-shouts as she drags her arse out of the bedroom at the back.

Demi grunts from the front on the sofa. "Of course you would be morning people! Total psychos!"

We both look at each other, shrugging. Demi really did fit in, apart from her lack of swearing, but we will rub off on her eventually.

It's like she belongs with us. She drags herself to the table, looking a bit green around the gills. She frowns at the tequila. "What the hell is this?"

"What the fuck does it look like?" Scar shoots back.

"Just neck it, then eat. Promise you'll feel better," I say as I start shovelling in my sandwich Scar groans as she stuffs bite after bite in her face. "Fucking hell, Scar, you're giving me a wide-on with all that moaning. Rein it in, will ya?!"

Winking at me and waggling her brows, she chuckles while taking another bite.

"You two are weird. Are you actually… you know, like, together? As in a couple…?" Demi quizzes.

"Nah, we dabbled when we first met, Scar still does every now and then, but I prefer dick. Just wish I could get it without the rest of the guy attached to it, urgh!"

"Dabbled? But not any more?"

"Nah, like I say, not me anyway. Why? You feeling bi-curious?"

She flushes again. "Erm… I mean well… not… possibly… maybe… no… yeah definitely no… thought about it… yeah, no… don't think so… yeah, it's a no… yeah, a definite no."

We both burst out laughing again.

"God's sake, here we go again." Demi rests her head in her hands on the table and just shakes her head from side to side.

We get ready and, after lunch, take Demi back to her place. Her scumbag boyfriend has taken all of the cash she'd saved, but everything else is there, and he's left her car, so not the end of the world.

Poor Demi, she's gutted. "Can't believe he took my cash! Argh! It took me a year and a half to save that, a grand gone like that. I hope he gets chlamydia and his penis falls off!"

Looking around the place, I can't see any spare keys. "I think you two should stay here while I go get some supplies, okay, guys? Can I take your car Demi to save me from going in the van?"

She tosses me the keys, and I head out and jump in her car. I google what I need and head in the direction of the hardware store on the edge of the nearest town of Ravenswood, then head further into town to grab us some food. I get back and toss the bags on the counter. "Let's eat, and then I can change the locks."

Demi looks at me suspiciously. "What? What do you mean by changing the locks? I can't afford to get someone in for that, Ray. Don't worry. It will be fine. I don't think he will come back!"

"That's what I went out for, don't worry, I've got all the stuff, so I can do it. It will only take about twenty minutes, so let's eat and get those locks changed. You're not having that fuck face waltzing back in here when he changes his mind, and the fucker will. They always do."

We eat, and then I change the locks. I have also brought a chain for the door and a doorbell that records anyone who comes even close to the door.

"Hey, what do I owe you? I appreciate you doing all that, and I will feel so much safer now, thanks to you guys!"

"Don't be daft. You don't owe us anything. I chose to grab that stuff. It's on me." I toss a stack of notes onto the table too.

"What the hell is that for, Ray?"

"Take it, stash it. It's yours. We have more than enough, so we would prefer you to have it."

"Oh my God. Guys, I can't take this. There must be at least a grand here. No, sorry guys, I can't."

"We're not asking you to take it. We're telling you to. There's a difference. And besides, I kind of like having you around. It feels like you need it more than we do!" Demi falls quiet, eyes glistening with unshed tears, bless her. She really doesn't know what to do with herself.

"Look, Demi, it's not a big deal. Just take it, put it somewhere safe, use it to pay bills, waste it on tequila, whatever you like, just say no more about it!"

"Guys, I don't know how to thank you, I can't believe it—"

Scar interrupts, "Right, now that's sorted, bagsy picking the chick flick! Grab some blankets and snacks, and let's camp out in the living room. Maybe tomorrow we could head to the beach if you're not working!"

I might be sick after bingeing on crap and too many chick flicks. We all fall asleep in a pile on the sofa.

Waking up with a stiff neck, I must have nudged Demi. She flies up, eyes wild, trying to figure out what's happening. "Fuck's sake, girl, chill!"

"Jesus, Ray, I had no idea where I was or what was happening. Holy hell, my heart's in my mouth!"

"When are you next at work?" Scar says without even opening her eyes.

"Jesus." Demi jumps a mile. "You guys are trying to kill me off... Not till tomorrow's late shift."

"Okay, let's get ready and hit the beach. Let's just go have some fun."

After getting ready, we head out to the van and back down to Castle Cove, pulling into the parking lot over the road from the beach. There's a restaurant, more like a bistro kind of place, a small nightclub, a bakery that sells coffee, and a small seating area with a cafe feel. There's a laundrette and a supermarket with a few other shops spaced out down smaller side streets.

It isn't the warmest day, so I send the girls down to the beach with the blankets, chairs, and supplies we need. I head along the main road. I grab what I need and then head back to the girls.

They've set up a nice little encampment with the blankets, some camping chairs and the small fire pit, and then they have the tequila and Demi's rolling a joint in front. I cock a brow at them both.

"Shit, it's gonna be one of those types of days, is it?" Chuckling, I hand out the coffees and pastries I've brought and grab the tequila up, adding a healthy shot to each coffee.

"Jesus!" Demi barks out.

Scar chokes on her gulp of coffee. "That's good, but bloody strong. My liver's gonna be pickled if we keep drinking like this. I can't cope!"

"Well, you're not gonna like my next idea then! I thought we could bum around here all day, then head to that nightclub over there later." I point a thumb in the direction of the parking lot. "Let's get totally wankered. What do ya say?"

Scar bumps her paper coffee cup against mine and Demi's, saying, "Clink! I'm in."

I shake my head. Another messy night it shall be, then. After a day of hanging out, getting to know each other better, and generally talking shit, we head back to the van, dropping all the crap we'd had at the beach off, then heading to grab some food at the bistro place. We settle on pizza and chips to soak up all the alcohol before heading back to the van to get ready.

The girls grab a shower then we all head into the bedroom to do their hair and make-up. "Fuck's sake, how long are you guys gonna take?" I ask, drinking my tequila.

"Come on, Ray. You haven't even had a shower yet!" Demi sounds so frustrated.

Laughing at her pouty face, I say, "Listen, babe, it will take me twenty minutes to get ready, thirty including the shower if I take my goddamned sweet time, so just give me the heads up when you've nearly finished, okay?"

Demi's mouth opens, a little shocked, turning to Scar. "Is she serious?"

"Deadly." Scar shrugs when the girls are nearly ready. I jump in the shower. They're just putting on their shoes as I get out.

"Come on, let's go fuck shit up!" I laugh.

Scar and Demi both have short tight mini dresses on. Although Scar's curvier than Demi, her tight dress still hugs Demi's body like it was made for her. They're wearing high heels, and their hair is in soft curls down their backs. Demi's silver dress looks phenomenal with her long, dark, almost black hair and tanned skin. She has a faint dimple on her left cheek when she smiles, and her dark lashes flutter around her dark hazel eyes. She's about five foot eight but has the same athletic build as me.

Scar has on a bright red dress, and she looks sexy as fuck in it. Then there's me. I chuckle to myself. I have on my black ripped jeans and black vest top with a checked shirt unbuttoned over the top.

I have put on my studded bracelet and choker and dark eye make-up. My hair slicked back in a high pony. I slide on my New Rock Trail boots which are my favourite things besides my weapons. They are one of the things I bought from home.

I slide my knife into my boot and twirl for the girls. They both laugh at my complete disregard for my femininity. I don't give a fuck. I think I look cute, and my boots do have heels, even though they are biker boots, with a chunky silver heel and a skull on the front, big chunky buckles up the sides, but they are totally badass, and totally me, so fuck it.

FMBs, that's what we call them back home—Fuck Me Boots. But with my lack of interest in men, they were more my Don't Fuck With Me Boots. I stride out of the van, followed by the giggly girls, mentally face-palming myself, locking the van and heading over to the club.

It's still earlyish, so not majorly busy as we stride in. We head straight up to the bar. Ordering us a few drinks, we neck them and head off to the dance floor. We party like it's going out of fashion. We've been getting a lot of male attention from the start of the night, so I stopped drinking a while ago, wanting to keep my wits about me.

Scar and Demi are trashed but still sexy as fuck, and guys just never seem to think when pretty girls say no, they mean it.

It must have been around midnight when the groping started to get crazy. I mean, the drunker guys get, the more right they seem to think they have to get handsy, so after a couple of suggestions to various blokes to kindly remove their appendages from my arse and from the girls, too, I finally lose my shit when one of them moves from me to grab Demi and try to kiss her.

I push him off her and snarl, "Keep your hands and lips to yourself, dickwad, or you'll be going home with your teeth in that fucking glass!" I nod to the almost empty whiskey glass he holds limp in his hand.

"Ooh," he coos back. "Aren't you a feisty little thing? Let's see how feisty you are choking on my cock."

The smile that spreads across my face must have been a sight to see, going by the grimace on Scar's face, but she still gives me the nod all the same, the nod that says, "Bring *her* out and do your worst, motherfucker."

"Go on, shithead, underestimate me. That'll be fun." He makes a grab for my hair. "Big mistake, motherfucker." I dodge his grasp, slapping his hand away, slamming the heel of my other hand up into his nose with an almighty crunch. The faint squeal that leaves his lips makes me fucking smile, and then I bring my elbow through to catch him again, spreading his broken nose sideways across his face, I spin around and punch him straight in the mouth, as his head spins to the side with a spray of blood across the dance floor. I'll be surprised if the shithead doesn't have whiplash.

He coughs, chokes and snarls on the tears in his eyes and the blood pouring down his face, and when he spits out, to my delight, there's a fucking tooth! Barking out a laugh, I kick out at him, landing it full front and centre in his dick, and as he drops to his knees, not knowing whether to clutch his nose, his mouth, or his dick, I finish him off with a roundhouse.

"Lights out, motherfucker," I say as I stand over his very unconscious body, bouncing on the balls of my feet and laughing like a maniac, spitting down on him, then glancing around to make sure his mates get the hint making eye contact with one of them, he raises his hands in submission. He and another handsy dude drag him off the dance floor.

One of the bouncers heads over to us, glaring at him and crossing my arms over my chest. "Don't even think about it, motherfucker." As he comes to stand in front of me, I jab him in the chest. The dude is a full-on brick wall of muscle, hefty as fuck, shaved head with tats up the sides and down his neck into his white shirt. "If you had been doing your job ten fucking minutes ago instead of feeling up the barely legal girl at the bar, then maybe, just maybe, I wouldn't have had to knock out that motherfucker! So I'm warning you now—"

"Hey, hey, calm down." He raises his hands in surrender, tapping his earpiece. "Boss says to get you… " He trails off, giving me a once-over. "Lovely ladies drinks, on him!"

Spinning around in a circle, flipping off "the boss" in the direction of any cameras I can see, I turn back to the bouncer.

Eyeing him the same way he had me. I cross my arms back over my chest. "We'll take a full bottle of vodka and two bottles of tequila!" Looking him up and down again, I say, "And none of that watered-down shit! Top shelf!"

Pressing his earpiece again, he nods. "This way… ladies."

We follow him over to the bar, and he leans across, speaking to the bartender, leaning back to speak in my ear. "Boss would like a word!"

"The boss can have as many words as he wants, starting with 'fuck.' He can also have 'douche canoe' followed by 'suck my dick' and ending with 'off!'"

The bouncer flinches as I hear a bark of laughter coming from his earpiece.

Turning to Scar and Demi, I say, "I'm gonna go speak to this boss guy. Wait here! Do not move, you hear me? Do. Not. Fucking. Move!"

I follow the bouncer once the girls have the three bottles of booze tucked under their arms and are perched on the bar stools.

We head out the back, pushing through the double doors and down a long corridor as we get to the end. The bouncer knocks on the door. "Sir!"

"Enter!" a slightly muffled voice comes from behind the door.

The bouncer opens the door but steps back to let me enter on my own. I eye the twat cautiously before stepping in. "I will wait outside to escort you back to your friends." The bouncer nods as he closes the door.

The man behind the desk rises to his full height. He's about six feet, ever so slightly shorter than me with my boots on.

"Please take a seat," the man behind the desk says, gesturing to the seat in front of him.

When I make no move to sit, he sits back down himself. He has dark slicked-to-the-side hair, not a hair out of place, clean-shaven, mildly handsome, I suppose, if you like that kind of thing, all sharp angles and harsh cheekbones, an almost regal face structure.

Dark eyes, which look almost black in this light, as I look down at him from across the table, but that is obviously the lighting, he is slimmer and more athletic build than the bouncer, but I can see he works out from the movements of his shirt across his body, as it goes taught across his chest and biceps as he moves and flexes. His fitted, crisp black shirt clings in all the right places with the top two buttons open and black trousers. I can't see his footwear because his legs are under his desk.

Priest

There's a faint rap at the door. "Sir."

"Enter!" Donny pushes the door open but steps back, allowing her to step in, telling her he will wait outside till we are done and take her back to her friends.

I rise to my full height. I'm six foot, making me ever so slightly shorter than her with her heeled boots on.

"Please, take a seat." I gesture to the seat in front of me. When she makes no move to sit, I sit back down myself.

"So, what do you want?" she snaps at me in what sounds like a British accent. She crosses her arms over her chest and pops her hip out. The scowl does nothing to hide her beauty, but it's a beauty you would find in a great white shark or a black mamba. More deadly beauty than a pretty girl kind of beauty.

"No need for animosity, miss… " I trail off, waiting for her to fill in her name, but she stands stoic, looking bored instead. "So, miss…" I try again.

"Business," she replies.

I cock a brow in her direction, sounding the name around in my head. "Business? That's an unusual surname."

"Yup!"

"So, Miss Business, may I call you that?"

Smirking, she adds, "My first name's Nonya."

I nod. "So, Miss Nonya Business." I grimace as the words leave my lips. She's playing with me, clearly. She struggles to hide the smirk on her face as the corner of my mouth twitches too. "What are you, twelve?"

Shrugging, she just stares me straight in the eye, giving me a look that says if I think I'm going to intimidate her, I don't have a fucking clue who I'm dealing with. She just grins back at me, tightening the folded arms across her chest.

"Well, Miss... Not important right now." I shake my head. "I have a proposition for you."

Cocking her head in question, she asks, "Proposition, you say, Mr..." She's using my own tactic against me, but she isn't expecting an answer.

"Priest," I reply.

Cocking a brow at me, she says, "So Mr Pri—"

"Just Priest," I interrupt.

She nods in understanding. "What can I do for you then?"

"I couldn't help but notice your... skills. Would you be interested in a job? I could use someone like you."

"What, you think my dancing skills are what you need? Nah, I'm good, thanks. Just passing through."

"While your dancing skills are impressive, I think we both know the other skills you exhibited on the dance floor are what you're actually in here for. Couldn't interest you in hanging around for a while?"

"Like I said, just visiting from the UK, not staying long, will be moving on shortly."

So I was right with the accent. "Shame!"

"Anything else?"

"Nope." Leaning across the table, I slide a blank-looking card along it towards her. "In case you change your mind."

She picks up the card and turns it over.

AFTERLIFE
666-732-7377

Sliding it into her back pocket, she turns to leave.

"Hopefully see you again soon sometime." The corner of my mouth kicks up into a semi-involuntary smile, and my eyes almost twinkle. I hope I'll see her again. Something about this woman speaks to my soul. She's a predator, that's for sure—beautiful, deadly, powerful. She feels like maybe a kindred spirit, like a missing piece, possibly kin.

"Ray." She smirks. "Maybe. Thanks for the drinks."

She two-finger salutes me, and I nod as she leaves the room, clicking the door shut behind her.

Call me intrigued. I open up the laptop and call Dice, forwarding him the video files of the bar fight and the office conversation, tapping out a small message. "See what you can find. Name, Ray. From the UK." If anything can be found about this woman, I need to know it all. I believe in fate, and fate has brought her straight to my door. I will make sure I see her again.

Ray

There's something about the look on this guy's face. Almost like when two predators meet and assess each other with curiosity, caution and respect before seeing who they truly are and recognising their similarities, then passing on their way.

The air in the room thins and sparks, and there is something about this guy that makes me feel sure our paths will cross again at some point, accidentally or intentionally. Either way, I look forward to it.

Heading back towards the girls to carry on the party, I can feel him watching me through the cameras. The place is filling up, but then it's the only place like this I'd noticed, so maybe there is nowhere else to go. I'm intrigued, but not enough to hang around in the middle of bumfuck nowhere.

Walking over to the bar, I turn to the girls. Scar's grinning like a fucking Cheshire cat. "Ah, our knight in shining armour!" she coos. I shake my head once slightly, and she gives me a tight-lipped nod.

"You know I'm more of a twat in tinfoil." I chuckle at her.

Demi has her hand over her mouth in total shock. "Who even are you?"

Scar smugly grins, slinging her arm around Demi's shoulder and whispering, "She's the scariest motherfucker in the room."

Demi looks at me again as I shrug, and she just nods, opening her mouth, then closing it again, then opening it and then letting out a sharp breath.

Scar spins her in her seat back toward the bar holding up three fingers. "Glasses," she mouths as I slide to stand in between them, throwing my arms over both their shoulders.

After staying in bed till almost lunch, we head down to the beach for a couple of hours before Demi needs to head off for work. Scar and I will check out Ravenswood for a few days and see what's there, as that's the biggest town around these parts.

Clearing her throat, Demi glances between us and nervously asks, "Ray? You know that shit that went down last night with that guy? How? Where did you learn to fight like that? It was hot as hell… scary… but scary-hot, too!"

I sigh. "Basically, my dad was a badass. He retired just before Mum had me and talked his mates into retiring too and running a business together back in England. My mum died when I was four, so they all stepped in and raised me.

"My dad, Pa Steven, Pa John, Pa Bernie and Pa Cade are into all sorts of weapons and martial arts, all ex-military. My Pa Bernie's married, so Ma Marie came too, and although she tried with the girly stuff, there was just too much testosterone.

"Pa Bernie and Ma Marie have two boys who I've always called my brothers, and then I was a twin, so there was my brother too. I ended up doing all kinds of mixed martial arts and weapons training, which I loved and still do. Living at the Adventure Centre was amazing. We had motorbikes, quads, axe throwing, crossbows, archery, a gun range, and paintballing. We also had a lake where we went canoeing, camping, and all sorts of Bear Grylls type shit."

"What's 'Bear Grylls' type shit?" Demi frowns.

Scar just bursts out laughing. "Basically, she could survive in the wild for years with nothing but a spoon and kill a grown man with the spoon in eighty-five different ways without breaking a sweat."

It's my turn to bark out a laugh. "Scar, you really do oversell my skills!"

There's a long silence as Demi stares between us, not knowing what to say. After a few panicked looks and a slow release of breath, she just whispers, "Jesus!"

And that about sums it up. We all just sit back and stare at the sea lapping against the beach, and a comfortable silence spreads across us as we enjoy the quiet for a few hours.

Dropping Demi at her place to get ready and grab her car to go to work, we head off to grab some stuff, and then we'll meet her to have food at the diner as we're heading over to Ravenswood tomorrow.

We're gonna stay there for a few days. It's only about twenty miles from the diner, but we probably won't return for a few days.

After food, we wait for Demi to finish her shift while we chat with George. We head back to the van to get changed and head over to the bar to blow off the cobwebs again.

As we walk over to the bar, Scar says how horny she is and hopes there are some fit guys in there to give her some eye candy for her lady spank bank. Her words, not mine, but the more I think about it, the more I feel a little horny too.

"Shit, now I'm horny too. If you hadn't mentioned It, I wouldn't be so. It's your fault." I punch her in the arm.

"Hey!" she snarls.

"What?" I smirk back. I grin at her. Demi asks why don't we just pull some guys at the bar and take them either back to the van or round the back of the bar for a fuck, you know, like classy ladies. Scar laughs at that and whispers in her ear, "Ray has issues!"

"Nu-uh! I don't!"

"Yeah, you fucking do if Jeremy is anything to go by."

"Fuck you, Scar. Don't bring Jer up again, okay?" We stop walking, and Scar crowds us both in her arms, leaning into Demi.

"Okay, okay, I'm sorry, my lips are sealed on the whole Jer shitshow or whatever the fuck that was." She holds her hands up in surrender, and I shoot her a filthy look. "See, the thing is, Ray loves dick but doesn't like the rest of what comes along with men. She's had her heart broken and now thinks if it's just sex, more like a transaction of sorts, you scratch my itch and only my itch and I'll scratch yours type thing, nothing else, then she won't get hurt. She won't let them touch her, so she has… difficulty following through. She likes to be in control… sex, no other touching, no kissing. Most men do not like that one bit. It leaves for very blue lady balls for this one!" She cocks her thumb, pointing it in my direction.

"Fuck's sake, you make me sound like a freak. I just don't appreciate guys being… gropy. That's all! It leads to too much physical stuff, and I've learnt it's easier to just fuck it and chuck it, hit and quit. So, I like to find someone who will let me get on with it and then never go back for a repeat. Well, not since Jer, anyway." I shrug at them both.

"When was the last time you fucked Jer? And have you fucked anyone since then?" Scar pouts at me.

"Nearly twelve months ago. It's a sore subject, so can we not, okay?"

Scar butts in, "And she won't sleep in a bed with a guy, she won't let a guy hug her or kiss her, bare minimum contact, just enough to get her rocks off, and that's it! Game over! End of story! Finito! No fucking feelings. She's like a black hole of emptiness. She's a fucking dude. That's what she is!"

Demi looks panicked. "Did something happen to you, like something bad?"

Wanting to get that pitying look off her face, I tell her, "Look, it's nothing like that. I've only had a couple of boyfriends who were total pigs. I learnt quite quickly that the more I give, the more I get hurt, so rather than setting myself up for a fall, I met Jer, who wanted to give me what I needed, and I learnt to take what I wanted, and it works for me okay.

"I don't have issues with men touching me… It's just… if it feels like it's going to be sexual, I put a stop to it." Shrugging, I add, "It just works for me, okay?"

Demi nods, and Scar blobs her tongue out very maturely. I flip her off. Rolling my eyes at her and opening the door to the bar, I glance back, eyeing them both. Fuck. I need a drink, a vibrator, and possibly a butt plug too, but mainly a drink!

After a few drinks and a couple of games of pool, Scar's flirting with a guy by the jukebox as Demi leans over.

"Ray, you know the sex thing?" I cock a brow at her as if to say what the fuck bitch, but she just leans in a little closer. "You see the guy behind the bar, the good-looking one?" Glancing over, I can see who she means. He's generically, classically good-looking, like high school jock good-looking hot, but not my type at all. At about my height with mousy brown hair and brown eyes, he's athletic looking but more in an I-play-sports-way than an I-go-to-the-gym kind of way. I can see the appeal, I suppose.

"Well," she says. "That's Dwayne. He runs this place. I went to high school with him. He's a nice guy, but I think he could… ya know… Be the kind of guy to… erm… go for the… type of sex thing… ya know… God, Ray, don't make me say it!"

I burst out laughing. "You mean he's the submissive type?"

"Yeah, that's totally what I mean!" The flush rises to her cheeks. I contemplate what she has said. I'm not getting any less horny sitting here, and maybe he could be what I need. Not Mr Right, just Mr Right Fucking Now!

"I will take that under advisement, thanks," I say, then gesturing to the pool table. We neck our drinks and head over there. Scar has the guy she has been talking to pinned to the jukebox with her tongue down his throat and her hand rubbing his dick through his jeans.

We play a couple of games till she comes back looking more frustrated than when she left. Looking at them both, I nod towards the bar, and Demi smirks as I say I'm heading over there for a little bit, and she leans into Scar to let her know I have found a potential victim.

Walking over to the bar, Dwayne's cleaning glasses as he glances at me. I lean down on my elbows, leaning right over so I can whisper in his ear. "You got an office?"

He leans back, eyeing me, but giving a nod, I ask, "Fancy fucking me in it?"

His eyes widen, and his eyebrows almost meet his hairline as he turns to the other guy and tells him to watch the bar. He goes to grab my hand, but I pull it away and say that I will follow him. We head through the door that says "Staff Only," down a corridor, walking past a door that says "Stockroom," and then one that says "Staff Toilets." At the end is the office.

He walks through the door, gesturing for me to go in. As I walk into the room, there's a desk at the side of me with a sofa opposite it.

I walk to the front of the sofa and tell him to slide his jeans and boxers down and then to sit. He eyes me warily for a second before doing as I ask.

"Condom!" I bark at him, an order rather than a question, as he nods to the shelves, gulping and taking a deep breath. I head over and find the shelf with tampons and condoms on. They must have been for the vending machines in the loos, so I grab a handful, stuffing them into my jeans pockets, then turn and throw one at him. It lands on the sofa at the side of him. "Put it on!" And he does as he's told.

"Good boy!" I walk over to him. His dick's hard, his face flushed, his pupils blown and his skin pebbles. He looks a little intimidated and a little scared. Now *that* I can work with.

I slip out of my boots and slide my jeans down. I have a skulls and roses tattoo going all the way down my left leg, which makes him smile, and he reaches out to run his hands down me as I stand In front of him.

"Don't touch." I slap his hand away, and he gasps, looking up at my hard gaze. I straddle him, grabbing his dick and thrusting myself straight onto him.

He gasps out as his head lolls. "Fuck." He goes to grab my hips. I slap his hands away, rocking back and forward on his dick.

"Don't touch!" I spit out as I rock backwards and forwards, concentrating on the feeling between my legs. I start rocking faster. I can feel the heat rising in me. His eyes shoot up to meet mine, staring into my eyes like they hold the key to my soul, but little does he know I don't have one. As I thrust over him, rocking my hips and concentrating on the friction, his breaths come out stuttered, and he leans in for a kiss.

Oh, hell no. Before I can think about it, I grab his wrist with one hand and his throat with the other. I hold him in a punishing grip as I continue riding him, chasing that feeling of going over the edge, but before I can come, his breath comes all raggedy, and he swells inside me, and before I can slow, he spills into the condom.

Sagging and panting against the back of the sofa, he doesn't make eye contact again. "Sorry… it was the throat thing… fuck… no one's ever done anything like that to me before. That was hot… that was amazing… that just threw me, and I couldn't stop it!"

I take a deep breath. I'm shocked as I sit there, feeling his dick deflate inside me. That was disappointing. I look down and then back at his face, which is flushed again with embarrassment. I climb off, getting dressed while he sits there panting, still out of breath, slick with a sheen of sweat.

"Don't worry about it." I turn and leave the room.

Just as the door swings shut, I hear him say, "Wait, just give me thirty minutes or—"

But I'm out the door and storming down the corridor, fucking blue lady balls and all. Fuck my life. I get to the door marked "Storeroom."

I glance both ways, then I dive in, grabbing two bottles of tequila and a bottle of vodka before shoving out the door into the bar, making a run for the exit, hollering, "Fucking leg, it bitches!" as I shoot across the bar.

They don't need telling twice as they see me barrel through the door. They're hot on my heels, and we run out the door. I get out into the parking lot and burst out laughing, still running with my ride or dies right behind me, no questions asked, just following me blindly. Hades, I love these dumb arse motherfuckers. We don't stop till we reach the van, and all pile in.

"B-bloody hell!" Demi stutters while she's struggling to breathe, and Scar's trying not to hyperventilate.

"Fuck you, Ray," she chokes out. "We're not fit like you. A bit more warning before we make a run for it would be good, and why the fuck are we still sitting here? Let's get out of here!"

"Nah, don't worry, ladies. He won't be coming after us!" As we sit in the van and get wasted, I relay all the gory details. Once they're done literally rolling around on the floor laughing their tits off at me, I tell them both to go fuck themselves, and Scar barks out, "You go fuck yourself. It's the best offer you'll get tonight!"

Demi blushes and chuckles. "You go… you know what yourself. You look like you need it. What colour are your lady balls?" They both crack up laughing again. Fucking bitches.

"Those comments weren't even funny, and this is on you, Demi. You referred the inferior goods!" But I join them, and we don't stop till we all have tears in our eyes and can't breathe.

Packing up and leaving Demi for a few days just feels weird, even though we haven't known her long, and we won't be far away. We head over to the diner for some food before getting ready to head off. We start a group chat while we eat to keep in touch, and then we say our goodbyes, sliding out of the booth, hugging Demi as we walk out the door. We just get to the bottom of the steps, and our phones bling.

Demi: Miss you guys already!
Ray: Seriously? We're not even in the van yet!
Scar: Knobhead!
Demi: Hey, I'm feeling all emotional and lonely, okay?
Scar: Okay, bitch, see ya soon.
Ray: Fuck's sake, knobhead, we're only gonna be gone a few days if that, and we're still not at the van!
Demi: Okay, love you guys. Don't die on me, okay? I need you! Xx
Scar: Okay, love ya bitch tits! Xx
Ray: Love ya both, you twat waffles! Xx

Finally, we make it to the van, looking over at the diner. Demi's standing in the window, leaning on it with her hands flat on the glass, mouthing, "Don't leave me!"

Ray: Twat!
Demi: LOL! Drive safe, psychos. xx

We get in the van and drive out of the parking lot. She's still plastered to the bloody window watching us go. Sorry, George, looks like you're gonna need a window cleaner and maybe a new waitress. Sorry, not sorry.

It becomes a little more built up as we drive nearer to Ravenswood. We head straight to the centre, park up and head out to see what's around. There seems more to do here, so we find a little coffee shop to the right of the central town square, which is also a parking lot. There's also a little book store, a hardware store which I'd used to change Demi's locks, a fancy gym, some clothing stores, a party planning place—whoever the fuck needs shit like that; I have no idea—next to a fancy wedding/ball gown dress shop.

There's a wine bar and a bistro, and there are a few empty shops, but the town has a design over the windows so you can't see in, which makes it look nicer than empty shops, I suppose. There's also a thrift store. I guess it's like a charity shop in the UK. This is all we can see from the main square. There's so much more beyond that.

We wander into the coffee shop to start looking into the local area. Checking through our phones, we find a few places we're after and head out to scope the area.

Ravenswood has everything we could need, but something's missing. Not sure what it is, we head back to the van to find somewhere to park up for the night. Maybe it might feel different after a good night's sleep and further investigation tomorrow.

Demi: How did it go today?

Scar: Not bad. There are a few options here, so gonna investigate more tomorrow. We will probably stay here for about four days.

Ray: Their apple pie sucks!

Demi: LOL! Nothing beats my apple pie. That's why George gets me to do all the baking!

Ray: You make the apple pie at George's?

Demi: I make all the deserts!

Scar: 'Heart eyes emoji' 'Laughing emoji'

Ray: 'Facepalm emoji'

Demi: Night, guys. xx

Scar: Night, knob cheese. xx

Ray: Night, John boy! Xx

After breakfast, I head over to one of the local bike garages on the outskirts of town. Scar stays in town as she wants to check out spaces for rent. I think she thinks if I stay, she needs a backup plan. I don't think I have any invested interest in staying. I just need to know I gave it my best shot. The garage I try says they have no work for a woman unless I want to make the coffee, ha ha fucking ha! But I'm good and don't throat punch or dick punch anyone, so I would say that's personal growth. However, I let the tyres down on their truck and two bikes outside, so there's that. I'm taking it as a win.

After that's a bust, I decide to check out the local gym. It's overlooking the central parking lot, and the second floor has big glass windows with a view of the whole square.

Talking to the manager about a job, he tells me they could use a Pilates instructor as theirs is on maternity leave, but other than that, they aren't the down-and-dirty kind of gym I spend my time in. They are more a commercial gym, with lots of shiny equipment rather than a cage and sparing. Regardless, I still spend a few hours there putting myself through my paces.

It's still a really good gym, but not somewhere I would want to work or work out regularly.

Once I'm done, I grab a shower and chat with a few of the guys at the entrance to grab a little more info. There's a little garage out of town which I'm heading to the next day, but there's also a boxing gym just out of town, which sounds more like my scene.

Pulling up at Barry's Bikes, I can see it's a bit run-down but clean. I head inside. It's only one small unit. When I walk through the doors, a spanner goes sailing past me and collides with the wall.

"Fucking hell!" the gruff voice mumbles.

"Yep, I should say so." I grin in reply as the guy's head shoots up from behind the bike.

"Shit, I'm so, so sorry. I didn't hear you come in!" He stands up, wiping his hands on a rag. "What can I do for you?"

"Hey, I was scoping out the area and wondered if you have a bit of cash work going?"

"What, like cleaning?" He cocks his head to the side, still wiping his hands.

"No! Like fixing bikes, duh!"

"Oh shit, sorry, caught me off guard. I'm having a crap day. This piece of shit bike is playing up, and I'm gonna miss my kid's birthday party. So I'm sorry, but unless you can service that pile of shit in the corner, then I can't help you."

"Okay."

"Okay?"

"Yep, okay!" I walk over to the pile of shit in the corner, rolling it out of the garage. I start it up. "Just gonna chuck it down the road before I start."

"I don't know what you're up to, but I really can't have you stealing that bike. I will call the cops if you try anything!"

"Here." I toss him the keys to the van. "If you don't want my help, just say. Otherwise, I will be ten minutes, giving this thing a road test first to see what I'm up against, okay?"

He waves at me in the end. I think he's hoping I'm gonna steal it, but five minutes later, I pull back in and get started, stripping it down and grabbing everything I need.

Less than two hours later, I'm done. Bike cleaned down and purring like a good 'un!

"Well, fuck me!" Barry says, wiping his hands on his rag again. He's just finishing up, too, and glances at the clock

"Shit, I can't believe it. Looks like I'm gonna be early!" Grabbing his wallet from his back pocket, he takes out fifty dollars, handing it to me. Shaking my head, I shove it back.

"Nah, call somewhere on ya way to the party and grab your kid a little something extra and some flowers for the missus." He shakes his head and tries to give me the money again. "Honestly, don't worry about it. Can I take your number, and if I need a reference, will you be happy to give me one?"

"That's it? That's all you want?"

"Yep, that's it".

"Thanks, I really appreciate it."

I leave my number and tell him that if he needs me in a pinch, I will be around for the next few days and head back to meet Scar.

Ray: Hey, how you doin'?

Demi: Bored!

Scar: Babe! You missing our crazy arses?

Demi: Yep. Please come rescue me.

Ray: 'Laughing emoji'

Demi: Rude!

Scar: 'Shocked emoji'

Ray: 'Middle finger emoji' 'Laughing emoji' 'Gun emoji'

Demi: What is it you guys say… ah, yeah, go fuck yourselves!

Scar: 'Shocked emoji'

Ray: 'Shocked emoji'

Ray: Knew you'd crack, Demi, that didn't take long! See you in a few days, talk tomorrow.

Demi: Can't wait.

Ray: You're gonna have to.

Scar: Doh!

Leaving Scar in town again as she has a meeting with an estate agent or realtor, whatever they're called apparently, I head to the boxing gym dressed in my workout gear. I park up outside and head in.

"Well, hey there. You lost, little lady?" An old guy is wrapping a young lad's hands beside the ring in the centre of the room.

"Oh, hey, old boy, I'm scouting the area, possibly moving here, so I'm seeing what work's around. You have anything?"

He ponders me while thinking, "What kind of work?"

I appreciate him asking rather than offering cleaning or bookkeeping. I mean, I can do both, but I wouldn't be moving here for those job prospects. "Trainer? Manager?"

He laughs. "You want that place in Ravenswood on the square. We don't do yoga or all that fancy stuff!"

It's my turn to laugh. "Ah, old boy, I think you'll be surprised at what I could teach around here!"

"That I'd like to see!" A voice from the side of me interrupts.

I turn to the side. There's a guy there who's about six feet tall. He's built with thick corded muscle wearing boxing gloves. He has dark blonde hair, not unlike mine, and a pretty boy face, probably about my age. He strolls over towards me, eyeing me from head to toe.

"Play nice, Ax!" the old boy tosses at him.

"I'm always nice, Papa," he says, winking at me.

I groan and cross my arms over my chest.

"Excuse my son, little lady. He gets his manners from his momma. So, sweetheart, what can you do?"

I actually kind of like the old boy. His terms of endearment aren't as insulting as I first thought. When he calls me little lady, he seems kinda nice. "I can manage boxing, but my strong point is mixed martial arts."

The old boy smiles, but the dick's quicker off the mark. "Ooh, I'd like to get you on your back on the canvas, princess!"

"I'm sure you would!" I deadpan. "Maybe I can knock some manners into you."

The old boy barks out a laugh. "That I'd pay money to see."

"A hundred bucks says I can beat you in three rounds. Old boy decides the winner. Whaddaya say, mouth?" I grin at the gobshite.

"Ah, a pretty little thing like you shouldn't make bets her body can't cash. That body could write far more suitable checks, like ones that involve those pretty little lips wrapped—"

"Axle!" The old guy stands up, glaring at his son.

Stepping closer, I say, "You win, and I'll blow you all you like. I win; I want five hundred bucks. Whaddaya say, mouth?"

"No rules! Three three-minute rounds unless I knock you the fuck out beforehand, but when you wake up, your mouth's mine. I ain't going easy on you cos you're a girl!"

"Show me the money first, then you're on, 'princess,'" I spit at him.

He heads across the gym and up a flight of stairs to the office.

"What the hell are you doing? He will pulverise you!" the old boy says, shaking his head.

Grinning at him, I say, "Don't be so sure. He's too arrogant for a start and too bulky. He's slow, and he might hit like a brick wall, but he's gotta catch me first. I was willing to box. He said no rules, so basically, he's guaranteed his downfall, but let's keep that mine and your little secret, yeah, old boy?"

"I really like you!" He smiles. "Give him hell! Beat him, and I will throw in another two hundred bucks just to see him taken down a peg or two!"

"You're on! Fancy strapping my hands for me?"

"Sure thing, sugar!" He winks at me. "Kid, you're gonna have to wait a bit. I think you might learn something here!" he says to the lad who he'd been wrapping when I walked in.

Axle's heading back down the stairs, cash in hand. I'm already getting strapped up. I have taken my leggings and T-shirt off and am in my sports bra and shorts set, barefoot. I slip in my mouth guard and grin at Axle as his brows shoot to his hairline. Yeah, motherfucker thought I was slim, but I'm ripped and covered in tats. I curl my lip and snarl through my mouthguard at him.

I start warming up beside the ring as Axle hands the money to his dad to hold, and he removes his gloves. His hands are already strapped inside. He toes off his trainers and steps into the ring.

I continue warming up a little longer when he snarls, "Are we doing this, or are you just fucking about doing ballet?"

I walk up to the ring. I grab onto the top rope crouching down before propelling myself straight over the ropes into the ring, ending up in the superhero landing just to take the piss.

Rising to my full height, I do a few stretches, shaking my neck out before saying, "You ready, mouth? No mouth guard?"

"You won't get near enough for me to need one. I'm glad you're protecting your mouth for me, though, princess. My dick's gonna look so good shutting you the fuck up later!"

Winking at him, I nod to the old boy that I'm ready, and he grabs his stopwatch that's hanging around his neck. "Three three-minute rounds, you both ready?" We both nod. "Fight!"

Axle comes at me, swinging haymakers left, right, and centre. I bob and weave, bouncing on the balls of my feet, staying light and fast. I'm not so arrogant that I think I can beat this guy strength for strength. I mean, pound for pound, I hit like a heavyweight. I've been training with my dad, my pas and my brothers my whole life. I know how to punch hard, fight dirty and take a hit.

Axle's slow, and his cardio's seriously lacking. In boxing, power isn't everything. Let's let him get a body hit in and see what he's working with. I dance around him, and when he goes to take a stomach shot, I raise my guard so he thinks he's sneaking in underneath my defences. I tense and brace for impact.

Just as I thought, he isn't bad at punching, but he's slow, real slow, so as he's drawing back from the stomach punch, I step into him, slamming him with an uppercut and catching him off balance, sending him to the canvas on his arse. I have already bounced away from him as he takes a second to realise what's happened. He shakes his head, rising to his feet and trying to shake the punch off.

"Time!" Old boy shouts as he takes Axle a bottle of water, and the lad passes me one.

"Fuck he doesn't look happy!" The lad laughs. "He likes to throw his weight around in front of us all. I've just filmed the first round so I can show my mates. He's gonna be so pissed. Make him look like an idiot in the next two, please!"

Grinning at him, I just nod.

"Ready?" The old boy steps back out of the ring. "Fight."

Axle comes at me again. This fucker really wants a blowjob. Well, fuck him. Not gonna happen. He swings a few punches grazing across my bicep with one and another gut punch, grinning at me.

"Not so confident now, are you, princess? Pucker up for me." He laughs.

I wait for him to be breathing out with his laugh, and his guard drops, and I get him good in the gut, a little winded. I then clip his cheek with a cross then jab him straight in the nose. *Crunch.*

"Fucking bitch!" he yells as I grin, bobbing to the side as his hands shoot out, one to his face to cover his nose and the other to punch me, but I'm not there. I punch him in the side of the temple, ringing his bell a little. He staggers to the side.

"Time!" Old boy shouts, bringing in the water again.

"Jesus, I'm fucking loving this!" The lad laughs as he gives me the water. "I've got fifty bucks on me. If you knock him out, it's yours!"

"How about I do it for free?" I grin back at him, winking as I slide my mouthguard back in. I've played nice, only punching, but he said no rules, so it's time to get creative. I back off and let him throw a few punches. He grazes my cheek, but I will barely have a red mark. He's getting tired, and he's slowing down. He lunges at me again.

I duck in front of him so the punch lands a foot above my head. I use all my force to thrust an uppercut right under his chin, and as his head reels back, I hit him with a left hook. I can see his eyes roll, and I drop down to the floor and sweep his legs out from under him, and he hits the deck like a sack of fucking shit.

I wait for him to jump up, but nope. Guess I'm not gonna get creative at all.

"Well, fuck me!" Old boy laughs as he climbs in the ring and rolls his lad onto his side, slapping him on the face and wafting smelling salts around.

Axle comes around with a jolt as I climb out of the ring.

"Money's on the stool, little lady. It was well earned." He winks at me as he's sitting Axle up.

"Thanks, old boy. I will take that as nothing is available at the moment on the job front! Axle, it was an absolute fucking pleasure!" Two-finger saluting, I give the kid my number. "Send me the footage, mate. I'm gonna enjoy watching that back."

"You barely broke a sweat!" He laughs.

I grin as I leave, it looks like I won't be offered a job, but fuck, that felt good. Heading back to the centre of Ravenswood to grab Scar, we've taken in everything we need to know. It still doesn't feel like somewhere I want to be. At this rate, I will be heading back to the UK, begging for my job back at the Adventure Centre, but at least I can say I've given it a shot!

After we explore the whole town, we have our bearings, and although it seems like the town has almost everything we could need, it just leaves me feeling a bit flat. There doesn't seem to be any kind of job here I could see myself doing. I want something exciting, something taxing, maybe a little dangerous. I think I have been spoiled in the Adventure Centre and family business. It really is a perfect fit. Maybe I will just enjoy the time here and go back home when it's done, chalk it up to be just the vacation it had started out being all along.

We head back to the diner. As we get out of the van, Demi comes running across the parking lot and throws herself into my arms.

"I missed you both." She laughs as she turns and grabs Scar dragging her into her arms too.

"Erm, Dem… I can't breathe!"

She releases her hold from our necks, laughing. "God, sorry, I just missed you so much!"

"Missed you too," we both say, throwing our arms around her shoulders and leading her back to the diner.

We take our usual booth and order our usual food with apple pie, as the last one I had was shit. We stay chatting with Demi and George until closing time, and as we head outside to go to the van, I hear a guy's voice shout, "Hey, erm, hi!"

Looking up, I mutter, "Fuck."

Scar and Demi look across the parking lot and see Dwayne standing there waving at me. They both look at each other, look back at me and chuckle to each other as they fuck off in the direction of the van, leaving me to tackle this shitstorm on my own. So much for having my back, fuckers!

Scrubbing my hand down my face. I look up at him as he walks over to me.

Once he gets in front of me, he looks down at his shoes and kicks at the floor, rubbing his hand up and down the back of his neck. I pop my hip and cross my arms across my chest, grinning at how nervous he is now he's right in front of me, that really shouldn't make me horny, but it does, and unfortunately, been there and done that.

"Hey, Dwayne, what can I do for you?"

"Err… hi, hey… Hi."

"So I think we've established that you wanted to say hi… and hey."

"Err, yeah… hey."

"Okay, Dwayne, good talk. Catch ya later, yeah?"

I turn and stride across the parking lot. I leave him standing there like the Mayor of Fucking Awkward Town. Fuck's sake.

I open the door to the van. Scar and Demi are sitting at the table near the window.

"Well, that looked fucking painful."

"No shit, Scar, that's a fucking understatement. He wanted to say hey and hi, and err. That was about the extent of the conversation… fucking facepalm emoji."

Demi raises an eyebrow at me. "Did you just say facepalm emoji?

"Fucking facepalm emoji!" Scar barks out in between her laughs and grins like a dick. I'm sure she's gonna piss herself.

"Yep fucking facepalm emoji! That just about sums that up!" We all just lose our shit at that, and I can't help but laugh till I get a fucking stitch.

After I compose myself, I get up and grab the tequila. "Fuck, I need a drink."

"Me too."

"Me three."

Grabbing the drinks, we sit down to talk. We tell Demi that we haven't found whatever it is that we are looking for yet, even though fuck knows what that actually is. There are still a couple of places we want to check out on the outskirts of Castle Cove and Heighton and around the outskirts of Ravenswood, but after that, we are gonna head to Gosport Harbour, which is an hour and a half up the coast then carry on travelling.

We chat a bit longer, then decide to head over to the bar for a drink. Apparently, we're now a democracy, and I'm outvoted two to one. Fucking facepalm emoji.

We head over to the bar, and those two fuck faces keep hanging back, so I have to go in there first. I mean, seriously. What are we, fucking twelve? Wankers. I take a deep breath, pull up my big girl pants, stride through the door, and walk straight up to the bar. "Hey, Dwayne, can I get two tequilas and a vodka? Make 'em all doubles, would ya? Cheers!"

"Yeah, erm… sure." Grabbing the drinks, I head over to where the girls are sitting. Placing the drinks on a table next to the pool table, we rack 'em up.

Demi's just breaking as two guys, biker types, stroll in, wearing those leather waistcoat things. From the patches on them, they are a fair way from home and not locals. Coming straight over to us, the taller one, an ugly motherfucker with teeth that look like a burnt-down fence, stinks of weed, and I think that's pizza sauce in his beard. Attractive! He purrs as he stands next to me. Demi's to my right at the end of the table, bent over, ready to break. I'm on the side nearest them chalking a cue, and Scar is sitting behind the table with the drinks

Prick number one, the twat with the burnt fence teeth and stale weed smell, smirks. "Look at what we have here, fresh pussy. Mmm. I can almost taste you from here, Come over here, sweet cheeks, and sit on my face, will ya?"

The smaller but stockier one, prick number two with greasy long straggly hair and a front tooth missing, cracks up laughing. "Yeah, come sit on my cock and look pretty. That's about all you're good for!"

He grabs my wrist with the cue in it, and I quickly glance at Scar, then Demi, and back to Scar. She gives the smallest nod. She knows what I'm getting at as we have known each other for years. She moves to stand between Demi and me, taking another cue from the rack: Scar's no fighter, and she probably won't need to be, but it helps to be prepared.

I look at prick number two, then down at where his hand is clutching my wrist. "Remove it!"

"What's that, sugar tits?"

Gritting my teeth with a snarl, I repeat myself. "Fucking remove it!"

"There's no need to be like that, sugar tits. You know you want it from a real man. I'm gonna fuck you real good, and you know you gonna be begging me for more!"

Flicking my gaze, I look over at Scar, and she's shoving Demi further around the table, putting it between them and the guys. Smart girl.

"Go on, arsehole, underestimate me. This will be fun!" A blank stare slides into place, followed by a feral grin as I put the chalk down, making my movements painfully slow. Then, I look him in the eyes and put my hand on his. "Last chance. Re-fucking-move it! Now!"

Barking out a laugh at me and getting right in my face, before he can move another inch, I smash my head into his nose, grabbing his middle fingers and yanking back as hard as I can, hearing the snap and then a high-pitched bitch squeal falls from his mouth. "You fucking bitch! You broke my fucking nose and fingers!"

Releasing my wrist, he grabs his fingers with his other hand squeezing them together.

Prick number one lunges for me, but I kick the bottom of the cue up into my other hand, wielding it around and slamming it straight across his face; then I bring it down across my knee, snapping it in two. I slam one end into prick number two's face, spreading his broken nose across it. I roundhouse prick number one in the side of the head, knocking him out cold.

Fuck, I'm getting really good at broken noses and knockouts. Maybe they're my signature moves.

I jump up onto the pool table, and as prick number two lunges for me, I slam the heel of my boot into his face.

"Lights out, motherfucker!" I jump down off the table and throw the cues down.

I grab Scar's hand, and she grabs Demi's. As we walk by the table, I snatch and neck my drink, dragging them behind me. We walk out of the bar, two-finger saluting at Dwayne as I go past. As we get outside, we run to the van and take off. Never mind the booze we've drunk. We just need to get as far away from here as possible. I'm not worried about myself, and I'm not one to run from a fight, but I need to make sure Demi and Scar are safe. We hightail it to Demi's apartment, taking back roads and side streets, making sure we aren't tailed. We lay low for the rest of the night.

"Ray, remind me never to touch you again," Demi says, half joking, half serious.

Pouting, I look over at her. "Ah, babe, you can touch me anytime, anyplace, anywhere!" I wink at her breaking the tension. We all just laugh again, because what else are we gonna do?

"Bagsy watching a chick flick!" Scar bellows out.

"Really?" We groan.

"Yep, bitch, we've had enough action for one night. I need a time-out!"

And with that, we head inside to watch whatever pile of shit Scar picks, because they're the rules, apparently! The world has gone to shit.

We hang around the area for the next week or so, keeping an eye on Demi to make sure there isn't gonna be any comeback from the bar fight. I'd gone over to speak to Dwayne the next day and given him my number and some cash for the damage in case those guys came back. He called the next day to say the guys had gone back to ask him who we were, but he said we were on a road trip just passing through, heading south. He knew they weren't local, so we shouldn't be running into them anytime soon, but we kept a low profile for a while, just in case.

Dwayne had made it clear he was hoping for a repeat of the other night, too, which wasn't fucking awkward at all. I graciously declined his offer, telling him he is a great guy, and as we aren't hanging around long, I don't want to start anything that I would have to end when leaving. I mean, he is a nice guy, and I'm not a total bitch.

After we thought it was safe to leave Demi, we returned to Castle Cove, then onto Heighton, and spent nearly a week with the family before continuing to Ravenswood. We dropped by to see Demi every other day and were constantly messaging back and forth. We found there were a few places around the outskirts of Ravenswood to check out, too, so we planned on hanging around another week before heading to Gosport Harbour.

I pull up at the first garage on the list. I screw my face up and don't even get out of the van, starting the van back up and driving away.

"I will take that as a no on this one."

"Yep, you do that, Scar." I glare across at her, mentally thanking her for stating the fucking obvious.

Heading a little further east, we reach the gym I wanted to check out. It's smaller than the one in Ravenswood Centre, but similar to the boxing gym on the outskirts, more of a martial arts gym come boxing gym than a gym with machines like the one in the centre. I leave Scar to do her own thing while I train myself ragged. God, I love working up a good sweat, beating the crap out of the bag.

One of the guys helps me wrap my hands and offers to take me out after. He's cute but a bit too old, maybe mid-thirties, but he definitely looks older. After the "bet" at the boxing gym, I decide a place that permanently smells like testosterone isn't the best place to find a job, so I just work out and keep my head down.

I just love the feeling of the burn in my muscles, and the stress relief from going a few rounds on the bag really helps focus my inner turmoil and incessant overthinking about finding the right place with everything perfect. Argh, does what I'm looking for even exist? It's addictive to just be rather than having to feel. When I get back to Scar, we grab food and then head back to the van for the night.

The next day, while Scar checks out a couple of properties and the local area, I check out the second garage on the list. I get out and chat with the guy running the place for about ten minutes, then head back to the van, shaking my head as I get in.

I don't have to meet Scar for a few hours, so I head to a little cafe on the highway and grab a drink.

When I meet up with Scar later, I tell her, "It's only a tiny place, they just didn't have enough work, and there's nothing else around here for miles, so that's a bust. Let's head and fill up with fuel; then, we can call it a day. We will call at the last one tomorrow, then head straight up to Gosport Harbour!"

"No worries, babe. If we don't find it, we don't find it! Don't worry!"

"I'm not worried, Scar. I was hoping to find something more than Pa Bernie and the family to make me feel like I belong somewhere. I think I'm just missing my other pas."

"Come on, Ray! We found Demi. Maybe we're just meant to be together and keep moving around. Don't stress. It's all good. We've only been here for a month. That's not long. We've got six-month visas, so chill!"

"Yeah, yeah, I know, just want something real. Something for just me. While I love the family business, it's been all-consuming my whole life. I just need a sliver of something that's just mine."

Pulling up outside the last garage, it's setback from the road with a massive high fence all around it and a huge parking lot between it and the road. I pull up to the front of the garage, and there seems to be a load of bikes around, which must mean they are busy, so I'm taking that as a good sign.

I jump down from the van and head to the front. There are two big double garage doors to the left, with a door with a large window covered over at the end. One garage door is open, and the other is closed. I pull in front of the closed one. As I step inside, there's a guy crouched down fixing a bike. There are another four bikes in there, but no one else around.

Without looking around, the guy shouts to me, "We're a bike garage, sweetheart! We don't do RVs, and if it's about a bike, take a number, as I'm up to my nuts in it, literally!"

"Well, that's good news!" I smirk back at him.

He stands, turning round to face me and grabbing a rag out of his back pocket, cocking his head at me in a questioning sort of way. "How the fuck is that good news for either of us? For me, I'm gonna be here till stupid o'clock, and for you, if you want something doing, you've got more chance of pigs tap dancing across the motherfucking parking lot!"

I huff and smirk at him. "Well, maybe I can be of help. I'm looking for a temp job just to get a bit of travelling cash, so what do you say? You need a hand?"

"What can you do?"

"On bikes? Anything you want."

"Can you even ride one?"

I smugly grin through this conversation. I don't know why, but I kinda like this guy. He doesn't mince his words, says it like it is, and swears like a sailor. Sounds like my kind of person!

"Yeah, of course I can fucking ride one and fix them like I was made for it too. There's not much that will beat me when it comes to fixing bikes! Period!" I sling my arms across my chest.

"Fine!" He steps in front of me and mirrors my pose.

"Fine?" I ask, cocking my head to the side, taking him in.

"Yep, fine! Shift that monstrosity around the back! Then come back around, and I will give ya something to do."

I reach out to shake his hand. "You won't regret it! I'm Ray, by the way. My sister Scar is in the van. Is it okay if she hangs around? She won't get in the way."

"Sure, I'm Dozer. Now shift that pile of crap. It's giving me a headache looking at it. It's got far too many fucking wheels for my liking!!"

I jump back in the van and drive around the side of the building and slam the brakes on. "Fuck."

"Hey," Scar shoots over at me. "I thought he said take it round the back? I've just drawn all up my face with my lippy, knobhead! What the fuck are we stopping for anyway? Ray, what the actual fuck?"

Scar's gaze falls onto mine, and then she follows my line of sight. "Well, if that's not a sign, I don't know what is," she breathes out.

"Fuck."

"Yep, fuck!" she repeats again, as clearly we hadn't said it enough. Looking to the side of the bike garage, there's another building set even further back from the road, which is why we hadn't seen it before and from the massive logo on the side of it. It's a motorcycle club, not a shocker, you may think, but when the logo is a massive Grim Reaper, a sword, a scythe and all, and the sign says,

"The Reapers MC, Ravenswood"

Then yep, fuck about covers it!

Driving around the back of the unit and parking up, I jump out of the van. I'm dressed in black jeans, a dark grey long sleeve T-shirt and combat boots. I slide my knife from the door pocket into my boot, just in case, and pull my jean leg down over it.

Right, let's get to work. I've got a feeling about this place. Not sure whether it's good or bad yet, but I definitely have a feeling.

Walking back around the front, I introduce Dozer to Scar.

Dozer's about the same height as me, clearly works out, maybe around ten years older. He's got brown eyes with a hint of gold running through them and brown hair with a golden sheen in the sun. His hair is shaved on either side but long down the back and middle, which he has in a ponytail at the base of his neck.

He's covered in tattoos all over his hands and fingers, climbing into his tight black T-shirt, out the neck and up the sides of his shaved head. He has a long neat beard that must be down to his pecks. He's wearing blue jeans, slightly baggy on the legs, grease and oil stains on his thighs, and the bottoms shoved into his biker boots.

Scar's wearing this cute sundress, white with yellow flowers all over it, buttoned all the way up the middle. It's a nice warm day, so she grabs a chair and sits at the front of the building. She pulls the dress up, tucking it up around her thighs for maximum leg showing, then she undoes the top buttons folding the top into a sweetheart neck, so it only covers her bra. It has shoestring straps, which she lets fall off her shoulders. She takes a wooden crate from near the door and rests her legs.

Chuckling, Dozer grins. "You okay there, princess? Can I get you anything while you wait? A cocktail? Maybe a parasol?"

"Nah, I'm good, thanks, Dozer. Aren't you a sweetheart?" She grins back at him, clearly ignoring his sarcasm.

He stalks back into the garage, shaking his head and muttering to himself something about she's gonna cause an accident looking like that around here. I follow him into the garage. His leather waistcoat is hung up, and it has "Road Captain" on it. Maybe I will have to learn what that means if I hang around. He leads me inside.

"You any good at electrics?"

"Yep."

"Electrics, as in rewiring the engine?"

"Yep."

"Well, okay then." He points to a gorgeous Harley Davidson Night Rod Custom and then leads me over to it.

I can see the seat removed and the whole wiring loom wrecked.

"What happened to it?"

"Woman scorned."

"Ah, say no more. I know we can be crazy arse bitches, but you guys really know how to push our buttons." I smirk at him, and he points me toward the tools. "I will get cracking."

"Now that's what I like to hear. It's 1 p.m. now. If you can get that bike going by the end of the day, I can give you enough to do till at least the end of the week. Just don't fuck it up more than it already is."

"Sounds good to me, and I'm not sure that's even possible."

Grabbing the wire strippers, volt metre, heat shrink, wire cutters and a crate, I sit down by the bike. It really is a gorgeous piece of machinery. The Harley Davidson is sexy as fuck in matte black, with red accents and chrome detailing. It's making me wet, just hoping to get a chance to ride it when I get it going. "Don't worry, beautiful." I pat at it, stroking the fuel tank. "I'm gonna take real good care of you!"

Looking at the bike, it looks like the said woman scorned had removed the seat, taken a hunting knife to the wiring loom, and just cut through most of it, so although it's a painstaking job, it isn't that taxing. After a couple of hours, Dozer heads out to test a bike.

I'm almost done. I just need to tape up the loom and tidy it up, so I start it up and tell Scar I'm gonna test it. She gives me a two-finger salute. I grab a helmet from the back wall and throw my leg over the bike. I shoot across the parking lot, out of the massive gates and down the long empty road, opening it up and flying down it. My jaw aches from the grin that's plastered across it.

Scar

"Well, hello there, princess!"

I glance over the rims and lower the sunglasses that I have my eyes shut behind. Well, fuck me sideways! Holy Greek god in leather and denim, just walking right up to where I'm sitting. He's about five foot eleven, with blonde hair, short on the sides and longer and top, with bouncing curls shoved back from his face, a short beard trimmed neatly, hazel eyes sparkling with mischief, one of those leather waistcoats things, tight black T-shirt and blue jeans tucked into biker boots. His leather waistcoat says "President" on it.

"Well, hello yourself." I grin from behind my glasses.

"What's a pretty little thing like you doing hanging around a place like this?"

"Me? I'm working on my tan. So what's a pretty little thing like you doing hanging around a place like this?"

He smirks at me. "You think I'm pretty?"

"I do have eyes." I wink at him.

"And they are mighty fucking pretty eyes at that, princess." He takes an appreciative glance over the rest of me. He smiles, licking his lips. "I'm Ares."

"Ah, as in the star sign? Or the Greek God of War?"

He beams at me, all blonde hair sparkling gold in the sun and twinkling hazel eyes that are looking for trouble. "God of War it is, then!" I smile to myself, then realise I said it out loud. I own it and smile up at him. Oh, he's gonna be my kind of trouble. Looking him up and down and loving the feast for my eyes, I tell him, "I'm Scar."

Dozer picks that moment to pull back in.

Ares's brow creases. "Where the fuck's my bike, Dozer?"

I relax into my chair, reposition my sunglasses over my eyes, and close them again. Pointing out the gates and waggling my fingers, I say, "Ray took one for a test ride or whatever."

"Who the fuck is Ray?" Ares snaps, his whole tone changing in a split second. Taking a step closer to me, he asks, "Is that your boyfriend or something, princess?"

"Or something," I reply, smirking.

Dozer clears his throat. "The bike is running then?"

"Of course!"

"Is it finished?"

I cock my glasses back off again, looking at Dozer. "Nearly!"

The next thing we hear, the bike comes back, and Ray pulls up, taking off the helmet she'd borrowed and shouting, "Holy fuck, I think I've just come in my pants!"

Ares crosses his arms over his chest, clearly pissed, glaring at Dozer. "What the fuck? Who the fuck? Dozer, start fucking explaining before I lose my shit!"

"Relax, Ares! Ray's my new mechanic." Ares relaxes at that while Dozer shrugs. "Nice work, kid!"

Ray beams at him. "Cheers, old-timer!"

"Cheeky twat, how bloody old do you think I am? …Don't fucking answer that!"

"So, princess," Ares purrs, "Fancy coming to the clubhouse for a drink or five while these guys finish up?"

"Sure, if you're buying. Hey, bitch face, come find me when you're done!"

"Fuck you, cunty bollock, don't do anything I wouldn't do!" Ray spits out at me as I laugh, standing and starting to walk towards Ares. He grabs my hand, tugging me along as we head to the clubhouse.

Ray: Good news. I've got a bit of work at a garage. It's a big place, and they're busy, so it might lead to something.

Demi: Ray, that's amazing! 'Fingers crossed emoji'

Ray: We'll be here till the end of the week. It's on the top side of Ravenswood, next to the Reapers MC.

Demi: Ray, I think you should forget about it. My brother told me to stay away from there. He says they're real trouble.

Ray: Don't panic, girl, it's fine. We're just checking it out.

Demi: Promise me you'll be safe and be careful. Don't let your mouth get you in trouble, okay? Just stay away from the MC.

Ray: Bit late for that. I'm heading over there now with the guy I'm working with for drinks. Scar's been over there for a couple of hours already, don't worry, I can look after us. We'll be fine.

Demi: Just please be careful, Ray. Those guys are trouble and into some seriously sketchy shit. Just keep in touch, okay? I'm worried about you both.

Ray: Will do, babe. Honestly, I've got this. xx
Demi: Okay. xx

Dice

Stalking into the bar from the tech room where I've been at my computer for hours, Priest, Viking, Tank, and Blade are sitting at our table. I scrub my hand down my face as I sit in my usual chair facing the door, my back towards the bar, opposite Priest.

"You find anything?" Priest asks before my butt even hits the chair.

"Not much." I turn and wave to Roach to grab me a drink.

"You're not still talking about Ninja Barbie, are you?" Viking laughs out.

"Get stuffed, Viking. You'll get it when I find her. She's one of us. I can feel it. She's our missing piece. I tell you, I'm sure of it. She's just a fucking ghost at the minute."

"Yeah, just what we need, a fucking missing piece. Who says there's anything missing? A fucking sister we didn't want and can't get rid of." Blade smirks.

"You'll see. Trust me, we'll find her!" Priest swears.

"What do you think's gonna happen, mate? You think she's just gonna waltz through that door and fit like a glove, be our sister we didn't know we needed? Or you just wanna fuck her cos she's hot as fuck?"

"Dice, you know it's not like that. You all do. I've told you how she spoke to me, and the air vibrated around us... I feel it. She's supposed to be with us!" Priest tries to reassure me.

"Priest, you know I love you, man, I truly do, but do you think you're having a stroke or an aneurysm or something? Because I think you're fucking losing it! And if you're not gonna fuck her, then I'm calling dibs. That video is so topping my spank bank."

Priest scrubs his hand down his face. "That's gross, Dice. You'll see, she's gonna be more than that. You didn't see it, guys. You don't know."

"Dude, you've not shut up about her for three weeks. Dice is doing everything he can. Cut him some slack, okay?" Tank tries to reason.

"It's okay, Tank. Look, I know Ray is not her real name. She's just about to turn twenty-three. Her mum died when she was four, there are some sealed court documents from when she was fourteen, there's an article about her brother being murdered at nineteen, and she was in a car accident on the same night, but then there are no records at the hospital or with the police about what happened to her, as in they're gone, not she wasn't there. Her dad died a couple of months ago from cancer. Other than that, nothing.

"I traced the RV lease and got most of her details off the driver's licence. That's how I got this info. She's part owner in some sort of Adventure Centre, fuck knows what that is, but I'm looking into it.

"I tracked the RV through street cams but lost it on the back roads out of Ravenswood. She's been around Castle Cove, Heighton and Ravenswood and hangs around Dwayne's sometimes, but by the time I get a hit and head over, she's gone. At the minute, she's literally is a ghost, but I will find her.

"I've set up an alert on my phone. It will ping if the RV comes across a video surveillance camera. Until that happens, unless she walks through that fucking door, mate, I'm struggling. I've hardly got anything! But I'm on it, okay? She keeps returning to Heighton, but there's not a lot there, so she disappears for days. She must know someone there somewhere, but I've not found where."

"Did you manage to clean up the footage from the club?" Blade asks.

"Yeah, I've emailed it to Priest."

Priest reaches into his pocket, grabs his phone and hands it to me to key up the video.

"Hey, you guys know who the smoke show is with Pres? I can't put my finger on where I know her from!" Priest scratches his head.

"Shit, they don't make them like that around here!" Viking grins.

"Where the fuck do you think you've ever met a girl like her? Seriously, man, you are totally having a stroke!" I laugh, jabbing at the phone, getting it to fire up. "There's no audio, but you'll get the gist!"

Placing the phone on the table and hitting play, you see the argument and altercation. The guy gets his ass handed to him, then they stalk to the bar, and when she goes to the office, she clearly doesn't give a fuck who Priest is and then goes back to the bar with her friends.

The guys are all shaking their heads. "She's fucking lethal!" Blade mutters under his breath.

"You're telling me!" Priest leans in. "You see what I mean? I mean, come on, you don't think she belongs with us? Guys, come on!"

"What are the chances of us actually finding her?" Viking asks curiously.

"If I can track the RV on video surveillance, then we can find her quite easily. It's only when she uses the back roads that I can't locate her, but she will pass through one before much longer. She's not far away. She's still somewhere on this side of Ravenswood."

"Hang on a minute, play that video back again," Blade asks.

I lean in, adjusting it and setting it back up before hitting play.

"Wait, pause it, back it up," he says again.

"That's her!" Blade points frantically at the screen.

"Blade, we know that's her. What the fuck you talking about?" I mean, seriously, is everyone having a fucking stroke?

"Back it up again. Stop it when she goes back to her friends," he sighs like I'm the idiot.

"What is it?" Priest leans over.

"The friend that's with her, that's her with Pres, I'm sure of it."

As we all check the girl and the phone and the girl again.

"I mean, it could be. She looks similar. I will try and grab a… holy fucking shit!" I mutter under my breath.

"What's up, Dice?"

Nodding behind Priest, we glance around and see her. It's fucking her. She's just waltzed straight into the fucking bar with Dozer. "What the actual fuck?"

No one says another word. Priest tracks her every move. The rest lean in, whispering, discussing the likelihood of any of this actually happening.

As soon as she sees her friend, her eyes lock on her, and she strolls over to them.

Scar

After about an hour or so, Ray and Dozer came in, eyes roaming for me. As soon as she clocks me, she locks on and doesn't look away. Ray has clearly showered but is still wearing a long sleeve T-shirt and jeans, just slightly different variations of grey and black.

Jesus, she really has no clue how hot she is. The I-don't-give-a-fuck attitude just makes her that much hotter. The T-shirt clinging to her perky tits and athletic body and her jeans hugging her curvy arse and hips and strong thighs and those bloody legs for days, even though she's only an inch taller than me, her body shape and toned physique make her look so much taller, like a model. She really does give me a lady boner some days. I know we don't roll like that anymore, but I've seen what she's working with, and damn. Some days she really makes me question our life choices.

As they walk into the bar, there's a pool table and darts board on their left with a couple of tables and chairs. There are five guys sitting huddled around one of the tables, one of them a guy who looks so out of place here, he locks onto her as she walks in, and his gaze follows her every move. He has dark, slicked-to-the-side hair and sharp features looking almost chiselled from stone or marble. He looks too clean-cut to be here, even though he's in a black T-shirt and jeans. They don't quite fit his look. He looks like he would be more at home in a suit.

There's a corridor going off behind the bar somewhere, and the bar is along the back third of the left wall. Half a dozen stools are at the bar, and two guys are sitting talking in the ones nearest the back wall.

There's another door on the back wall near the bar and a fireplace to the right. At the side of the fireplace is a raised area with a couple of booths, and we sat in the one nearest the fireplace. Although it isn't lit, it's still way too warm for a fire!

There are two booths beside us, and a couple of girls, well, really, they look like two-dollar hookers sitting there. One of them is almost sucking off the guy that's with them. A few other guys are dotted around talking, but it isn't overly busy.

Ares follows my gaze and laughs. "Club sluts."

I scrunch up my face at him. "Nice!"

Ray and Dozer come over to say hi, smirking Ray glances between Ares and me.

"You looking after my sister, Boyband?"

Cocking a brow at her with a confused look on his face, he asks, "Boyband?"

"Yeah, Boyband," she huffs out.

"Where the fuck did that come from?" He still looks confused.

"I'm gonna grab a drink. You guys want anything?" Clearly ignoring Ares's question before asking her own. Typical Ray. We all say no as she walks over to the bar. She orders a drink. Ares shouts over to the guy behind the bar that her drinks are on him. The young guy looks about seventeen at most. He's scrawny, a bit shorter than Ray, and he has darker skin, maybe Mexican, with black hair, buzzed, and dark bug-like eyes. He introduces himself as Roach, grabbing her the tequila she's asked for. She tilts her glass to Ares in cheers and downs it.

She taps the glass again, and Roach tops it up. Before she can take a swig, a guy with greasy-looking long black hair and a bit of a beer belly hanging over his jeans sits beside her with his back to the bar facing us. He puts his left hand on her left thigh and squeezes.

"Fuck," I mutter under my breath.

Ares looks over at me. "What's up, princess?"

"I just need to go and stop Ray from laying that guy out." He doesn't remove his hand, just slides it up her thigh, gripping tighter, and I can physically see her tense from here. He leans over to her ear, but I can hear what he says. He isn't quiet about it at all.

"Out the back now, and suck my cock, then I'm gonna fuck you against the wall and come all over you while you beg for more, and if you're a good little club slut, I will let you suck my cock clean after."

Cringing, I stand up to head over, but Ares puts his hand on my arm, shaking his head. Besides holding my hand on the way here, he hasn't touched me at all.

I look down at him in panic. "If I don't go over there and get him away from her, this will not end well! You need to let me go!" I try to move away as Dozer stands before me, blocking my way.

"Guys, please, seriously, you don't understand. I need to stop this. We don't want any trouble!"

"He's a hang around." Ares shrugs. "He's a nothing and a no one around here, just a wannabe. Let's see how this plays out; you've got me intrigued."

Blowing out a breath, I sit back down, and Dozer steps to the side, not taking his eyes off Ray. The guy keeps his left hand on her thigh and reaches around with his right to grab her arse.

I twitch as if I'm gonna get up again, but Ares puts his hand on my thigh, gripping in warning to stay put. All three of us stare at Ray and the guy.

Ray slowly turns on her stool so she's almost facing the guy and grinds her teeth at him. "As lovely as you think that offer is, I'm gonna confirm your request is denied. Now, kindly remove them!" she snarls.

"I'm assuming you mean my pants, sugar." He laughs as he squeezes her arse, then releases it, sliding his hand up her arm, grazing her tit as he goes, then sliding his hand behind her neck.

"Fucking. Remove. Them," she grits out again. I shift again, and Ares grips my thigh firmer as Dozer puts his hand on my shoulder. I'm physically vibrating. Ray slowly turns her head to me, a stone-cold blank stare plastered across her beautiful face. I know what she's asking. Can I do this? Can I lash out? Can I break bones? Can I kill him if I need to? I'm her voice of reason in this situation, she's looking to me to give her an out, to stop this, to call it off, but I can't. I look at Ares and Dozer, and then I do the only thing I can to help my sister. I nod in acknowledgement of all her unasked questions.

Everything seems to happen in slow motion after that point. This eerie grin spreads across her mouth, causing me to shiver in the guys' hold. They both tense slightly but remain firm. She turns back to face the slime ball and leans ever so slightly towards him. The dick totally misreads the sign. As he leans in for a kiss, Ray draws back her head and nuts him straight in the nose, blood exploding out everywhere.

He lets out a shriek, grabbing the attention of everyone in the bar. No one moves to help him. They just all stare. The guy who had been tracking Ray's movements leans into the circle of guys, and they all lean forward to listen to him, and he whispers something, then all their gazes shoot around with interest.

At the same time, she grabs his left hand, which is resting on her thigh, and yanks his middle two fingers back. *Crunch*. Fuck, that sounds like they're broken. His hand from behind her neck grabs for her face as she grabs onto his wrist, still holding his fingers in her other hand and twisting violently. There's another almighty crunch and another squeal. That's his wrist fucked up. He goes to punch her. I'm positive she's just broken his wrist, so I'm not sure what he thought he was gonna achieve as he staggers off his stool.

Ray blocks his punch, causing him to gasp. Yep, his wrist is definitely broken. She still holds onto his left fingers, wrenching them back the whole time as she blocks his punch and punches him in the throat while she knees him in the bollocks. He grabs his bollocks with his right hand, cupping them as if he can make the pain stop, tears streaming down his face, mixing with the blood already streaming from his nose over his mouth and down his chin.

Hitting the floor with his knees dropping his broken fingers, she punches him in the side of the temple knocking him to the floor.

"Lights out, motherfucker," she snarls over him as he hits the deck. She spits on him, wiping the back of her arm across her mouth and wiping her hands down her jeans. There are a few muttered "Holy fucks" and a couple of "Shits" called out and some wide smiles. I'm sure the dark-haired guy says what sounds like, "Told you," but I can't be sure.

Ares rises, barking out a laugh. Stepping forward to Dozer's side, he nods at Ray smiling, and I see the tension roll away. Then, looking at the five guys huddled around the table watching her every move, he barks, "Take out the trash and make sure he gets the message!"

Ray's eyes track Ares's to the guys at the table, and there's a weird wide-eyed look which spreads across her face for a split second before it's gone again in an instant, an almost confused recognition maybe.

Turning to Roach, Ares shouts, "Don't just stand there gawping, Prospect! Give the lady something to wipe her hands on and pour her another fucking drink!"

Then he bellows, "Prospect! Clean this fucking mess up!"

Two of the five guys are already dragging the slimy fucker out of the bar, with two of the others opening up the door. The fifth guy at the back, a tall fucker with long blonde hair in a ponytail tied with a length of leather wrapping a couple of inches around it at the base of his skull and a mid-length beard almost reaching his chest, looking like an honest to God Viking, he turns back. Piercing blue eyes sparkle with amusement as he takes in Ray standing there with that blank bloody stare again. He winks at her and smirks as she gives him a feral smirk back. Nodding to her, he steps out of the bar with the others and the door slams shut behind them. The two guys at the bar just turn back to their drinks and carry on talking.

Ray bends down, picks up the stool the slimy guy had been sitting on, and sits back down on her own stool. Roach hands her a damp towel and pours her another tequila leaving the bottle on the bar for her. Another guy comes rushing in from the corridor with a mop and bucket and starts mopping the floor.

Ares sits back down next to me as Dozer takes the seat on the other side. "I think I'm gonna enjoy having you ladies here for a while!" Turning to face me with a totally genuine smile, he grabs the back of my neck, tilting my gaze to him with his thumb pushed under my jaw before devouring my lips and pressing his tongue in my mouth. Well, fuck me, that escalated quickly. He doesn't let up till we're both out of breath and panting. He rubs his thumb across my bottom lip as he leans in and licks it.

Locking eyes, he whispers, "Perfect!" We hold each other's gaze, making my breath come out really harsh. God only knows how long we sit there, lost in each other's gaze, then the door slams open, and the five guys come in laughing and shoving each other. The tall Viking guy glances over at us, and Ares nods at him while he nods back with a smirk, then nods towards Ray, who is still sitting at the bar. And Ares gives a swift nod, then turns to face me.

"So, princess, how much trouble are you two gonna cause me?"

With a nervous laugh, I reply, "I've no idea what you mean!"

Barking out a laugh, he kisses me again like he needs the oxygen directly from my lungs. Fuck me. I'm a puddle and in deep fucking shit!

Breaking apart, I look over at Ray. She's smiling up at me, and I wink as she winks back. The Viking dude leans next to her, whispering something into her ear, grabbing the tequila off the bar and stalking over to the other four.

Ray rises from her stool, looking back at me, gesturing in their direction. I smile back, and off she stalks after him. I'm confused. He's definitely not her type. She's normally into dark-haired guys, for one, but when she gets over there, she snatches the tequila from his hand, takes a massive gulp and wipes her mouth across her sleeve; handing it back, he claps her on the shoulder, but she just smiles at him, an honest to God smile.

Ray hates guys touching her. One of them leans over and grabs her behind the neck, leaning in and whispering something in her ear, she barks out a laugh at whatever he says, and he steps back, but those guys introduce themselves to her and shake her hand. One high-fives her, and another fist-bumps her, then the Viking throws his arm around her shoulder and pulls her into a side hug, and they both walk over to the pool table to play. WTAF?

She must feel safe with them and not a speck of sexual tension, which she normally picks up on straight away, so even with the sheer size of them, she isn't remotely intimidated.

Ares looks at my pained expression. "Hey, princess, what's up?"

"Nothing, just keeping an eye on Ray."

"Don't worry, princess. The boys will look after her. I trust those guys with my life." He points over to them. "The blonde one with his arm around her is Viking."

Shrugging, I reply, "Figures! I can see why."

Laughing, he carries on, "The one next to him is Dice, then Blade, Tank and Priest. They're part of my inner circle. They're known as The Fucked Up Five."

"Nice, she'll fit right in!" Turning, I grin at him, and he kisses me again, fuck he's so hot!

Ray

Sitting back at the bar, a Viking-looking dude with "Vice President" on his cut swaggers over, leans next to me and whispers into my ear, "Come on, little 'un, Priest has been looking for you. Come have a drink with us... you're gonna fit right in. We're The Fucked Up Five, and apparently, you're our newest member!" He grabs the tequila off the bar and stalks over to the other four.

I rise from my stool and look back at Scar. I nod in their direction. She smiles back, and off I walk after him. I snatch the tequila from his hand and take a massive gulp. I wipe my mouth across my sleeve, then roll my lip ring through my teeth, handing it back, he claps me on the shoulder, but I just smile at him. I like him already.

I normally hate guys touching me, but then Priest, his cut says, "Secretary," leans over and grabs me behind the neck. "Told you I'd see you soon, Ray!"

I bark out a laugh in reply, and he steps back, but the other guys step up and introduce themselves to me. One shakes my hand and tells me he's Tank, "Tail Gunner," or whatever the fuck that is. He's as tall as he is wide at five foot nine, his biceps are as big as my face, and he has hazel eyes and warm golden brown hair. He looks like he's covered in the most beautiful, colourful tattoos and scars from what skin is visible.

One high-fives me and introduces himself as Blade, also known as "Captain." His dark brown, almost black hair and dark brown eyes compliment his chocolate brown skin. He's covered in tribal tattoos and piercings.

Another fist-bumps me, nodding. His name's Dice, "Sergeant at Arms." He's five foot eleven and looks to be mixed race, some Asian maybe, with jet black hair, shorter on the sides, warm dark brown eyes and warm tan skin. He winks and grins at me while stepping back. Then the Viking looking one, all blonde hair and blue eyes, he's the tallest at around six foot two, throws his arm around my shoulder and pulls me into a side hug. He's called Viking, apparently.

They steer me over to the pool table to play. After playing pool and darts for most of the night, their personalities start to shine. Priest doesn't swear, Tank doesn't say much, mostly grunts and laughs but will talk for extended periods when he's passionate about a topic before returning to grunting again.

Dice seems quite flirty, but it doesn't fully hit as flirty, as if he isn't trying it on. There's something there, and he's totally hot. Definitely my type looks-wise, with his dark hair. There's just something missing, though, Priest would have been my type, too, but he's too clean-cut for me. Viking's loud and leary, right up my street. Blade's calmer than Viking, but still funny. Together they all gel and bounce off each other. It's easy to see they have been friends for a long time, like me and Scar. That bond's hard to miss and naturally flows through them all. I'm definitely gonna spend more time getting to know these guys for as long as we're here.

Scar

Ray heads over to us at around 11 p.m., nodding to each of us in turn. Dozer has already left, telling Ray to be at the garage at 9 a.m.

"Alright, knobhead, Boyband?" She smirks. "I'm gonna head back to the van. You coming, Sis?"

"Sticking with Boyband, eh?" His confused look in her direction only makes her smugger.

"Yep, if the cap fits, slap that fucker on!"

He scratches his head. "It's like you're speaking another language. I have no fucking idea what you're saying!"

Laughing, she turns and walks away,

Looking over at Ares, I say, "Thanks for tonight. I should head off. I had a right laugh, though. Cheers!"

Standing and sliding out of the seat, he grabs my hand. "I'll walk you out!" He holds my hand all the way out of the bar and around the back of the garage, where Ray has already disappeared into the van. As we get to the van, I turn to say goodnight.

Before the words have left my lips, he spins me around, pushes me up against the garage wall, and then kisses my lips, sliding down to my neck, nipping and licking across my collarbone. A moan slips between my lips as he pins me to the wall. One large rough hand grabs my waist, and the other slides down to my thigh, the roughness of his hand instigating small electric pulses through every touch, and he starts sliding it up under my dress.

I gasp as his touch meets my pants. He looks into my eyes, grinning, sliding my hands into his hair at the back of his neck. I know he can feel how wet I am. Fuck, I want him so bad, but I'm trying to be chill about it. Next, he's circling my clit through the fabric of my pants as he kisses me again.

I think I'm losing my goddamn mind as he slides his fingers around the fabric, stroking them through my pussy. I moan into his mouth, and I can feel the smirk appear on his lips. I lift my leg and wrap it around his hip, pulling him closer as his fingers push inside me.

"Princess, fuck." He starts pumping his fingers in and out of me, rubbing my clit with his thumb. Using my leg that's wrapped around his hip, I grind against him, trying to get some friction or traction or fucking something.

"Fuck! Ares!" I pant into his mouth as he swallows my cries. He circles my clit firmer and faster, pumping his fingers in the most delicious way. As we break apart from the kiss, gasping for air, he flicks across my clit again, burying his fingers right inside me. My head slams backwards, and he bites down on my neck. He catapults me over the edge, and I'm freefalling. I'm coming, seeing stars and struggling for breath. He keeps circling, flicking and pumping, dragging out my orgasm until my legs are shaky, and I breathe harshly. My thigh drops from around him, and we stand gasping, chest to chest, staring into each other's eyes, just breathing in each other's breaths.

My eyes shoot up as the van door swings open. Ray stands there, clapping. "Nice moves, Boyband."

"Fuck," he breathes out, resting his head against my shoulder with his back to her.

"Jesus, Ray … you're a fucking arsehole, you know that?" my voice comes out all breathy and sexy.

Winking at me, she slams the door, locking it and shouting through it, "I'll see ya tomorrow night, guys!"

Flipping the bird to the van door that's now well and truly locked, I say, "Fuck, Ray, stop being a dick and let me in!"

Ares grabs my hand, pulling me back into his arms. "You can stay with me if you need to."

"She's only messing. If I knock, she'll let me in."

"Okay, let me rephrase that. I want you to stay with me."

Looking into his eyes and biting my lower lip, he searches my face for any sign of a no, and when there isn't one, he turns and walks back towards the bar dragging me behind him.

I shout insults at Ray and the van over my shoulder as I'm dragged away.

"Wow, I don't understand half those swear words! They are swear words, right?" He says, dragging me right past the door to the bar.

While I'm laughing, I ask, "Hey, where are we going?"

"I thought it would be better to go in the other door rather than dragging you back through the bar for everyone to see." He shrugs his shoulders.

Laughing, I shake my head. "Ah, I see. Rather not let anyone know you're slumming it! ...Ouch!"

My back is immediately pushed into the side of the building as he spins, crowding me and getting in my face. There isn't much height difference, so I'm looking into his eyes, and I can see the rage.

"Is that what you really think? I thought taking you this way would be less embarrassing for you!" He jabs his finger at me. "I was trying to be a gentleman. I don't want people thinking you are just some club slut. Easy and fair game!"

Pushing off the wall, I channel my inner Ray and get back in his face. I snarl, "Don't worry about my reputation, sweetheart. I don't have a fuck to give when it comes to what people think of me! I'm good! And don't worry. I will save you the trouble. I'm going back to the van." I shove past him and storm back across the front of the building!

"Fuck." Then heavy quick boot steps are chasing me down, sounding behind me, but I ignore them and carry on.

"Stop."

Still, I carry on.

"Wait!"

I keep walking briskly.

"Fuck's sake, Scar, I'm sorry, okay? I was just trying to be a decent guy, a nice guy for a change."

Putting his hand on my shoulder and bringing me to a stop, he turns me around, holding both my shoulders at arm's length. "That'll teach me to try and play the nice guy, huh?"

Stepping into him, I cup his face with my hand as he closes his eyes, and I take a deep breath, really looking at his features. When he opens his eyes, I'm staring at him. "I never asked you to try and be something you're not. I never asked you to play the good guy. I never asked you to pretend. Just be you!"

"Really?"

"Yeah, really!" He grabs me and drags me in for the filthiest kiss. Then he takes a step back, holding my hand out before bending and stepping forward at the same time. He then throws me over his shoulder, smacks my arse and growls, "I'm taking you to my room, and I'm not letting you out till morning and maybe not even then!"

Then he storms back towards the bar, kicks the door open, and storms through. In front of everyone, he heads into the corridor. As he swings into the corridor, I look up, and every pair of eyes is on me. I give the dirtiest grin I can and wink. That's when the catcalls and wolf whistles start, and that's all I hear until I'm thrown on the bed, and the door is kicked shut behind us.

"Holy fuck! Spank me again!" I grin up at him.

The dirtiest, smutty laugh falls from his lips as he climbs up my body and kisses me like his life depends on it. Breaking the kiss, he looks down at me, stroking back a strand of hair, leaning up on his arms and taking his gaze down me, then smirking, he starts flicking the buttons undone one by one until my dress is totally unbuttoned. He pulls it away from my body and sits back. "Fucking hell, princess, let me just look at you!"

Adjusting his dick, he goes to lean back over me, but I raise my foot, putting it on his shoulder, stopping him dead in his tracks. "I think you're wearing far too many clothes for this situation."

I lick my lips as he reaches between his shoulder blades and grabs a handful of shirt, and drags it over his head in one swift, hot, sexy as fuck motion, throwing it on the floor and then unbuckling his jeans. I raise up onto my elbows so I can admire the view. He undoes his fly and slowly shoves his jeans and boxers over his hips, freeing his impressive dick, springing out from behind the fabric. He shuffles his jeans off while kneeling between my legs and kicks them to the floor, leaning forward and resting his hands on the side of my shoulders.

I look down the length of his body as my mouth waters. He has a chest tattoo of who I think is Ares. It looks like a Spartan, maybe? There's a boar and Greek patterns, a beautiful woman on one side, and the Reaper club tattoo on his right bicep. They are stunning and done in blacks, greys and whites with subtle colours entwined through them, his sculpted chest is divine, and his stomach muscles and his Adonis belt are mouth-wateringly delicious, and then there's his dick. It's definitely eyeing me with interest, looking back up at him and smirking.

He huffs at me. "Now who's the one wearing too many clothes?"

I push my chest up, reach a hand behind me, and unfasten my bra. His mouth is on me, biting down on my nipple through my bra before I finish undoing the clasp. I arch into him even further, and he flicks my tit out of the cup, licking and sucking it with intent. I drag the bra with my dress down my arms, wriggle it from under my body, and throw it off the bed, leaving me in just my pants.

Pushing himself up, he takes me all in. "Fuck, I don't know where to start," he gasps out, his pupils blown and his voice becoming all gravelly.

"Then let me!" Pushing him off me onto his back, I slide down between his legs and nip at his dick with my teeth!

"Nope!" Is all he says before flipping me over and pinning me to the bed.

"Nope?" I question him.

"Yep, nope! I'm not having you taking over and then me blowing my load like a twelve-year-old." He slides down my body, licking and caressing as he goes. He stills and settles between my legs, rubbing his fingers over the fabric of my pants.

"Fuck," I pant and arch my back at him.

Grinning from between my thighs, he doesn't break eye contact while shoving my pants to the side and running his tongue through my wet lips, drawing out a gasp from me. I can feel his lips kick up in a smirk before plunging his tongue inside me a few times and then replacing it with two fingers while sliding his mouth up to suck my clit.

I buck off the bed, and he pushes me down with his hand on my torso. Holding me in place, he slides his fingers in and out, causing slight tremors from my already sensitive clit and the orgasm he already gave me, sliding and stroking my inner top walls punishingly, sucking my clit into his mouth and rolling his tongue around it. I'm overstimulated and loving every second.

"Fuck, Ares!" I pant out.

"Fucking hell, Scar, I love the way my name sounds in your husky voice." Leaning back down and licking through my wet lips again, he whispers, "Say it again, princess."

"Ares!"

"Again!"

"Ares, fuck…"

"Again, princess!"

"Ares, please… Fuck, Ares… Ares, I'm… I'm gonna… Fuck!"

Clamping down my thighs on him and grinding myself against his face, I lose it, fireworks shootlng across my vision. I grip his hair in my fist, holding him there while I grind down on his face. I hope he has gills and can breathe through them, or this will be one hell of a way to suffocate. He holds his tongue against my opening, letting me come straight into his mouth, then he licks me slowly from back to front, groaning while devouring every last drop, panting so hard I think I may pass out, he licks me again, and if he wasn't holding me down, I think I would shoot off the bed.

"Shit, that was … "

"Yep!" He nods. "I need to feel you do that again!"

He dives right in face first between my legs, having still not come down from the first orgasm. With a few licks and sucks and more than a few nips and bites, I'm off again, my vision darkening as I gasp for breath, rocketing into my third orgasm, my mind fuzzing, my breaths ragged. Can you pass out from an orgasm? I think I'm about to find out! Looking into his beautiful twinkling hazel eyes, he smirks up at me. "Again?"

I grab a handful of his hair, dragging him up my body. "Arsehole! Fuck me now before I pass out."

Sliding straight inside me, I gasp as he thrusts in until he hits my cervix, causing a full-on body tremor.

He gasps out, "Fucking hell, Scar, Jesus!"

He just stays there, fully settled, staring into my eyes, panting, both lost in the moment. Leaning down, he kisses me. He starts moving steadily to start with, then breaking the kiss, he leans up with more conviction, slamming into me over and over again. Fuck, I can feel another orgasm building, my toes curling. I don't know if I can hang onto consciousness again. I barely made it last time. Relentless, he pounds and pounds as my ears start to ring and my vision dots with black spots. I blink to try and clear them, but it's no use as it hits for the final time. I scream his name as he grunts mine, and suddenly, I'm falling over the edge and dragging him with me.

Spilling inside me with the force of a freight train as he gasps, "Fuck, condom!"

"Shit!" I gasp. Staring into each other's eyes, he lets out a shaky breath. I pant, trying to think straight. Jesus, what the fuck was I thinking? I'm never this careless. Jesus, Scar, you utter twat. I'm mentally berating myself in between panting out breaths and trying to steady my heart and stop it from pounding out of my chest.

"Hey, Scar… you okay?" I blink at him and take in a deep breath, nodding.

"I can't believe we did that! Fuck, what were we thinking? Jesus!" I scrub my palms into my eyes, breathe out again and slam my head back into the mattress.

Ares reaches up, pulling my hands away from my face, his dick still buried inside me. "Hey, shit, I'm sorry. Fuck."

I shake my head. "It wasn't just you. I've clearly lost my mind!" Cupping my cheek, he leans in and kisses me. It's so tender in comparison to the way he's just fucked me. It takes me by surprise.

I close my eyes and breathe him in, letting him calm me, looking back up at him and letting out a sigh. "Hey, I'm covered in the birth control department. I'm clean. We got tested before we came out here."

He lets out a shaky breath. "I've only fucked one person since I got tested, and we always used condoms, but maybe we should get tested just to be safe!" We both take a deep breath. I twitch as I feel his dick start to harden again. I look him in the eyes, contemplating what I should do now. "Sorry, can't help it. You're fucking gorgeous." He leans down to kiss me, and he starts to pull out.

I wrap my legs around him. "Well, it seems a shame to waste it now we're here."

He smiles down at me. "You sure?"

Grinding my hips and grinning, I waggle my eyebrows at him. "Well, we're here now!"

"I knew you would be the best kind of trouble, princess," he breathes into my neck as he slowly starts thrusting his hips in and out in slow, frustrating moves, grinning into the crook of my neck and licking and nipping at my collar bone. He pulls back, looking into my eyes like he's about to steal my soul.

"I want to hear my name on those lips for as long as you'll allow me." He thrusts into me as if he's trying to force me through the bed.

I gasp up at him. "Fuck me like you own me, Ares!"

And he does, and then again, just to prove it.

Ares

That moment before you're fully awake, where you're not quite with it, and everything still feels warm and happy…

I stretch and feel the ache in my balls and the tenderness of my cock. Jesus, it chafes, but in the most worthwhile of ways.

I had spent most of the night buried in the most beautiful woman I had ever seen. Stretching again and smiling, I reach out to drag her closer, only to find the bed empty. I open my eyes, the smile slipping from my face. Yep, the bed is definitely empty. I slide my hand across it. It's cold too. Sitting myself up, I can feel the tight pull of my stomach muscles.

Glancing around the room, I get out of bed and pad to the bathroom, knocking on the door. There's no answer. "Morning, princess."

I push the door gently, shoving it back all the way. It's empty.

"Fuck."

I check the clock. It's 7.30 in the morning, and we didn't pass out till at least 5 a.m. Scrubbing a hand down my face and heading back to grab some clothes, I see the note on the top of the drawers under my wallet.

THNX

S

X

...Well, fuck me, that stings! I drag on some clothes and head out to look for her. As I walk through the bar, it's deserted. I stomp out the door and across the parking lot, ducking round the side to head to the RV at the back of the garage.

I stop dead. It isn't there! Where the fuck is it? That must mean Ray's gone too. What the actual fuck? She's supposed to start work today. Fuck, I know Dozer won't be here till about 9 a.m. at the earliest, so I head inside to get a shower, and at 8.45, I'm pacing in front of the garage, checking my watch every thirty bloody seconds. What the fuck is wrong with me?

I hear the rumble of a bike as Dozer pulls in, taking one look at my face. "Fuck, Pres, you okay?"

"Yeah, I'm good, mate. What time's Ray supposed to be here?"

Dozer looks down at his watch. "Told her nine, so she shouldn't be long." He glances away and then back again. "She not in the van?"

"No! Van's gone."

"Fuck's sake, she best not let me down. I booked extra in today, thinking I'd have her here." He scrubs his hand down his face he stares at me. "I haven't even had a fucking coffee yet. It's too early to deal with the fallout if I have to cancel jobs, fucking hell!"

He kicks at the wall. My head spins around as I hear the sound of a car coming up the road, shit, that definitely isn't the RV. The car pulls right past us and around the back.

"Who the fuck is that?" We stomp around the corner as we can't see through the reflection on the glass. As we get halfway around, we're met by Ray.

"What the fuck?" I spit out. "Whose fucking car is that?" I bark at her.

"Morning, Boyband! If I'd known you'd be here, I would have grabbed you a coffee! Morning, old-timer! Here!" She thrusts a coffee in Dozer's direction, ignoring my question, then grabs the bag from under her arm, looking in it, then at me, then in it again, before setting her gaze on me. "Doughnut?"

I turn around without answering and storm back to the clubhouse. Fucking hell, I want to punch something, and I'm gonna have an annoying reminder of last night for at least a few days as my cock is chaffing in my jeans something rotten, and my boxers are fucking damp from thinking about her. Fuck my life!

Ray

Laughing, I hold the bag out to Dozer. "Doughnut?"

"Sure, thanks." He shakes his head, grabs a doughnut and shoves it into his face. "What's his problem?"

"Ah, you know about yay high"—I gesture slightly smaller than me—"blonde, big tits, curves for days, beautiful blue eyes and pouty lips, she has a habit of getting under a guy's skin!"

"Nah, no way, Pres isn't like that."

"What happened to the bird who wrecked his wiring?" I walk back around to the garage.

Dozer fills me in. "Shay? They were together for a while, a few months or so. She was what we call a club slut. Sorry, they're here to bag a guy to raise their status. They always have their eyes set on the Pres, one of the inner circle, or his officers. There were a couple in last night, but since Shay is gone, they've been scarce. Shay was no different. She just got lucky.

"She thought they were gonna shack up together, even though Pres never promised her anything. He's never been into fucking around like some of the others. They go from one girl to the next or two at a time, but he likes to stick to the same one, not for any other reason than he doesn't like fucking multiple girls that are also fucking multiple guys, so he picked one and stuck with her.

"I don't even think he liked her all that much. It was just a fuck, but she started getting ideas above her station, bossing some of the guys and some of the wives around like she was some big shot, so he cut her loose. That's what happened to the bike!"

Grimacing, all I can think to say is, "Oh."

"Have you seen Scar this morning?"

"Yeah, we went to meet a friend at the diner for breakfast. I left them there with the van and borrowed Dem's car as they needed to use the van for something." I shrug.

"Dem?" he asks, definitely thinking she's a dude. "Did she seem off?"

"Nah, she was fine. She said she was tired and a little sore from fucking all night but said it was totally worth it!"

"Jesus, Ray, you could have just said she was fine. So what makes you think she's his problem?"

"Because she's my sister, I know her, and I know how men get when they... sample the goods. Honestly, she's like some kind of siren, maybe even a succubus... they just can't seem to get enough! Don't tell me you haven't noticed how fucking hot she is. Who knows, but I bet you now that he's had a taste; he's gonna be hounding after her!"

"Yeah, she's a pretty girl, but I will take that bet. I bet she will end up chasing him."

"You're on, old-timer, shall we say $500? I bet he'll be chasing her!" Shaking on it, we finish our doughnuts and head into the garage.

I finish the day five hundred dollars better off. We didn't need to see Scar. We saw Ares a total of eight times that day, even though he never asked about her. Dozer said he might usually call in once, maybe twice a week, never multiples in a day, so Dozer's pretty convinced I'm right, and there's no way on this earth I'm gonna hang around on that bet!

As we finish for the day, Dozer says we don't have to start till 10 a.m. tomorrow, and as it's Friday, he asked me if I want any work next week. I take his number, say I will speak to Scar tonight, and let him know in the morning. I head out before Ares can make another appearance, as it's getting really fucking awkward!

Arriving at Demi's, I crash on the sofa.

"Jesus, Ray. You're filthy."

Smirking and raising my brows, I add in a suggestive tone, "I know, right?" I wink at Demi and chuckle to myself.

"Argh! Get your dirty ass off my sofa and get in the shower. Dinner will be ready in ten."

Jumping to my feet and saluting, I head into the bathroom. Once I've finished, I head back to the kitchen.

Scar's at the table, nose buried in her phone. "What the fuck you doing, bitch tits?"

She looks up at me. "What the fuck do you mean, dick face? I think it's fucking obvious I'm on my fucking phone!"

"Not that, twat waffle. You and Boyband?"

Slowly putting her phone down and turning to face me, she asks, "What do you mean?"

"What did you do to him?"

"I didn't do anything to him! ...Well, I did... I did lots of things to him... All really dirty... Dirty things, and he did plenty right back... hmm... Why, what's up?"

"He's been a right twat all day, he's been by the garage eight times, and Dozer says he barely sees him normally." I point at her. "You did something, didn't you, with all that!" I gesture to her whole body.

Demi looks really confused, but Scar just flushes and stays quiet.

"Come on, Scar! Spill!" I hound her.

"Can we at least eat first?" She flushes again. So after we've eaten, we go in the living room, and Scar explains what they did and how they passed out from all the fucking. Then she got up and left, leaving him a note to say thanks, and that was it.

"Holy shit!" I laugh. "Girl, you got under his skin good and proper. You totally dude-checked him!" By the look on her face, it's a mutual feeling. "Fuck, you like him! You really like him! You fucking panicked, didn't you? Ha! Fucker, I knew it! You like him. You wanna do stuff again, don't you? I knew it! "

Demi had been quiet this whole time, then blurted out, "How do you guys do that? Know what each other's thinking without saying it?"

We both shrug. "We've been friends for a long time, nearly nine years. We know everything about each other."

"Speaking of knowing everything about each other, don't forget we're going to Uncle Bernie's this weekend," Scar reminds me.

"Argh, do we have to?"

"Yes, Ray, we have to."

"Argh, this is gonna be the worst! Demi, you're coming with us!"

"Wait, what? ...I thought you loved your Pa Bernie and the family?"

"Oh my God, I do so much, but this weekend will be... fucking horrific!"

Scar laughs, shaking her head at me. "You're such a fucking drama queen. It will be great, and you know it!"

"Blah, blah, blah, fuck you, Scar!" I stomp off to lie on Demi's bed, leaving the door open so I can hear them still, but sulk like a toddler.

"What's wrong with Ray? It's not like her to be so... moody." I hear Demi ask.

"It's her twenty-third birthday this weekend, so we're having a pool party at Uncle Bernie's. She just hates all the fuss and attention. Also, it's the first one without her dad and away from the pas, which will only make us amp it up to torture her. She'll love it, really."

"No, I won't. It will be terrible!" I shout back.

"It'll be entertaining, and it will be great. You'll get to meet Bernie and Marie and Bran and Dane. I think Dane is bringing his girlfriend so we can torture her too. She'll be all like, 'Argh, don't splash me, don't get my hair wet. Ah, no, my mascara!' You'll love it!"

Scar's probably fanning her face, being all dramatic, which makes me crack up.

"Wait, you sure they won't mind me coming?"

"Nah, they said to bring you. It will be great. Pack your swimmers!"

Sulking on the bed, I decide to stop being a little bitch and stroll back into the kitchen. I love my birthday, I just don't like all the fuss, which just makes them go mad to try and torture me. Also, I miss my dad, my pas, and home, but I know I will have a great time, so I just need to suck it up. I need to find out what's happening with Scar and Boyband!

"Hey, bitch face. Spill on you and Boyband! He gave you the feels, didn't he?"

"Fuck, guys, I'm so screwed. He's amazing, and I wanted to stay with him, but I knew he would just blow me off like guys do, so I thought I would just save him the hassle. All I thought was, 'Treat him mean; keep him keen!' Fuck my life. What am I gonna do? I really want to see him again, but I don't think he will be interested!"

"I'm at work tomorrow. Why don't you drop me off but then come back to get me later, so at least you've got an excuse to be there without it looking like you're hanging around to see him?"

"What the fuck am I doing? I normally don't give a shit about guys, but he really got under my skin! Fucking facepalm emoji!"

That's it. We all burst out laughing. Fucking facepalm emoji looks like it's here to stay. Sometimes, it just sums everything up!

The next day Scar drops me at work but leaves me on the road and fucks off. She's coming back about four, and then we're gonna pick Demi up as she's at work till six.

Scar backs in front of the garage. Before she even has it in park, Boyband's striding across the parking lot towards her. She's hanging out the window talking to me, and I can see him stalking across to the other side of the van, pulling the door open. She flinches and spins to see him getting in the front next to her.

"Erm, hey… what you doing?"

"Erm, hey yourself, and what does it look like?"

Wow, this is awkward as fuck. I bail.

"I'm still busy, Scar! I will be out in about an hour or so, okay?" I shout over my shoulder as I disappear back into the garage.

Scar

"Okay…"

"So, I had fun the other night… I thought you did too?" He looks out the front window avoiding my gaze.

"I did, Ares. You know I did."

"So why did you bail? And the note, Scar! Fuck, the note. That fucking stung!"

"Are you pissed that I left a note? I thought it would be best to leave something rather than just leave. If I'd known you would get pissed at that, I would have just gone. We had fun, Ares. I don't know what I did to piss you off, but I'm sorry, okay?"

"Fuck, Scar, I didn't mean… Fuck, I can't think straight when I'm around you. I like you. I thought you liked me, but then you fobbed me off with a note saying thanks! Fucking *thanks*."

"I put a kiss on it!"

Huffing out a laugh, he says, "Yeah, you put a fucking kiss on it!"

"What do you want from me, Ares?"

"What do you mean?"

"You know, what are you expecting here? We had fun, don't get me wrong, a lot of fun, but we're not staying around here forever. We will be moving on soon enough."

"Moving on?"

"Yeah, Ares. We're here from the UK on a road trip. You know that."

"Yeah, but I thought… " He trails off and looks out the window again. "Do you wanna hang out while you're around then?" he questions.

"What do you mean, like friends with benefits?" I laugh.

But he nods.

"Oh…"

Glancing up at me, then back out the window, then back again, he offers a tight-lipped smile. "Wanna come to my room? We can talk for a bit and figure this out!" He gestures between us.

"Okay, come on!" I shout over to Ray that I'm going to the bar for a bit and for her to come and find me when she's done.

Heading straight to his room, he holds the door open for me as I walk in. Shutting the door behind me and flicking the lock, he spins to face me, then takes the two strides to where I am, one hand grabbing my waist and the other fisting the hair at the back of my neck, yanking me towards him. He slams his mouth into mine, and I groan and melt into him. Reaching one hand to his arse and grabbing, I reached the other up to pull his face closer.

"Fuck, you're beautiful," he whispers into my mouth as we both pant and come up for air.

I stare into his eyes. "I can't do this with you, Ares. I'm sorry." I go to pull away, but he holds me close.

"Scar, talk to me."

"Ares, you're dangerous, I'm... I'm leaving at some point soon, and I don't wanna get into this, whatever this is. I need to walk away now!"

"Scar, don't be like that. Let's just have some fun while you're here."

"You mean let's fuck while I'm here, then hope you don't get bored before I leave? Then when I go, it's an easy out?"

"Fuck, that's not what I mean at all. I like you. I like spending time with you. I wanna see where this goes!"

"Ares, where do you think this is gonna go? I live in a different country. We're not staying here." Pulling me back towards him and kissing me like his life depends on it, he smashes his mouth back into me again, easing me back towards the bed. The next thing I know, we're both naked, and he has his head buried between my thighs.

"Fuck, Ares... " I trail off as my orgasm rises. Heat spreads up my chest and down to my pussy.

My eyes glaze over, and I start to see stars. I'm a goner. I mean, how the fuck did this even happen? We were talking with our clothes on, for fuck's sake.

Then he's licking and sucking and biting at my pussy and pushing his fingers in and out. He leaves me with total disregard for any previous thoughts. Fuck, I want to stay here like this, with him.

While I'm coming down from my orgasms, he peppers kisses up my body, smirking, reaching my lips, kissing me almost gently and whispering against them.

"Say you'll stay."

"Ares…"

"Scar, say you'll stay, at least for a little while!"

"Okay, you've got"—I look down at my watch—"eighteen minutes, then we're leaving."

"What the fuck? Eighteen minutes?"

"Yep, well, seventeen now!"

"Fuck."

I smile at him. "We're going to visit family for the weekend. We need to pick a friend up, so I need to leave here in seventeen minutes. I can come back when Ray comes to work on Monday if you wanna carry on 'talking.'"

"Seventeen minutes, eh? Now that I can work with!" He slides down my body, licks all the way through my pussy, then back up, sliding straight inside me with a shudder and a groan.

"Fuck, Scar, what am I gonna do without you for the whole weekend?"

Shrugging, I wrap my legs around him. "Do you wanna think about that now or fuck me while I'm here?"

The way he slams into me, I take that as we are done talking and hold on for dear life, slamming into me over and over again. He makes me go dizzy, my eyes water, my throat dries, and there are spots before my eyes. As he comes with a loud groan, I spasm around him in a daze, panting and breathing in each other's breaths. He closes his eyes, touching his forehead to mine. "I don't think I will ever get enough of you."

I gently kiss him, then smack his arse. "You're gonna have to. Time's up, lover!" Shit, why the fuck did I say that? I blame my orgasm brain for my questionable vocabulary.

Shoving him off me, I laugh as he groans. I lean down and kiss him.

"See you Monday, yeah?" winking as I grab my clothes, throw them on and walk out the door.

I hear the faint "Yeah," as I pull the door. Fuck, I did not think this through. I'm walking through the bar when Ares's come decides to make an appearance down my leg. Great. I move as quickly as I dare, and when I'm outside, I run for the van, diving in the back and into the shower. Ray and Demi will have to wait a little while.

Demi

Pulling up at Ray's Pa Bernie's, I start to feel nervous. I mean, what if they don't like me? What if I feel uncomfortable? What if I'm left alone and don't fit in? Jesus, I think I'm sweating.

"Shit, girl! You okay? You literally look like you're about to puke or pass the fuck out!" Ray looks at me with concern in her eyes. I give her a small smile then she ruins it with, "Fuck, you're not pregnant, are you? If you're gonna hurl, don't splash the van!"

I shake my head at her. I just can't deal with her.

"Come on, bitch tits!" Ray grins, grabbing me and dragging me towards the door. "Come meet the rest of the reprobates!"

Walking straight in, she raises her finger to her lips and skulks through the house, hanging onto my arm with Scar at my back. As we come into the open space, we see a woman in the kitchen, and she holds her finger to her lips again, shushing her too. The woman shakes her head, giving me a small wave, and points outside.

We appear out on the deck. I can see the back of an older guy standing by the edge of the pool, talking to a younger version of himself. Ray drops my arm and screams, "Incoming!" making me have a heart attack. She runs full pelt at who I'm now assuming to be Pa Bernie. He spins around as Ray leaps onto him, knocking him into the pool, both of them fully clothed, with her wrapped around him. As they come up for air Scar touches my arm making me jump.

I remove my hand from my mouth. "Jesus! Is he okay?"

Scar laughs. "Nope! None of them are, Demi. They're all nutcases, deranged, slightly bonkers, and they all have screws loose; however you want to put it, they're all completely fucked up. I'm the only sane one here. Well, I suppose you now too!" She nudges me with her shoulder. "Come on. I will introduce you to Aunt Marie first. She's not as batshit crazy as the rest of them. I'll ease you in gently, okay?"

We head back into the house, ignoring the screams, shouts and splashes that sound like Bernie's trying to drown Ray.

Walking back into the kitchen, Scar first introduces me to her Aunt Marie. She makes me feel so welcome. It's lovely. We help get the food ready to take out for the BBQ as we head outside. Ray and Bernie have put their swimming stuff on, and I can't help but stare.

Ray's almost covered in tattoos, all up one arm and down the opposite leg, and her whole back is covered.

They're stunning, and while I stare a little longer, Ray catches me and tosses me a wink. I smile and take the food over as they're just about to fire up the grill. I'm introduced to Bernie, and I have to say he's really handsome for an older guy. He has a few tattoos, mainly military ones, and he's so funny. Then I'm introduced to his youngest son, Dane, who seems quieter than the others, but then that's not hard. They're lunatics, after all.

We're getting ready to sit down while we wait for the food. There's a holler from the door, we all shoot around, and the sight of him takes my breath away. He looks similar to Bernie and Dane, but damn, he's stunning, and while they both have hazel eyes and dirty blonde hair, he has grey-blue eyes like Ray and Marie, although Ray's are bluer.

"About time you made it, fuck face!" Ray yells from her seat next to me.

"Fuck you, arsehole!" Brandon smirks. Holy hell, I think I'm sweating. He's to die for. I mean, fluttering going on everywhere, in all sorts of inappropriate places.

He comes up behind me and rests his hands on my shoulders, and leans down to speak near my ear.

He whispers, "You're sitting in my fucking seat, arsehole. You might wanna move, like now!"

My mouth drops open, and I spin around to face him. "Oh my God, I'm sorry… so sorry, I didn't know I was… sorry, I'll move."

He laughs and looks at me with the most beautiful grey-blue eyes. Still beside me, he moves his hand around to cup my face.

"Not you, beautiful! …My dickwad of a sister." He nods towards Ray, who's currently flipping him off as she smirks at me.

"You should see your face, Demi. Shit, he's an arsehole, but that was priceless!"

Looking around the table, I shake my head. "Facepalm emoji." And that's it.

Ray and Scar literally wet themselves. The others look at me like I'm insane, and it's at that moment that I feel at home with these people.

"Why don't I sit with you, beautiful?" Brandon pulls up a chair between Ray and me, and I blush. Ray smirks and Bran winks at me, and damn, I think even my lady bits are starting to sweat. Well, that's what I'm telling myself, anyway.

After eating, we all play a few pool games, and then Marie and Bernie head to bed early so as not to cramp our style.

Apparently, Dane's girlfriend left a while ago. I don't even remember her being here, so it's no great loss, she's a cheerleader type, and I'm glad I'm not the one that didn't fit in.

Dane and Scar sit at the table while Ray and Bran mess around and beat each other, but he keeps casting glances my way. It's making me all flustered, heading over to sit with Dane and Scar. I want to understand the dynamic, as it confuses me.

Speaking to Dane, he fills me in. "It confuses everyone, especially at school. Ray and her twin Bas were the eldest, then Bran's a couple of months younger, and I'm nearly two years younger than them. At school, Bas said he wasn't related to any of us. Ray said we were all her brothers. Bran and I refused to have Bas as a brother, so Bas was our cousin, but Ray is our sister. Ray calls our dad Pa, and we called her dad Pa, but really all five pas are all our dads, so as far as we're concerned, Ray is our sister, and we're her brothers, and Scar is our sister by default." He shrugs. "We grew up together, but Bas was … difficult, so the three of us stuck together. Bran, Ray and I are closer than Ray and Bas ever were, and Bran and I love Ray as much as we love each other, so we're family. That's all that matters… you okay?"

Dane looks at me, and my eyes are glassy with unshed tears. He puts his hand on my shoulder and squeezes slightly, smiling at me. I tell him how beautiful it is that they have each other.

"I have a half-brother. We are close, I suppose. Well, I thought we were till I met you guys. I want to be close to him as I feel so lonely sometimes, our dad and Colby's mum had died just before I was born, and Colby came to live with us. He was always in trouble and ended up in juvie when he was a teenager. He moved when he got out, so I barely see him, maybe once a month, unless he's working away. Then it might be two or three months before I see him.

"He doesn't get in touch, only to arrange to meet, then he will meet up for an hour or so, try to give me money, then I won't see him again. I love him so much I just wish he would see me more, I want what you guys have."

I'm grabbed from behind into a big wet hug. I don't know how long Bran and Ray had been there, but Ray is hugging me like it's her job!

"You've got us now! Sorry, not sorry! You're stuck with us. Do you want me to kick his arse for you? I will!" She kisses my cheek and moves to sit on the other side of me, squeezing my thigh.

Bran drops his arm around me and whispers, "Do you fancy a swim, beautiful?"

I turn to look at Ray, but she just smirks and rolls her eyes.

"Did you just roll your eyes… out loud… at me…?" Bran sounds horrified.

Ray replies, "You better believe your arse, twat waffle!"

Then it descends into madness as they proceed to just insult each other back and forth till I'm dizzy.

"Cunty Bollock."

"Shit flicker."

"Butt muncher."

"Cockwomble."

"Douchecanoe."

"Dickwad."

"You've got a face like a clumsy beekeeper."

"Beauty's only skin deep. It's not your fault you were born fucking inside out!"

"Well, you fell out of the ugly tree and hit every branch on the way down."

"Well, you fell out of the stupid tree and hit every branch on the way down."

"Hey!" Bran says, sounding hurt. "No fair. You know you can't repeat an insult. That means you lose and have to do the forfeit."

"Fuck," Ray mutters under her breath. "Fine!"

"Okay, Demi, as you're our guest and the most beautiful girl in the room—"

"We're outside, fuckface," Ray interrupts.

"Okay then, in the world! You can choose her forfeit."

Scar grins. "Make it a good one, babe. You know she would stitch you right up." I do know this, Ray's awesome, but she's also ruthless and fights dirty.

"I need some time to come up with something. I'm gonna go for a swim with Bran and think about it!" Standing from my seat and reaching out my hand, he grabs it and pulls me towards the pool, flipping Ray off over his shoulder and sticking his tongue out.

Hell, if I wasn't down for this playful thing he has going on. He's hot, and I hope Ray won't be so cross that I'm totally crushing on her brother, but how did she say it? Oh yeah, sorry, not sorry!

Smirking to myself, I follow Bran around the pool, turning back to look at Ray. She winks at me, and I think she's giving me the green light, and I'm gonna take it.

Bran's everything I could ever want, and whether that's just for today or for longer, I'm down with either.

I feel his arms come around me as he feathers a kiss on my shoulder, "You really are the most beautiful girl in the world."

I feel myself smile a real honest to God smile. I know for however long these people are in my life, I'm gonna cherish them, and when I see my brother again, I'm gonna make him make more of an effort. I want what these guys have but want to be a part of this too. Bran leads me to the hot tub, and as we get in, the others suddenly become tired and all fuck off. Perfect!

Bran

I wake up to the smell of vanilla and chlorine and the feel of a warm body next to mine. It's been a long time since I had a girl in my bed, even though we didn't do anything; well, we didn't fuck, and we obviously did a lot of kissing and touching, but it didn't feel right to fuck her, not yet.

Demi seems like a really cool girl, and I want to spend more time with her, which is why I slammed the brakes on last night. If I'd fucked her, I would have just binned her off today, and I actually want to get to know her. She must be special for Ray and Scar to take such a shine to her. They never let any other girls in their group. I bury my face in her hair and breathe her in.

I whisper, "Morning, beautiful." I kiss her neck, and she moans. I nip her, then lick over where my teeth marks are as she shudders.

"Morning." She grins, rolling over and burying her face in my chest. I hug her tighter and drift back off to sleep.

"Incoming!"

"Fuck!" is all I get out as a body dives into us. I have Demi shielded in my arms, so I take the brunt of the attack, but she still winces.

"Too early," she mutters into my chest. The next thing, she's squealing and trying to get out of my grasp. Diving off the bed, she yells, "Did you just lick me?"

I look at her, confused, and then at my sister, who's still on top of me. The smuggest grin on her face tells me she did!

"Fuck, Ray, you have seriously fucked up boundaries, and I've got a raging hard-on, so please get off me!"

"Eww, you're gross!" she says, wiping her mouth.

I stick my arm out of bed, waving it at Demi, "Come back to bed, beautiful, I promise you can kill my sister later, and I will even help you bury her body!"

As Demi reaches for me so I can drag her back in, Ray interrupts our train of thought.

"No can do, motherfuckers." Ray stands up, feet on either side of me, and starts jumping up and down. "Get out of bed. We have shit to do!"

"Argh, fine." I roll out of bed, walking towards the bathroom as Ray jumps down off the bed, and I shut and lock the door behind her and run at Demi. She squeals as I tackle her to the bed and throw the covers over us. "Now, where were we...? Morning, beautiful!"

I devour her mouth, kissing her like I'm a starving man, loving how she melts into me. I let myself think I could get used to this. Our breaths become stuttered; I slide my hand down her neck, over the swell of her breast. She writhes against me, grinding into my hard body with her petite frame. She really is gorgeous.

Breaking the kiss, I slide my mouth down, palming her breast, flicking the bikini top down so her nipple pebbles between my thumb and my finger, kissing, licking and biting down to her nipples.

I suck one into my mouth as I move my hand down her stomach to her pussy, pinching her clit between my thumb and finger, then sliding one finger inside her, then swirling it around her clit, then two fingers, then three, as I lick across her lips. I then plunge my tongue into her mouth, making the most beautiful moan push into mine. She arches her back to try and get more friction, and I circle her clit harder, dipping my fingers inside her and rubbing her clit with my thumb. She's panting and flushed. I don't think I have ever seen anything more beautiful.

I pull back from our kiss slightly so I can see her face, her eyes wide and sparkling, her lips pouting and swollen from my kisses. I keep teasing her clit she gasps.

I shoot her a wicked grin and ask, "Will you come for me, beautiful? I wanna see you shatter for me." Gasping again, she nods and writhes against my hand, letting out a sharp breath.

"Bran... Brandon... Bran!" She arches off the bed, grabbing my wrist and holding it against her, grinding her hips into it, thrusting her head back and her tits in my face. I bite her nipple, and she freezes.

Tensing and biting down so hard I think she might break a tooth, she holds her breath, and I keep thrusting my fingers and rubbing her clit. "Look at me, beautiful. I want to see you."

"Bran… " is all she can get out, tensing up again.

Staring straight into my eyes, straight to my soul…

"Fuck! Fuck!" I curse as she pants and struggles for breath. Cupping my cheek, she looks worried, frowning at me.

"Did I do something wrong? Bran, I'm sorry!"

"Shit, no! Fuck, I'm so fucked!" Gasping, she shoots up and pulls the covers up around her.

"Do you… do you have a girlfriend? Is that it?"

"What?" Now I'm confused. "No! No, I don't. What makes you think that?"

"Just you seem angry with me, and then you said you were, you know… you were *fucked*," she mouths.

I laugh a humourless laugh, reaching up and tucking her hair behind her ear, then stroking her cheek. I lean in to give her the gentlest kiss I can.

"Nah, beautiful, I don't have a girlfriend … I know I'm fucked as I don't think I can let you go now!" I rub my thumb across her cheekbone and staring into those beautiful hazel eyes. "I want you, Demi, more than I've ever wanted anything! Will you see me again after this weekend? I don't want to not see you again after this weekend!"

She smiles at me like I have just offered her the moon on a stick. "I'd really like that, Bran. I really like spending time with you!"

BANG… BANG… BANG…

"Get up, motherfuckers. You're gonna miss the cake!" Ray screams through the door.

"Cake?" Demi raises a brow. "It is still morning? Isn't it?"

"Yeah. We get cake for breakfast on our birthdays, and we all just grab a spoon or some shit and dive in, but she can't start till we're all there, so she will be pacing outside the door like a caged lion. Grab a quick shower, and I will grab you some clothes."

I lay out some joggers and a vest of mine because girls are way cute in your clothes, and as she gets dressed, I have a quick shower myself, throwing on an almost identical outfit as Demi. Although it's massive on her, it looks way better.

I hold her hand as we go downstairs and out to the table, everyone is sitting waiting, and I pull Demi's chair out for her as my mum raised me to be a gentleman. She slides into it, looking rather guilty and so cute. Dad cocks a brow at me, and Mum punches him in the arm. I slide into the chair beside Demi and put my hand on her thigh, squeezing it. She smiles at me, taking my breath away. It's like everyone else just disappears, and it's just me and her. I want to make her smile like that every day. It sets something alight inside me, and it makes me want to be a man worthy of her. I'm not a bad guy. I just sometimes do questionable things in the name of the "family business," I just hope I can show her more good than bad.

"Choose your weapons." And just like that, the moment is broken.

"Fuckers!" I point at all the spoons in different sizes, from teaspoon to tablespoon, and the pile of forks. "Pick one, and then Ray will blow out her candles, and then we can eat."

Demi nods, grabbing a fork. I wink at her. I grab the same. "Nice choice!"

And then it's like feeding time at the zoo!

Ray

After a fab weekend, I have to go back to work, so leaving Pa Bernie's is hard. I really did miss them. I'm so happy to be so close to them now, but what is gonna happen when we have to leave? We have been here for about six weeks already!

Heading to the van, Bran asks if he can take Demi home, making out like it's out of my way, and I suppose it is, but I think they are both smitten, so I'm not gonna hate on him.

Scar has told Boyband she will come back with me Monday morning, so here we are, pulling up around the back of the garage. As if he has a homing device on my sister, there he is, stalking across the parking lot.

"Yo, Boyband. Sup?"

"Do you even speak English, Ray? I mean, fuck's sake!" Swiping a hand down his face, he walks around to Scar's side of the van, and as she gets out, he drags her into an intense kiss.

"I fucking missed you, princess," he whispers, but not quite enough. I'm just about to take the piss as I see Scar's hand shoot up.

"Fucking shut it!" She glares at me.

I mime locking my mouth with a key and throwing it away before locking the van and heading to work.

"Hey, Dozer, what you got for me?"

"Hey Ray, thank God you're here. How long can I get you for this week? I'm fully booked, what about next week? Word spread around the guys that you're fucking good, and now I've got bikes coming out of my ass! We've got a full house of services going on today."

"Nice! I've just dropped Scar off to spend some time with Boyband, so depending on how that goes, I'm sure I can definitely do this week and probably next week unless he fucks it up."

"Maybe she'll fuck it up." He shrugs.

"Ah, Dozer, my man, you seriously have a lot to learn about women. Come on. I will throw you a bone while we get to work!"

Turns out Dozer is married, and his wife's called Beauty. Well, actually, she's called Shirley, but everyone calls her Beauty on account of her being with Dozer and him being somewhat of a beast.

Hey, I don't make these names up. What can I say?

At 4.30, Viking turns up asking if we can look at his bike as he has a job tomorrow, and it doesn't feel right. Dozer's just packing up, and I've already finished, so I tell Dozer to head off, and I will sort it and lock up.

Viking asks if he can stay, and we chat while I work. After a couple of hours, I get to the bottom of it, and he's really happy.

"Come on, little 'un. I think I owe you a drink or five."

"Fuck it. You're on! Let me wipe my hands and tidy up, and I'll meet you over there."

I walk in, and The Fucked Up Five are all sitting around their usual table, but they have dragged me a seat over. I wave over at Scar, then join the boys. We laugh and joke and drink and play pool and darts, the guys get talking about hunting and camping, and I'm in my element.

I tell them bits about my childhood and my pas and my non-standard extracurricular activities, and they tell me there's a campsite they use where we could take the bikes too and stay for the weekend and do all kinds of stuff like that, so we make a plan for a couple of weeks time as I will need to borrow a bike.

"Is there a gym around here, anywhere or nearby?" I ask Viking, but Priest jumps in and says he will come to get me after work tomorrow and show me where it is if I fancy sparring with him.

As it turns out, they have one on the grounds. The land that backs onto this was an old fishing retreat, but when the MC brought the old farm and fixed it up, the noise scared the fish or something, so they bought that land, too. They use the lodges that surround the lake for families if they need to stay or bikers from other clubs. They all have one each. Apparently, a couple of the guys have started to renovate the lodges to live in rather than the clubhouse.

Dozer's supposed to be doing one up for him and Beauty to move into, but he hasn't got much done with work being so busy. Maybe now I'm here, for a little while, anyway, he can make a dint in it.

There's a big aircraft hangar size barn which they converted into a gym which is just up the track at the back of the clubhouse.

After a good few hours of drinking with the boys, I head back to the van to clean up and grab some food, as I haven't eaten since I finished work. As I get out of the shower, there's a knock on the door. I throw on a hoodie and leggings. I pad barefoot to the door, swinging it open.

"Roach? Hey, what you doing here?" It's only about nine-ish, but still, it's late for someone to be popping into the van. Roach is a prospect, apparently, which means he wants to be in, but he isn't, so he does all the shit jobs no one else wants to do while trying to earn his place. He's a scrawny guy who looks like he's at least part Mexican. He has big, bug-like eyes covered with long dark lashes and the hair on his head is shaved. He looks about seventeen at most.

"Hi erm, Ray… I… " Trailing off, he looks at the floor kicking the bottom step.

"You okay, kid?"

He looks up at me, shakes his head and starts to walk away.

"Sorry, I'll catch you tomorrow or some other time… "

Stepping out of the van after him and placing my hand on his shoulder, I ask, "You wanna come in for a drink? Whatever's wrong, you look like you could use one."

"I'm good... I don't wanna intrude... I shouldn't have disturbed you, just forget I came, okay? It's not important. It's just silly, really."

"Hey, come on. I've got tequila. If you don't wanna talk, at least have a drink."

Looking back at the clubhouse, then back towards the van, he nods, and I gesture for him to go in ahead of me. Taking a seat at the table, he looks really uncomfortable as fuck, so I pour him a shot. He necks it, then stares at the glass, I fill it again, and he knocks that one back topping it up for the third time he just keeps staring at it like it's gonna give him all the answers, but I know from experience that it won't.

"Come on, kid. You made it this far. You've done the hard bit. Now spill! Why are you here?"

He sighs. "At the club or at your RV?" he says, looking at me. He actually seems quite shy.

"Tell ya what, why don't you start at the beginning? Tell me a bit about yourself. Let's skip the heavy shit and start out as friends. So, you tell me something about yourself. Where are you from?"

Taking a shaky breath, "I'm originally from Puerto Guarda. It's a small town off the coast of Mexico."

Looking up at me, I can see the fear in his eyes, so I reach out and touch his arm.

"Hey, you don't have to tell me shit if you don't want. Just tell me what you need. What brought you to my door?"

"I heard you and the guys talking about training and the gym. I've asked them all to help, you know, make me stronger, train me, but none of them has the time for me, you know, being a prospect and all. I'm not one of them. I hope to be one day, but not yet. I want to get stronger. I just don't know what to do, and after how you took that guy down and the mess you made of him, I—"

"You want my help? You wanna train?"

"Erm… yeah… I understand if you don't have time or you don't want to, I just… "

"You just wanna fit in?"

He blushes and nods. "I need to learn to defend myself. I've got nowhere else to go, I've got no family, I can't fail here. I need this place. I've got nothing else!"

I arch a brow and read between the lines. "Defend," this kid said. "Defend." Something's up. "Who do you need to defend yourself against? Is it someone here? Is that why you came to me"

He takes a deep, shaky breath and necks his drink, his hand shaking. Looking at me, he nods. "Casper."

"Who the fuck's Casper?" I haven't even heard the name around the place. It doesn't ring any bells, but poor Roach looks terrified.

"He's the other prospect."

"The skinny guy, mid-twenties, pasty white, dull dark brown hair and shifty eyes? Casper?" I bark out a laugh, and Roach flinches. "Hey, I'm not laughing at you; it's the name. Casper, as in the ghost. He is kinda opaque, isn't he? I've seen milk with more colour than him!"

Roach huffs out a laugh. "Yeah, s'pose."

"So what's the story with you two then?"

"I turned up here about a year ago. I was homeless, an illegal, I had been trafficked when I was thirteen, and the guy who had brought me had died after about two years or so. I robbed him and took what I could before anyone came looking, and I fled. I was on the streets just over a year before I stumbled upon this place.

"Priest and Dice were on guard that day and bought me in. I've been here ever since. Casper showed up about six months before me, so he took me under his wing, but something's not right, and he's been throwing his weight around more these last few months. He's getting more cocky, and the way he speaks about some of the guys here… I don't know. I don't wanna be a part of whatever's going down with him, so I've tried to distance myself from him. I don't trust him."

"You trust me?"

"I don't know, kinda… I just need to talk to someone, and although they've accepted you while you're here, you're not one of them either, so I thought you would… I don't know… understand where I'm coming from." He shrugs. "Maybe I'm wrong. Maybe I'm just over-sensitive. That's what Casper says. Maybe he's right, maybe—"

"That's a lot of fucking maybes, kid." I pour another drink and, sitting back, I contemplate what he's saying.

"Does he hit you?" Bowing his head and twisting the glass back and forth between his fingers, he nods. "A lot?" Again he nods, lifting his shirt. His ribs are black, blue, yellow, and green, all different variations of ageing bruises. Even against his caramel skin, they stick out.

"Fuck Roach! Okay, here's what's gonna happen. Tomorrow Priest is taking me to the gym. I will scope it out and develop a programme for you. I have a job for you!"

Looking at me questioningly and assessing my gaze, he says, "Okay."

"Good, so tomorrow I want you to find out who uses the gym and when and what times these guys are creatures of habit. We wanna go when no one's around so Casper doesn't get wind of anything, okay?" He nods and looks kinda hopeful. Poor kid sounds like he's been through so much.

"Give me your number!" I put his number on my phone and message him back. "Come on. It's gonna be okay. Alright, I will keep my eye on you. Try not to be anywhere on your own with him, and message me when you know what the guys' gym schedules are, don't make it obvious, though, and don't worry about asking Ares, Dozer and The Fucked Up Five. I will quiz them, okay? Just casually ask around the others and let me know! Okay, now get off to bed, kid. you're gonna need plenty of rest, and over the next few days, we will start training, okay?" He smiles at me, leaves the van, and heads back towards the clubhouse.

After the conversation with Roach last night, I wake early and need to burn off some of the energy that has me on edge. I decide to go for a run. It's what I do to clear my head back home. Coming out of the van, Ares strides towards me.

"What up, Boyband? You shit the bed?"

"What the fuck does that even mean, Ray?"

I laugh at him as I start to stretch. "What you doing here so early? Where's Scar?"

"She needs some bits. Said I'd grab 'em for her."

"Aw, aren't you a sweetheart!" I joke. "You got the keys?" He nods, and I set off behind the clubhouse. There's a path leading into the woods. To the right, a big open field is behind the garage and clubhouse.

Following the path up between the trees, I could have been back home. The caw of the ravens drifts around me, making me smile, and the slight breeze blows my ponytail around. It keeps me cool but also encompasses me in a smell almost like home, the morning forest damp with dew and twinkling in the morning light. It really is beautiful out here. After heading along the path, there's an aircraft hanger-like building which I assume will be the gym.

There's a path straight up or to the left, heading straight up through the trees. It isn't long before I find a barn. They'd said it was farmland, so it isn't surprising. Carrying on up through the woods, the track veers off to the left then I come to a fork, left or right. Heading to the right, the trees thin, and I can see the fishing lake and lodges to the right and an old overgrown parking lot to the left.

I head over to the lake, jogging around it to take it all in. It's a massive body of water, almost in a heart shape. There are ten lodges spaced around it, and it is surrounded by grassland and trees. There's a gap in the trees, and I can see along the massive open field to the garage in the distance.

There's a large building. It looks like it would have been the reception area, tackle hire and possibly rec room or something like that for the fishing place. There's another fork as I carry on, so I head left this time. There are just masses and masses of open farmland and forest for miles, setting a steady pace. I'm enjoying the scenery. It's beautiful out here and makes me feel at home.

The caw of the ravens, the rustle of leaves in the trees, the smell of the outdoors, the breeze allowing me to smell the forest, and the fresh air making my lungs expand easily... I could have so easily been in England at the Adventure Centre. I've nearly done a full circle around the fields till I come to another fork. I can see some buildings through the trees, so I decide to be nosy.

The track's big enough for a car or van but is a dirt road rather than tarmac or concrete. As I get through the trees, there's a large fence, almost eight feet, with rusty razor wire circling all through the top. As I get closer to the fence, I can see another lake and three massive aircraft-like hangers with about eight large barracks, maybe lodges. There's a large open space between the building and the lake. It all looks contained within the large fence and looks like a disused military base.

Heading back to the path, I take the right fork heading along a thinner track, further down the track where it continues along in front or goes off behind me to the right, so I carry on bringing me out at the gym.

Interesting. I could do a full loop around the whole MC. It must be possibly twelve miles. I've been out nearly two hours and had a nosy around the lake and military-looking base, so it wasn't a bad run.

Heading back to the van, I have about twenty minutes to get my arse ready for work and grab some breakfast. I grab my phone and text one of the guys I'd met who they call Barbie. It turns out it was Barbie as in barbeque. He's the guy who does all the cookouts and mans the grill when they have gatherings. He had been a military cook, so he can handle it, but he's actually the "Accountant," I suppose you would call him.

Ray: Hey, Barbie, it's Ray. Are you at the clubhouse? I need a favour.

Barbie: What do you need, Ray?

Ray: Tell me to fuck off if you want, but I'm just heading to work, and I'm starving.

Barbie: 'Laughing emoji'

Ray: That's definitely not a fuck off. 'Fingers crossed emoji'

Barbie: Fine, but you'll owe me. What do you want?

Ray: Barbie, I will love you forever, and how much can I take the piss?

Barbie: Just tell me what you want. At this rate, you could have made it yourself!

Ray: Cheeseburger, lettuce and tomato, a bit of mayo, chips by chips, I mean fat fries, and a chocolate shake.

Barbie: For breakfast? Fucking hell, you don't want much do ya? Dozer said he couldn't service my bike for another week, two, maybe.

Ray: Barbie, if you bring my food to the garage when it's ready and drop your bike off, I will love you forever and do it today.

Barbie: You are a fucking legend. See you shortly!

Strolling into the garage and setting up, Barbie delivers my food thirty minutes later.

Groaning around a mouthful of food, I say, "Fuck, Barbie, will you marry me? Seriously, this is fucking amazing!"

Barbie lets out a chuckle. He's in his early forties, possibly, maybe even late forties. He's a broad fella, not ripped like some of the guys, but he still looks solid, just not defined. He has dark hair thinning on top, speckled with silver, bushy eyebrows and an infectious smile that crinkles around his almost golden eyes. When he laughs, I can't help but smile. He is a bit smaller than me, probably five foot eight, with a darker skin tone.

Dozer's giving me daggers. "Where the fuck's mine?"

"Sorry, man, you couldn't do my bike for a week, maybe two. Ray's gonna do it today." He shrugs.

"Is that so, Ray? And when do you think you're gonna get time for another fucking service on top of what you already have in?"

"Careful, Dozer, your green-eyed monster's showing, might wanna shove that little fucker back down, and don't you worry about me, old-timer. I'm all over it! Barbie, I fucking love you, man. The marriage proposal still stands. Text you later when the bike's done!"

Strolling back into the garage with my food, moaning like a prostitute on a good day, I can still hear Dozer talking at Barbie, which makes me smile, and the burger makes me happy dance all the way to my toolbox.

Priest's waiting for me when I finish work. Barbie has just left after collecting his bike, and Dozer has finished early, so I'm just locking up. "Said I'd see you again sometime." He laughs out loud.

We'd seen each other pretty much every night since I'd been here, but never alone. He clearly wants to talk about the club incident, and I know the rest of The Fucked Up Five know what had gone down as Viking had told me so.

"That you did." I laugh back. "So, you run the nightclub in Castle Cove, then?"

"Well, I'm the frontman, but it's run by the club. We launder our money through it. It's a legit business."

"So you told the others we already met." It isn't a question. I know he has.

"Yep, my brothers and I have no secrets. As soon as you walked in with Dozer, I recognised you. The night you left. I sent the footage to Dice, he's our computer whizz, but he couldn't find anything on you. I've been trying to track you down for weeks, scouring video surveillance footage and street cams trying to track you through your driving licence. Dice said Ray's not your real name, so he struggled a bit, and then you go and waltz right in through the front door!

"I was just showing the boys the footage at the club and telling them what I'd seen you do when the trash walked over to cop a feel, and I knew when I saw that look on your face what was going to happen.

"I just told them to watch, and watch they did. That's why we came to get you and took you into our group. I think you're gonna fit right in with us. I recognise that what's inside you, we all have it."

"Stalker much?" I laugh.

"Not normally, but you"—he points at me—"are something special!"

"So you know my real name then?"

"Nah, well, Dice does, but he wouldn't share."

"Am I supposed to believe that? You just said you have no secrets? And I'm not staying, Priest. We're just passing through. I mean, I really like you guys, you're all great, but a few weeks, maybe, and we're moving on."

"We'll see!" He grins at me, throwing his arm around me. "We're the same, the six of us. Fate brought you to us, Ray, and I'll be damned if I let you go!"

I stop and turn to face him. "We are the same, Priest. I feel it too. Unfortunately, that doesn't change the fact that we're only in the States for six months, and we've already been here well over a month. It's inevitable we will leave sooner or later regardless of how I feel about the people here and this place." I give a sad, twisted smile, then continue on towards the gym.

"Don't worry, Ray, fate always finds a way!"

I smile at him as we walk towards the gym. I see something in him, too, the first time we met a kindred spirit, maybe. I feel comfortable with him and with the others, too, maybe too comfortable. Only time will tell.

We will still have to leave at some point. I'm not going to think about that just yet. I just need to get my head back in the here and now. Enjoy my time here for what it is, and for fuck's sake, don't get attached!

Staring back at Priest, he's dressed in sweats and a vest. He's about thirty-six, so one of the older guys around here, but I haven't noticed many of them look much older than he is. He looks like a priest, all clean-cut and holier than thou, with his perfect sharp angled face. I haven't heard him swear; that's okay, though. I swear enough for all of us, with his dark slicked-to-the-side perfect hair, he's the vision of regal holiness. The only tattoo he has is the Reaper one on his right bicep. Well, that I can see, anyway, but I will bet my soul that's the only one. He intrigues me. What is a guy like him doing in an MC? Colour me curious.

After finishing up at the gym and sparring a little too hard—I caught Priest in the mouth and split his lip—we head to the bar. The guys all take the piss out of Priest, but he takes it like a champ telling them he would like to see the outcome if they went a few rounds with me, which they all laugh off. Funny that! No takers.

Blade

I'm quieter than normal tonight, kind of distant. I have a few things on my mind, nothing major, but enough to have me distracted. Ray slides in beside me. I have my butterfly knife, and I'm flicking back and forth in my hand, and rolling it around my thumb, doing tricks with it. I find it helps ease some of my stress and allows me to be a little spaced out, using it as a distraction. The constant of it trailing back and forth through my fingers and around my thumb and back is therapeutic.

She's staring at me. I can see her in my periphery as I glide my knife through my fingers and around my thumb. It's like an extension of myself. It's so fluid.

"You good?" She clears her throat at the side of me.

I smile at her. "Hey, Ray! Yeah, I'm good, just… you know, not feeling it." I shrug.

She shrugs back. "Give me a second. I need to run to the van and grab something. Can you grab some chalk? I've gotta game we could play."

"Well, that's not cryptic at all." I laugh, and she gets up from her seat and takes off.

Strolling back into the clubhouse carrying a box under her arm, she puts the box in front of me. She picks up the chalk and starts drawing a target on the wall near the dart board, then pacing back, she draws a line on the floor.

"The fuck you doing? Pres will freak if he sees you defacing his clubhouse." Tank laughs.

She shoots back a smirk, huffing. "Boyband? He would have to unbury himself from Scar's vagina long enough to notice first!"

With that, we all roar a laugh that makes me genuinely smile. I really do like her.

Shoving the box towards me, I eye it curiously. "These what I think they are?" She nods, and the grin that spreads across my face must have been a picture. Opening the box, I whistle. "Oooh, damn. These are nice!"

I take one rainbow-bladed throwing knife out of the box and toss it in my hand. They're weighted lovely. They sit in my hand perfectly, and they feel fucking sexy. "These I like!" I smile again, tossing one up and down and catching it, flipping it over in my hand.

"So let's play. You gotta throw 'em from the line. The lowest score does a shot and so on."

Smug grinning at her and nodding to the board drawn on the wall, I say, "You're on."

She grabs a bottle of tequila from Roach and some glasses, and we get down to it.

There are twelve knives in total, so this is gonna be fun, dangerous and potentially messy! My kind of game! It's a close game. I lost the first. Then she lost the next two. Then I lost the next, then she lost the next two, or did I lose the next? Who knows? I think we were both just drinking without losing anyway.

"This is too easy." She laughs out. "Shall we make it more interesting?"

"What you thinking?"

"Shall we set them on fire?"

"You fucking serious?"

"Sure." She grins, feeling her pockets, I'm assuming for a lighter.

"How the fuck are you gonna get metal to light?"

"Well, duh, we're gonna have to use something flammable to put on them." She rubs her chin, thinking. "What about petrol? I can grab some from the garage."

"How about we put a fucking pin in that idea, nutjob, and come back to it at a later date, K?"

She mutters, "Pussy," under her breath before tossing another blade at the wall.

After nearly two hours of playing her stupid, amazing-as-fuck game, we pack up. I give her the biggest hug and whisper into her ear, "Cheers, Ray, I needed that."

She kisses my cheek and tells me, "Anytime! Maybe we can figure out how to light the blades on fire next time to make it a bit more interesting beforehand, so we are prepared."

Leaving her with that thought, I head off to my room with a stupid grin. Maybe she is that missing piece we keep referring to her as. She just seems to know when I need my spirits lifting, and there she is, a full-blown distraction. I'm not even sure what was bothering me now I look back.

Ray

Roach gets back to me a few days later, and we arrange a time to meet at the gym. When we get there, I have written down a few pages of workouts for him to do and show him how to use all the machinery. It is state of the art, and they have an octagon, pads, weights, and every machine you can think of.

I weigh and measure Roach and explain we are gonna keep track and see how he progresses. While we warm up, I tell him a few basic nutritional tips and then put him through his paces, testing what I'm working with.

After an hour, he's knackered but has the biggest smile on his face. He gives me a hug and thanks me, and I realise that I don't seem to mind these guys touching me.

It doesn't seem to freak me out. I'm kind of thinking I have found my people. That makes me a little warm and tingly inside. But my inner dickhead screams at me not to get attached. I need to move on and find my place. How will I know this is it if I don't try anywhere else? Fucking stupid inner dickhead!

Dice

I'm in the gym just warming up as Ray comes through the door, looking like she's run up here as her warm-up.

"Hey beautiful, you come to see a real man work out?"

"Sure have, Dice. In fact, he should be here any minute!" She actually laughs at me, actually fucking laughs.

"Bitch!" I grab at my chest. "Wounded, absolutely wounded!"

She just gives me the biggest grin as if to say good and slings her bag off her shoulder.

"So, who you meeting, hot stuff?"

"Just taking the piss, Dice. I'm on my own." She smiles at me with a real genuine smile. "Fancy a game of spar and secrets?"

"What the fuck's that?"

"It's where we spar, first one to get to ten points gets to ask a question and the loser has to answer honestly, five points for a headshot, three points for a body shot and one point for anywhere else! What do ya say?" She grins with a wicked glint in her eye.

"Fine! But that sounds like you just made it up on the spot!"

She just shrugs at me and grabs some gloves out of the cupboard. Stepping towards each other, we tap gloves and then dance around, being cautious, gauging what the other is capable of. I mean, I totally have the advantage as I've seen her fight twice now, so I should win.

Leaning to punch her, I get her arm and bark out, "Ha, one point to me!"

She jabs me in the mouth. "Five to me, dickhead!"

I dab at my lip with my glove as she hits me again in the temple. "Hey, not fair!"

"Another five to me, knob cheese!" She gives the widest grin.

"You're fucking mean!" I laugh. "Right, what's your question?"

She thinks for a second, then hits me with, "Are you gay?" She cocks her head to the side and gazes straight into my eyes.

Stumbling back, I say, "What the fuck would make you ask that? Fuck off… this game's fucking stupid… fuck you, Ray!"

I spin and start tugging frantically at my gloves, trying to rip them off. Fucking bitch, who the fuck does she think she is, asking shit like that?

"Dice," she whispers as her hand comes into contact with my shoulder, tugging me around as I'm still struggling with my gloves. She reaches for them and removes them for me.

"Sorry, I was just curious. You don't have to answer if you don't wanna. I shouldn't have asked. I didn't mean to upset you. Dice, I'm sorry!"

I stride towards the wall, then turn my back, and slide down it resting my elbows on my knees when I hit the floor and scrub the palms of my hands into my eyes.

"Why couldn't you have just asked something stupid like have I ever killed anyone or do I collect stamps but no, straight for the jugular. Fucking hell, Ray. Why would you ask that?"

She shrugs at me. "It just seems obvious, so I thought rather than guess I would just ask straight out, but by your reaction, I'm guessing you're not out."

Too fucking observant, that one. Doesn't assume that she's wrong, just that I'm not out. Fuck! It isn't a question, more of a statement. I can't look at her, but a weird part of me just wants to be honest with someone who doesn't know me, doesn't have any expectations, someone new, who I can show who I actually am without holding anything back!

"No!" I breathe. "I'm not out." I open my eyes to look at her. "You won't say anything, will you?" I grab her hand. "Promise me, Ray!" I squeeze. "Promise me you won't?"

"Dice, I promise. I would never… okay?"

I release the breath I was holding and screw my eyes up tight. I'm trying not to freak the fuck out when she pushes my knees down and climbs over my lap, straddling me.

She wraps her arms tight around me. "I know what it's like to keep a part of you hidden, Dice. If you ever wanna talk, I'm here!"

Then she just hugs me and holds on till I wrap my arms around her and hug her back. Fuck, I'm freaking out, panicking and verging on some sort of nervous breakdown, but also, a wave of relief falls across me.

I told her, I told someone. Well, she asked, and I didn't lie, and the world didn't come crashing down around me. It didn't end or stop spinning, and I wasn't smited from high, cast out, or any of it… yet. I just got one of the best hugs I've had in a long, long time, and I grip her like I think she's the answer to my prayers, and if I don't hang on, she might disappear. I don't think I can actually survive if she disappears. I'm sure she's all that's holding me up at this moment.

After what feels like an hour, I remove my buried face from her neck, but looking at the clock behind her, it has been forty minutes. I just stare at her face, really look. I don't see any animosity, repulsion, disgust, malicious intent, hate, abhorrence or loathing, just something that looks more like understanding.

She's stunningly beautiful, if you like that kind of thing. She's breathtaking, and the way she's looking at me gives me hope that not everyone will see me as I think they will.

"You wanna talk?"

I shake my head and nuzzle into her neck again. I can't remember the last time I'd been held. She wraps her arms around me again and starts stroking lazy circles on the back of my neck up into my hairline.

"When I was little, I was a bit wild. I had a side of me that, when I tapped into it, was calm, quick thinking, so matter of fact and closed off, precise in everything she did, and I would slip in and out of that personality with no problem. But as I got older, more people noticed this ruthless, almost cutthroat side of me, and I had to dampen it down, hold it caged, and restrict its appearance. I became that side less and less. My dad and my pas tried to get me to be less restrictive, saying it wasn't good for me to keep such a tight hold on her.

"I'm almost smothering her into non-existence, but my dads thought if I carried on, it would come crashing down around me, and I would end up in prison or dead.

"Before I came here, they wanted me to learn to let her out again so it wouldn't strain me, and find somewhere I could be both sides. That's who you saw on the video and in the bar. *She* takes over, and, well, you saw what *she's* capable of."

I reach up and tuck a stray hair behind her ear. "You really are beautiful, ya know?"

She barked out a laugh at me. "Seriously! That's what you got? I tell you my secrets, and you hit me with you're beautiful?"

"It's true!"

She shakes her head at me. "So what do you wanna do?"

At that moment, the door swings open, and Viking and Priest walk in. Priest looks shocked, and Viking just grins.

Ray leans in and kisses me on the lips, then stands up. "Thanks for the workout, Dice. Maybe we can do it again sometime?" She struts over to her bag and swings it over her shoulder. She swings her hips like it's her motherfucking job and heads out the door!

I blow out a breath. "Fuck, she's something else!"

"What the fuck you playing at? I thought… you and Ray? That doesn't even make sense… What the hell, Dice?" Priest spits at me. Viking's still just grinning at me.

And as I get to my feet, I manoeuvre my dick and groan more because she has been sat on it for about an hour, and I think it has gone numb, but I think they take it as I've fucked her, but I wasn't gonna argue or tell them they were wrong. One person knowing is enough for now.

I sweep my own bag up. "Later, guys!" I nod and swan out of there without a care in the world on the outside. On the inside, I'm panicking like a motherfucker.

As I walk back over towards the clubhouse, I notice the RV lights are on, and I head over there, knocking on the door. It swings out at me, and I step back.

"Wanna drink?" she says as I step in. I'm not over this conversation yet, and I just nod because fuck I really need a drink. She pulls out two mugs, and I frown, and then she fills them with tequila.

"Jesus!" I laugh.

"Thought you might need it!"

We sit at the table and just drink till most of the mug is gone. "What am I gonna do?" I ask, as I have no fucking clue.

"What do you wanna do?" she asks, seeming genuinely interested.

"I have no fucking idea, Ray. I mean, what does this even mean to me? I could lose my home, my brothers, this club, fuck! I could lose everything, and for what? I don't even have a partner or someone to fall back on. It's just me!"

She reaches her hand over and slides it into mine. "You're not alone, Dice. I don't believe for one minute that you will lose your home, brothers or this club, and you won't lose me!"

"You've made it clear that you're leaving, Ray, so if I lose everything here, then it's inevitable that you'll be gone soon too!"

"Yeah, I'm leaving, but if you lost everything here, which isn't gonna happen, but say you did, what's stopping you from coming with me? I have a place for us to live, a job that's fucking awesome at the Adventure Centre, and a family that will accept you no matter what, so don't ever think you're on you're own! And if you ever need a wingwoman, I'm your girl!"

I snort a laugh. "You'd come to a gay bar with me?"

"I'll have you know I've been to quite a few gay bars, and lesbians love me!"

I bark out a laugh at her. "You're fucking ridiculous!"

"So, you ever had a long-term boyfriend?" she asks, cocking a brow at me.

I shake my head. "I've never been able to, really… I've never even dated a guy. I didn't realise I was gay till my mid-twenties, and I was already part of the club as a prospect, so I kept my head down. I've been here from the start. I went on a job, and we had a night off. I got with this girl who took me back to hers, but she passed out.

"I was putting her to bed when her brother walked in and tried to kick the crap out of me. He thought I was trying to take advantage. When I told him what had happened and that I didn't really like girls anyway, it turned out he was bi. We just ended up together for the rest of the week. The guys saw me leave with the girl. They just assumed I was with her, and I spent the week with him at gay bars. That was the only relationship I ever had. I still hook up with him every once in a while, but other than that, it's always been random hook ups. The job doesn't allow for relationships, or maybe I didn't through fear of losing it all." I scrub my hand down my face. "You know what I really want?"

"What?" She smiles at me.

"I want someone to hug me like you did earlier. I can't remember the last time someone hugged me, and I wanna kiss someone properly rather than just a quick make-out as foreplay. Most hook ups don't even bother with that, as it's normally a quick fuck or blowjob behind a club, in an alleyway or in a car, there's not normally a bed involved, and I want to hold hands and walk down the street, and I want to have someone, and I want to not be ashamed or afraid of who I am. I just wanna be enough, Ray! I just wanna be happy and have someone to love and someone who loves me."

She walks around the table and slides into my lap again, straddling my thighs, wrapping her arms around me and stroking the back of my hair.

"Shall I tell you a secret?" I nod as she licks her lips. "I don't like to be touched by guys. I get antsy. I can't bear it, but people think something traumatic happened, but really, it's because the relationships I've been in ended badly, and I found that the more physical contact I gave, the more it hurt me in the long run, so I stopped giving it out. Really, I would love to have what you want too. A person and someone who loves me for all of me, the good, the bad and the downright terrifying, so if you wanna wingwoman to be by your side and find you that, then I'm your girl!"

She leans in and kisses me as the door swings open, and we both gasp and swing our gaze to the door as Ares and Scar are there.

"Well, shit!" Ares grins.

We both look at each other and the position we've found ourselves back in, and both burst out laughing. Well, fuck. I will have a job convincing anyone I'm gay now. Ray leans in, kisses me again, squeezes me in a hug, and slides off my knee.

"I suppose you wanna drink, Boyband?" She smirks at him and starts pouring out the mugs of tequila.

"Jesus, you two, fucking mugs of tequila, what are you, animals?"

We both grin at each other and just start drinking again. Fuck, my head is spinning already, but I'm not sure if it's the tequila or the life-changing conversations or just Ray. She does kind of have an effect on me.

I feel like she sees the real me. She seems to crave the same affection I do, so I'm gonna keep her close until I'm ready to be honest with the world. For now, this is just mine and Ray's secret.

Ray

Heading into work the next day, I feel shit. It was well late when Scar and Ares had left, and Dice had hung around a little longer but fell asleep, so he had to do the walk of shame, which is totally fucking hilarious as now he has finally admitted to himself that he's gay, the whole club seems to think we're fucking, and in fairness, we haven't even tried to set them straight.

It's nice for me to actually have that contact and touch that I was so dead against, and I know it's fake, but because I know he doesn't want me sexually. It feels easy to get it from him because it definitely isn't sexual. I feel like I'm not losing myself. It feels natural to be so tactile with him. Maybe that's what I'd needed all along, a fuck buddy and a gay best friend, two separate people giving me exactly what I need. Now I just need to find another fuck buddy, another Jer, if there is such a thing. I wonder if Dwayne would be up for a bit of fuck buddying. As I stroll into the garage, I whip my phone out.

Ray: Hey, my saviour of all and bringer of sustenance, how the devil are you?

Barbie: The usual?

Ray: I fucking love you, you know that, right?

Barbie: Yeah, yeah! Thirty minutes, okay?

Ray: You're the best!

Thirty minutes later, the person I love most in the world at this very second walks in. "Thank fuck. Barbie. My stomach is starting to think my throat has been cut. I owe you one, big man!" As I plant a kiss on his cheek.

"Hey, hey, don't go getting me into trouble with that boyfriend of yours!"

"Eh?" I cock a brow at him. "Boyfriend?"

"Yeah, you and Dice. The jungle drums have been thumping this morning."

I burst out laughing before schooling my features. "Fancy being my dirty little secret then, Barbie? I won't tell if you don't, and I don't see a ring on this bad boy!" I wiggle my fingers at him, grinning.

He shoves me playfully on the shoulder. "Ah, Ray, if only I were twenty years younger, I might take you up on that." He titters and stalks away.

"How the fuck do you get that old bat to be nice and deliver food and great food at that? when we ask for anything that's not on an official cookout, we might get a frozen burger in a bun—"

"Cob!"

"What?"

"Cob, Dozer! It's a fucking cob, not a bun or a roll or a fucking bap. It's a cob!"

"I don't care what the fuck it is. How the fuck do you get it is what I want to know. Are you fucking him as well as Dice?"

"Ah, old-timer, wouldn't you like to know?" I smirk as I groan and lick my fingers before walking away, slurping on my shake. Fuck, this is amazing. I think the burgers are homemade. They're definitely not frozen. I think he makes the shake with ice cream. Fuck the calories. It's delicious. I will just have to go for a run in the morning and the gym, too, but who cares!

Feeling like a less hangry version of myself and totally sated and content, I crack on with work. The day literally flies by. I'm just packing up for the day when Priest arrives, looking a bit shifty.

"Hey, you okay?" I ask.

"Yeah," he breathes out. "I was wondering if I could ask you for a favour." He looks down at the floor and then scrubs his hand up and down the back of his neck.

Stepping towards him, I reach out and take his hand. "What's up, Priest? You seem rattled."

He huffs again. "It's the club. I've had a lot of stock go missing, and I've watched and rewatched the CCTV footage, but I can't find out what's happening. The staff know most of the guys, so they won't do anything while we're all around. I'm wondering if you could help. Maybe pretend to come to work for me and see what you can dig up. If you don't mind and you don't have plans with Dice, I would really appreciate it, Ray. I'd owe you one!"

"Yeah, sure. Tonight? What time do you need me?"

"Is eight okay? That way, I can get someone to show you the ropes before it gets busy!"

"Sure, don't worry. I'll get to the bottom of it! I'll see you later!" I lock up and head to the van to shower and get ready.

We knock at the door, and it swings open. Donny strides in with me.

Priest nods to Donny. "Thanks, Donny. Remember, you don't know her, never seen her before, okay?"

"Yes, Boss, sure thing." Donny nods and steps out of the door, shutting it behind him.

"Thanks, Ray, you're doing me a massive favour. I really appreciate it!"

"No problem at all, Priest. Can I have a look at the CCTV cameras so I know what areas they cover? Then I can get out there. I'll sort it. You know I will." I give him my feral grin. "Just what do you want me to do when I find out who it is?"

"I'll leave it to your discretion, Ray. I trust you'll know the best course of action when the time comes."

"Aye, aye, Captain!" I wink as I stride back out the door.

Donny takes me to the bar and introduces me to Sonya, who will show me the ropes. After about fifteen minutes, I think I have the hang of it, so I crack on, keeping my eye on a few of the staff near me, but they all seem like okay people as far as people go.

After about forty-five minutes of being there, I notice the glass collector paying a bit too much attention to where the other staff are, and I've seen him check his phone, then disappear a few moments later before returning with a grin on his face.

Next time his phone goes, I nod to Sonya, mouthing, "Bathroom," and she nods. I skulk around the corner just as the glass collector slides out of the stock room with a bottle of vodka between his arm and his body and heads towards the back door.

I hide in the shadows as he checks around to see if anyone's about before he pushes out the back door propping it open with the cigarette bucket filled with sand for the staff that smoke to stub them out in.

As he exits through the door to the alleyway behind, I step into the doorway. Another voice says, "How much?"

"Twenty dollars a bottle. It's good stuff!"

"Fine," the other voice says, just as I reach through the door and grab the bottle from him, resting it inside by the door and kicking the weasel in the back out into the alleyway. He squeals as he crashes into the other guy, and I step out the door with them and kick it shut behind me.

"You fucking bitch! Who the fuck do you think you are?"

"I'm your worst fucking nightmare, kid. Let me inform you that you no longer work at this establishment by order of the management. Also, take your cock sucking boyfriend with you and leave while you've still got the chance!" I stand in the closed doorway with my arms crossed over my chest, giving them both the death glare.

The other guy raises his hands in submission. "I don't want any trouble. I just wanted some cheap spirits… I'm gonna just go, okay?"

I nod, and he backs away slowly.

"Are you fucking kidding me? This bitch ain't nothing. We can take her, man!" he shouts after his friend.

"Looks like it's just you and me, shit brick! Are you gonna do this the easy way or the hard way? You choose!"

He reaches down, grabs an empty beer bottle from beside the dumpster, cracks the base, and points it at me. "I want my shit out of my locker. Then I will go!"

"Well, you see, the thing is, I don't give a flying fuck what you want. What's gonna happen is you're gonna walk away now, or you're not, and when I say you're not, it will because you're unable to, so last chance, cunty bollock. What's it to be?"

"Fuck you, bitch!"

As he lunges at me, I grab his wrist with the bottle in it and swing him around, breaking either his wrist, his arm, or both, but my fucks have runneth dry, and I have no more left to give. Keeping hold of his fucked arm, I pull him towards me, raising my knee and going for his balls. With a grunt, he drops to the floor. I grab the front of his top, lift him off the floor, and punch him back down again. I step back and wait for a second, but there's no movement, so I lean in and take his locker key and cash from his pocket. I kick him and roll him over so he won't choke on his tongue and make my way round the front of the club.

I push past the front of the line. Donny's there checking IDs. "Where the fuck have you been?"

"Taking out the trash, but the door locked behind me." I shrug and walk in. I stalk to the staff room and raid the jumped-up little twats locker. There's a tin with $820 plus the $65 I pulled from his pocket. I frisk his jacket, but there are only some house keys in it, so I go to the back door, throw his coat over him, grab the vodka, and make my way to Priest's office.

"Come in!"

"Hey, it's me. I'm done!" I say as I walk in.

"What do you mean you're done? You've been here"—he looks down at his watch—"all of an hour!"

"Yeah, soz it took so long, but I got locked out, so had to walk around to get back in. Here's the vodka I stopped him from getting, $885 he had on him and in his locker. I've cleared his locker out, and he's currently taking a nap in the alleyway out back." I shrug at him.

"Fucking hell, Ray!"

I just grin at him. "Need me for anything else?"

"Nah, I think we're good. Can you get back?"

Priest had brought me in but dropped me down the road, so it wasn't obvious that I'd come with him.

"Yeah, I'll message the guys and see who can grab me!" I reach into my pocket and shoot a group text, smiling as Priest's phone pings.

Ray: Can anyone grab me from Afterlife?
Dice: On my way, beautiful. x

Sliding my phone back in my pocket, Priest scowls. "Everything okay?"

"Yeah, sure!" He looks confused. "Thanks again, Ray." He counts the money and slides $385 at me. "Thanks again. You're a legend!"

"I don't want that. I was happy to do it for you."

"I know, but please take it. It will make me feel better. You've saved me a fortune, okay?"

"Okay, fine. By the way, I'm quitting, and I'm gonna have a drink while waiting for Dice."

He just nods as I walk out of the room. Closing the door behind me, I grab my jacket and helmet. I walk over to the bar and order a tequila from Sonya. When she puts the drink down, she gasps, "Where the fuck have you been? You're supposed to be working. Get your ass back around this bar now!"

Grinning at her like the motherfucker I am, I laugh. "I quit!" I throw $20 on the bar for the drink and $165 in Sonya's hand. "Tip!" I wink at her, and she blushes, closes her hand around it and stuffs it in her bra.

I nod and wander outside, sitting on the wall while I wait for Dice.

"That's gotta be the shortest employment in the history of Afterlife!" Donny laughs.

I'm sitting on the wall leaning back slightly, swinging my legs as I smile at him. "I like to be memorable, Donny. I'm sure you won't forget me!" I wink at him as Dice pulls up in front of me.

"Hey, beautiful, fancy heading somewhere fun?"

"Hell yeah!" I say, yanking my helmet on and sliding on the back, wrapping my arms around his waist as he squeezes my hand and then sets off!

Dice

She winks at Donny as I pull up in front of her. "Hey, beautiful, fancy heading somewhere fun?"

"Hell yeah!" she says, yanking her helmet on and sliding on the back, wrapping her arms around my waist as I squeeze her hand, then set off!

Fuck, I love this girl. She doesn't ask questions; she just says, "Hell yeah!" and dives on the back. I sigh to myself. Why can't she have a dick? If she did, she would be perfect for me. If she was a he, for fuck's sake!

Heading up the coast, about a forty-minute ride, I pull up outside a hotel. She slides off the back, removes her helmet and grins at me.

She leans up and kisses my cheek. "Ah, babe, have you brought me on a dirty weekend? Just a hotel room and sex on every surface? Wow, best surprise ever!"

I punch her in the arm. "Dick!"

She bursts out laughing. "Yes, dick all weekend, can't wait. Show me to the bed!"

"You're fucking ridiculous, you know that?" I shake my head at her but can't hide the massive grin. I don't think I've smiled this much in... ever! Wow, that's depressing.

"Fancy having a little fun?" She grins.

"Sure, why not!"

"So the rules are—"

"Wait. You're making rules up to have fun? Seriously?"

"No, idiot, for the game. Firstly, you must stay in character. Secondly, whatever is said, you have to go along with and can't contradict and thirdly, whatever happens, don't laugh! Okay?"

"Sounds stupid, but fine!" I grin at her. She's like a kid at Christmas, bouncing up and down on the balls of her feet.

As we walk into the hotel, the doorman opens the door for us, and she says in a more overly posh British accent than her own, "Why, thank you, young man."

Dude must have been at least fifty. She strolls straight up to a handsome guy about her age at the reception desk. "We'd like a room, young man, for me and my... houseboy Nigel here." She gestures towards me as I incline my head. Fuck, if I know what's going on right about now...

"What's the name, ma'am?" The guy behind the desk glances up from his screen.

"Davenport, but could you be a dear and put it under... Smith? If my husband finds out I've 'borrowed' one of the houseboys again, I shan't half make him a frowny face!"

"Erm, of course, ma'am, not a problem. How will you be paying for the room tonight?"

She winks at him. "Cash, of course, you silly sausage, mum's the word!" She taps the side of her nose and winks again. "Do you know how old I am, dear? Guess. Go on, see if you can, poppet."

Smiling at her like she's a special kind of special, he says, "Twenty-four?"

She barks out the biggest laugh making me jump. "Oh, Nate." She digs me in the ribs. "How precious, this young whippersnapper thinks I'm twenty-four. My husband really is a genius. Guess again, young man!" Leaning in, she winks again. "I will give you a clue. You're nowhere remotely close. Please guess again."

"Thirty?" He winces.

She just laughs again. "How absolutely wonderful! Shall I tell you how old I am, darling, young whippersnapper, you?" She leans over and pinches his cheek. "I'm fifty-eight. My husband is a plastic surgeon and has nipped, tucked and tightened everything, and when I say tightened, I mean… tightened." She looks down at her crotch and then back at him, smiling. "Everything!"

He takes a big swallow and stares at her tits, then back to her face. She slides her hand up his arm. "You know, Noel here is my favourite house boy as he does all the bum stuff, you know, putting stuff in… And out… And in again, and he even lets me put stuff in… And out… And in again too, but a young man as handsome as you could really give him a run for his money. I don't suppose you would be interested in a new job, would you? How many houseboys do I have Nathan?"

I start counting on my fingers. "You have... twelve, ma'am, well, eleven, really, as Dmitri is still awaiting surgery after your last... role-play incident."

"Ah, poor Darren, that was unfortunate, but I'd just had my BBL and needed to test it out. It was just unfortunate... it was a ten out of ten from me, I'll tell you, sonny!"

Leaning in and stroking his arm again, she whispers, "I'm having another boob job in two days once I'm healed. I don't suppose I could entice you to want to take them for a... test drive?" She raises her eyebrows at him, then she runs her finger over the top of the mound of her tits, leaning in so he can get a good look down her cleavage. "We could call it a job interview if you like? Are you opposed to pegging? Nathaniel here loves it, especially when I pull his hair and spank him. Is that something you would go for? And also, once a month, we have Naked Tuesdays while my husband's at golf all day, and we basically have an orgy. What fun!"

"Erm... I'm... it's... " The poor guy's sweating and looks like he's seriously considering it for a second before Ray steps back.

"Anyway, I'm wetter than an otter's pocket, so I mustn't dawdle. Come on, Norris, mummy needs her legs behind her ears in less than five minutes, or I'm going to get spanky, and not in a good way." She snatches the two room keys off the counter and heads to the elevator.

The poor guy goes red.

I grin at him. Leaning over, I whisper, "Naked Tuesdays, we get to play hide and seek with each other's rude bits and stick them wherever we like. Gerald is a really good hiding place. He will always hide three," I wink and stride away, arriving at the side of Ray as the lift doors open, and we step in.

She throws me against the side of the lift, lifts her thigh up to my waist and starts kissing me and yanking at my shirt as the doors slowly close. Once the doors ping shut, we both burst out laughing.

"Oh my God, Ray, you're fucking bonkers. That poor guy!"

"I bet tomorrow he'll fancy a new career. Now, what are we actually doing here?"

I flush a little. "There's a gay bar around the corner. Fancy being my wingwoman?"

"Hell yeah, quick tidy up, out in ten?" she asks, and I nod because we don't even have a change of clothes, so what the fuck are we actually going to the room for.

Dropping the helmets off and Ray's jacket, Ray dives into the bathroom, shouting, "Squaddie wash!" Whatever the fuck that is.

As she walks out of the bathroom, she yanks the hair thingy out of her ponytail and runs her fingers through her hair. I've never seen it down before. It's all different blondes and so shiny it looks soft as it lays down her back to almost her waist.

"I just need to put my make-up on." She laughs, grabbing some gloss, lipstick, or something out of her jacket pocket, slapping it on, and shouting. "Woo, woo! Let's go get some dick!" She punches the air.

Shaking my head, I just laugh at her. She really is ridiculous, and fuck, I love her. She makes me feel like a kid again.

She throws her jacket on the bed. She's wearing these amazing silver-heeled biker boots with buckles up the side and a skull on the front, skintight jeans with a rip in one knee, which are a faded grey that really shows off her long toned legs, a tight grey long sleeve low-neck tee, which the girls are just peeking out of and it clings onto her whole body for dear life, and a black and white checked shirt over the top. She's stunning and sexy as hell, if you like that kind of thing, and it would be so much easier if I did, because fuck, she's wild and fun and gets my heart racing in ways it hasn't done for years, but alas, the lack of dick is an issue. Maybe after a few drinks, I can forgo it and take her for a spin. Who knows?

Heading out the door we reach the lobby, and the guy from earlier cocks a brow at us. Ray rushes over to him.

"My word, dear boy, Nelson has just informed me of a bar around the corner where I can find him a gentleman to do things with while I watch. How fascinating. If you have a break, would you like to join us?" she purrs at him.

He's totally eye fucking her, and I smile as I saunter over, adjusting my dick in my jeans, sliding my arm around her shoulder and licking her face. She shudders in my hold and lets out the filthiest moan that, were I straight, my dick would have been jumping out of my jeans.

"Now, now, Nick, don't go wasting that talent on my face, dear boy. At this rate, we will be heading back to the room, and I will miss out on all the debauchery you promised me at the other establishment!"

Winking at the guy, I turn her towards the door. "We can't have that, Mrs Davenport, now can we?" As I slap her ass and shout, "To the sex rooms!"

She jumps to my back, yelling. "Tallyho! Giddy up, Ned!" I jog out of there like my life depends on it. Dropping her to her feet the minute we're outside, I grab her hand and drag her to the club. We are still laughing as the queue comes into view.

Stalking straight to the front of the line, I smile at the doorman, the first guy I ever fucked all those years ago. That's why I come here. If I don't find anyone, he's always my backup. "Dice?" He smiles at me. "It's been a while!" As he leans in and gives me a hug.

I just smile at him.

"You around later?" he asks, flushing slightly before looking confused as I'm still holding Ray's hand.

"Maybe." I grin at him. I don't want to fuck him off totally. We head inside, and Ray drags me over to the bar. "Six shots of tequila," she fires at the bar woman.

"Fucking six? Who are the rest for?"

"Dice, it's nearly midnight. We've got some catching up to do," shoving three in my direction while necking hers, then gesturing the same again at the bar woman.

"Fuck, this is gonna get messy. What time are you at work tomorrow?"

"I'm working late, so I don't have to be there till twelve! Fuck yeah!" She bellows the last bit.

"Jesus!" She's a bad influence. Necking the six shots, she grabs my hand and drags me to the dance floor. I fucking love dancing but never have anyone to go with, and seeing as Ray is my new favourite person, I can't wipe the grin off my face.

After a little while, the buzz of the tequila kicks in, and I grab her hand, pulling her against my body and grinding against her. I pull her in and whisper in her ear, "You'd be my perfect guy if you were one." I breathe across her cheek.

Looking into my eyes and gazing into my soul, she says, "You'd be my perfect guy if you weren't into sucking dick and taking it in the arse!"

I burst out laughing and squeeze her tighter. "Fuck, I love you!"

"Love you too, knobhead, but grinding against each other isn't gonna get you laid, so come on! To the bar!"

She grabs my hand and tugs me around while I'm laughing again. I don't think I have laughed so much in my whole life since this wild girl stormed into my world and upended everything I thought I was and everything I thought I wanted.

As we get back to the bar, she orders another six shots, and as we are necking them, a guy sidles up behind me. He's hot, with dirty blonde hair, my height, slim but muscular, totally my type. He starts stroking my arm and whispering in my ear, I glance over at Ray, and she nods to the cage with the pole in it near the stage.

When there aren't any acts on, people can dance in there. As she stalks over, there's a guy already in there dancing like he has a broom shoved up his ass, and he's dancing to a totally different song than the one playing for the rest of the club, but she grabs him and drags him out which makes me laugh.

"Ah, you like that, huh?" The guy rubbing all over me whispers in my ear. Before catching where I'm looking and glancing over, Ray's now swinging around the pole like some kind of pornstar pole-dancing expert, looking sexy as fuck. "Is that your ... friend?"

"Yeah!" I say to him, but it comes out all breathy.

"Wow, she's mesmerising!"

"Yeah, she sure is!"

"Are you two together?"

I turn to face him, shaking my head. "Nah, she's my best friend." At that moment, I realise she's the only person in the world who truly knows me. I haven't even shared this with my brothers through sheer fear alone. She makes me feel happy and brave and strong and enough.

"I'm bi, if she wants to join us? She looks like my kind of fun."

I frown at him. I don't want him looking at her like that, not because I'm jealous, but because I feel really protective of her.

"Nah, neither of us would be into that!" I state flatly. He just nods and carries on watching. She's fucking amazing, as flexible as hell, even though she has practically drunk her own body weight in tequila. After the song ends, she gets down, and more than a few people are clapping as she leaves the podium.

Stalking over to me with a sway in her hips, I can't help but smile.

"You wanna get out of here?" the guy asks.

"Sure!" I smile at him, turning to Ray and nodding at him.

"I'm gonna head back now, too, so stay and have fun. I'll see you later." Ray leans in to kiss my cheek and whispers, "Knock him dead, hot stuff!"

I laugh as I pull away and grab her hand. "I'm walking you back first!" And the guy just follows behind us, making it to the outside of the hotel. The doorman swings the door open.

"Catch ya later!" She turns and struts through the door, but as she gets inside, she starts doing this weird walk that looks like she'd had five guys in her ass, and when I look up, the reception guy's watching her, his cheeks flush slightly. I put my hand in front of my mouth to stop the laugh, but I have to look away. She's fucking ridiculous.

I get tugged away without realising as he clearly gets impatient with me, staring after Ray. He has hold of my hand and drags me around the corner of the hotel into the alleyway.

There's a dumpster halfway up, and he walks us past it. After we are far enough past it to not be seen, he pushes me against the wall reaching the front of my jeans and opening them up, sliding his hand into my boxers and grasping my dick. Rolling his hand up and down, he drops to his knees and cups my balls while licking his tongue along the underside of my shaft.

I fist my hand in his hair and lean back against the wall. I cock my head back and close my eyes, sighing.

He's good at what he's doing, and I try to focus on the feel of him taking me into his mouth as he gently squeezes my balls while taking me to the back of his throat, pumping and twisting his hand at the same time. It feels great, but it also feels so… empty. I want more.

Pulling him up, I undo his jeans and shove them and his boxers to his ankles, I spin him round so his front is to the wall, and I'm behind him. Sliding a condom on, I spit in my hand and slide it around my dick, sliding it between his cheeks while I push him forward into the wall. He puts his arm on the wall and rests his head against it as I slide in, gritting my teeth as I'm met with a slight resistance before I slam myself in. Fuck waiting. He grunts out in shock as I pull out of him and slam back into him again. He gasps at the intrusion, but I grab his hips, slamming into him again. He reaches around and starts pumping his own dick while I continue my assault on him from behind.

I grunt as I slam in harder and faster as he pants and grunts with every thrust. "Wait, slow down!" he gasps out, but I'm raging, and I don't know why.

I'm so angry. It comes over me all of a sudden, so I take it out on him, slamming into him again. He tries to turn to face me, but I shove him back to the wall pounding into him again.

He rocks back against me. "Fuck, Jesus," he spits out, and I'm pounding like a maniac. I've got him pinned against the wall, and I'm not holding back. He's pumping his fist harder and faster, trying to keep up with my thrusts, but I shudder, and I'm done. Done with this. Done with him. I'm just done! He's panting and still chasing his own climax as I pull out, rip the condom off and throw it at the dumpster. I rip my jeans back up and turn to walk away.

"Wait, please don't leave me half-done. Come on, man!"

"I'm done!" I say coldly as I stomp away back to the hotel.

Once I reach the lobby, I stalk straight to the elevator, not making eye contact with anyone. I storm up to our room and let myself in. I can see the body shape in the bed as she's left the table lamp on for me. I strip out of my clothes and walk over to the bed. I slide in, wrap my arms around her and nuzzle into her neck, kissing the side of her face.

"Hey," she whispers, and I roll her over onto her back and slide over the top of her so I'm between her legs but holding myself off her body.

She blinks up at me, but her eyes aren't really focusing. "You okay?" She runs her hands up my shoulders and runs them through my hair. I sigh out and relax, laying on her, resting my head on her chest. She wraps her arms around me and holds me like she knows this is what I need. I let out a sigh of relief as I finally start to relax. "Wanna talk about it?" I shake my head against her, and she strokes lazy circles along my neck and shoulders.

"Will you let me try something?" I shyly ask without moving my head from her chest.

"Tell me what you need, Dice."

"I need to kiss you. I mean, really kiss you. No messing, just … I need to know if there's something between us. I'm out there getting my dick sucked, then fucking that guy, and all I can think about is you, but fuck, I don't know what that means."

"I don't think it means what you think it does, Dice. I know I've stirred shit up for you by finding out your gay, and I know it can't be easy trying to fit that into your life now and try and see where you now fit—"

I put my fingers against her lips, shutting her the fuck up as I know she can talk for England, literally. "You don't have to. I don't want it to be weird, I don't want it to spoil whatever this is I've got with you, but you're my best friend, you've made me feel shit I've never felt before, you make me feel strong and confident in who I am, you make me feel alive and I fucking love you.

"If I weren't gay, I would marry you and have gorgeous babies. I would be with you forever. I just need to try and see if I'm bi, because if I'm not for a girl like you, then I'm definitely gay, and I need to start to own that myself before I can expect other people to.

"You're perfect in every way except your lack of dick, and I need to just try… so I know."

She runs her fingers through my hair and down my face cupping my cheeks. "I don't know, Dice. I'm not normally comfortable kissing guys… I just … You sure about this?"

I huff out a release of frustration and close my eyes. Next thing I know, her lips are on mine, gentle and unsure at first, and then she slides her tongue across my lips, and I open them for her. I slide my hand against her side, inside her shirt and slide it up, cupping her breast in my hand and squeezing slightly. She lets out a slight moan and rocks against me. I grind myself into her and slide my own tongue against hers, kissing her like my life depends on it. I pinch her nipple between my finger and thumb and roll it between them, making her gasp and grind into me again.

We devour each other's mouths as my dick becomes rock solid and grinds into her. I can feel her heat, and she's wet, and I think I can do this. I think I can fuck her. She's so beautiful and funny and sexy, and she's everything I want to feel. I kiss her and grind into her even harder, and she gasps again. I slide my hand back down and hook her pants to the side, and I slide my fingers between her lips, and she bucks beneath me, as I slide two fingers in her and groan as she shudders.

I nip at her neck and kiss along her jaw, and she gasps and grinds onto me. I circle my thumb around her clit, and I grind into her again. I'm lost. I'm so desperate to feel. I can do this. I start to pump faster and rub my thumb against her clit harder and faster as I slide another finger in. She gasps and grinds into me, and her breaths stutter as her back arches off the bed. She's the most beautiful thing I've ever seen, and then she starts to come and grabs onto my wrist, riding my hand unashamedly till she comes with a muffled grunt.

I slow my thumb, moving slower till every shudder passes, and as she gasps for breath, she whispers, "What the fucking hell was that, Dice? I thought you said a kiss!" She pants as I lean up and gaze into her eyes. She bursts out laughing and shakes her head as I roll onto my back at the side of her.

"Fuck." I scrub my hand down my face. "Jesus, woman, that's some magical pussy you have. I lost all sense of myself and wanted so badly to bury myself in you back then!"

She barks out a laugh. "Says the gay guy who's just given me a fucking epic orgasm. What the fuck, Dice?"

"Fuck Ray, have I just fucked everything up? I mean, I fucking love you, and in the middle of it, I thought I could do it. I thought I could throw all caution to the wind and fuck you, and it would solve all my problems, and if there was ever a woman who could fuck me straight, Ray, Jesus, it would be you, and my dick was definitely harder than with the guy I just fucked, shit… what the fuck's wrong with me?" I try to roll away from her, but she straddles me and lays on my chest, pushing herself up to gaze into my eyes.

"Dice, you're gay. It's okay to be gay, it's okay to be confused, and it's okay that you just gave your friend the best orgasm she can ever remember having, but it's not a problem. You're not less because you're gay."

I breathe out a laugh.

"And it's fine to be yourself, and you need to learn to love yourself as you are, then you won't want to hide that side of you. Dice, everyone loves you. You just need to love yourself enough to believe that."

I squeeze her tight to my chest and kiss the top of her head, just breathing together for a second before. "So, best orgasm, hey?"

Then she punches me in the ribs. "Oww!" Then we both laugh again. "Shit, I'm sorry I got carried away. I thought I could kiss you, but then … it felt so good that I just got confused and lost to what I wanted. I thought it was you, when actually I think I want what I have with you with a partner, someone who I can do all the goofy shit with and kiss and hold hands and fuck… fuck, Ray. I'm so sorry."

"You know what'll make me feel better?" She grins down at me.

"More orgasms?"

She punches me again. "Hades, you're such a dick!" She rips the covers off and jumps on the bed in her long sleeve T-shirt and her underwear. "Room service!"

"Ray, it's nearly five. They don't even start serving breakfast till seven, and nice tats you got there. You got any more?"

"Yes, tonnes, now come on!" She grabs my hand and drags me from the bed to the door, snatching a key card and sliding it in the front of her underwear.

"What the fuck you doing with that?"

"Does it look like I have fucking pockets in this outfit, and we don't wanna get locked out while we go raid the kitchen, do we now, dickhead?"

As she drags me out of the room, breaking into a run, dragging me behind her, I'm only wearing my boxers, and we're both laughing like loons while we run barefoot down the corridor to find the kitchen.

We get off the lift on the second floor and head down the stairs so we don't end up in the middle of the lobby, skirting around the corners and hiding behind plant pots. She drags me along till she finds what she's looking for.

Once we reach the kitchen, she darts inside and heads straight to the fridge, whisper-yelling, "Grab us some forks or spoons or something!"

I run to the other side of the kitchen to look for the cutlery. The kitchen door swings open just as she's shutting the big walk-in fridge with a massive cheesecake in her hand with fruit all over the top.

We both drop to the floor, crawling towards each other behind the large centre island.

Two guys walk in. "Fucking Rory, text me last night about this fifty-eight-year-old bird who came in with her fucking house boy or something wanting him to join them. Her husband is some big-shot plastic surgeon, and she has a body to die for and barely looks in her twenties. Offered him a job and everything!"

"Fuck off, John, as if! Rory's talking bullshit!"

"Nah, man, look! He sent me a pic from the security footage!"

"Fuck, I wouldn't mind becoming a house boy if I got to bang that. Fifty-eight, you say? I still don't believe it!"

We're staring at each other, holding our breaths. Ray's biting her lip with tears running down her face. I have one hand across my mouth, trying to keep myself quiet, but Ray never lets that fucking cheesecake go. She starts crawling towards me with the cheesecake held out before her.

As the two guys who walked in head to the back of the kitchen, she leaps up and sprints towards the door, swinging it open and darting out of it.

"Shit!" I whisper as I get to my feet and shoot off after her. As I get into the stairwell, Ray's there waiting for me, tears streaming down her face. "Fuck, that was close." I waggle the two spoons at her. "Race you back to the room!"

And off I run, but she laughs and runs after me. We don't stop till we get to the elevator and throw ourselves in it. When we reach the room, we sit on the bed and devour half the cheesecake before collapsing into a cheesecake coma and falling asleep.

The room phone rings, and I jump up in a panic, grabbing the phone. "Hello?"

"Hello, Mr… erm… Davenport? This is Rory from the front desk. I've requested a late checkout for you and Mrs Davenport. Your checkout is at 11 a.m." I look at my watch. It's already ten! Shit! "I'm off shift now, but I've left my number for Mrs Davenport to call me about the… test drive next time she's in town. Please tell her it would be my pleasure, and I hope to see her as soon as she's feeling better."

"That's lovely, Rory. Thank you, I will pass that on to Mrs Davenport for you, and we will be in touch."

"Who the fuck is that?" Ray snarls from under the covers.

"Your new house boy, he's left his number at the desk. Check out at eleven. Call him for the… test drive!"

She snorts and slides out of the bed. "Fuck, I'm knackered. I need some sleep, and I've got work, and this was a horrible idea!" She walks over to me, kissing my cheek. "Thanks for an awesome time and orgasm, but mainly time!" Then she stalks into the bathroom and flips on the shower. I find myself grinning like a madman. Even though I'm not straight, I managed to give her an epic orgasm. Yay me!

As we arrived to check out, Ray puts on that stupid voice again.

"Mrs Davenport, room 418. We would like to check out."

The young woman at the desk says, "Ah, yes, Mrs Davenport." She leans over and slides an envelope across the desk to Ray. "Thank you for staying at the Friedmont Hotel. We hope you enjoyed your stay."

"We did. Thank you so much, young lady." She turns and sashays away towards the door! As we reach the bike, she laughs, ripping open the envelope and in it's a letter.

Dear Mrs Davenport

Having you stay with us at the Friedmont Hotel was an absolute pleasure.

As per your offer of a 'test drive' when you're next in the area, I would love to oblige you. Hopefully, your stay with us has been as memorable as you are! I look forward to 'coming' with you next time.

Rory

665-658-7730

"Holy shit." I laugh out loud. "Come on, let's get you back, Mrs Davenport before we end up with a stalker!"

"Hey, did you pay for the room?"

"Shit, no, didn't you?" I grimace at her.

"Nope. I was too busy being Mrs Davenport!"

"Fuck, then let's get out of here!"

Slamming our helmets on and diving on the bike, we speed off back to the MC. By the time we pull up at the garage, my cheeks are sore from grinning all the way back!

As we pull up in front of the garage, we get off the bike and put our helmets on the handlebars. Ray wraps her arms around my neck and pulls me into a hug.

Whispering in my ear, she asks, "You good?" I nod as I squeeze her tighter. "Look, your sexuality… it's no one's business, and if you don't want people to know, that's up to you, but missing that part of yourself hurts you, trust me. I've been keeping part of me restricted for years, but the people who love me know that part of me exists and support me. If you want to share that with the boys, you know they'll support you too. Just love yourself, okay? You're amazing just the way you are." She leans in and kisses me on the cheek, squeezing me tighter.

She starts bouncing on the balls of her feet. "You know I love you, okay, but right now, my favourite person in this whole minute is on his way over!" Pulling back and staring at her, the excitement's unmistakable, she's literally vibrating, and as I step out of her embrace, she skips over to him, throwing her arms around his neck and kissing him on the cheek!

"You fucking legend, Barbie. I'm gonna have to put a ring on it soon before some other woman comes and steals you away from me!"

"Fucking hell!"

I jump, not realising Dozer's now standing beside me. "How the fuck's she managed to get everyone round here wrapped around her little finger? I mean, fucker never brings me anything."

Ray steps away from Barbie's hug with the bag with her food in one hand and the milkshake in the other. "I'm just adorable!" She winks over at him, and all of us laugh at that.

"You really are precious!" Barbie smiles across at her, and she gives him the widest grin while flipping Dozer and me off.

"Dice, I love you, Barbie, I love you more. Dozer… you not so much!" She blobs her tongue out at him. "I'm gonna go get changed for work, Dozer. See you soon!" As she happy dances around the back, munching on her burger, I shake my head at her as she goes.

"So she loves you, huh?" Dozer asks.

"She loves me more!" Barbie grins as he turns and walks back across the parking lot. I can literally hear him whistling. I mean, he's been a grumpy fucker as long as I've known him, but Ray seems to have an effect on, well, us all.

"Why the face?" Dozer nudges me with his shoulder.

"Eh? What face?"

"You know if she says she loves you, she means it, right? I'm sure she loves Barbie in a different way, man, don't take it to heart."

"It's not that, mate … I was just thinking it's gonna suck balls when she leaves."

"Leaves?" Dozer questions like he has no idea what the fuck I'm talking about.

"Yeah, they're only here on a six-month tourist visa. When that runs out, they'll be going home and possibly moving on before that. They're supposed to be travelling. We're lucky they've hung around this long, in fairness!"

"She's leaving?" Dozer looks like he's trying to divide the square root of pi by itself, leaving a deep furrow in his brow with a sigh. "She'll stay for you, though, won't she?"

I shake my head. "We're not together, Dozer!"

"Well, you're fucking, so that's something, right?"

"Dozer, we're not fucking. We're just friends."

"But you've been out all night together, and you're in the same clothes as yesterday!"

"Yeah, we went to a club up the coast, then stayed in a hotel, but nothing happened. It's not like that."

"Shit," he curses before shaking his head. "Could you fuck her?"

"What the fuck, Dozer? No, I'm not fucking her to manipulate her to stay!"

"Well, I'm sure one of the other guys will. I mean, she's stunning. I'm sure someone can help out!"

"Fucking hell, Dozer! There's gonna come a time when she's gonna leave, and it's gonna be shit on all of us. I really don't think the club will be the same when she goes. We won't be the same when she goes!" I shrug at him then we both just stand there, taking it all in. It isn't until her voice cuts through my thoughts and jolts us back to reality.

"What the fuck's wrong with you two?" She's showered and changed, and her hair's still wet, thrown into a messy bun on top of her head. Her cheeks are pink where she's scrubbed at them while in the shower, and she smells like the forest and citrus fruits, and I breathe it all in, sighing.

She steps forward, sliding her hands around my neck and pulling me in. "You okay?"

"Yeah, just thinking."

"What, both of you?" She looks over at Dozer, confused.

"Yeah." He nods. "Can I get one of those?"

Looking slightly worried, she lets go of me, kissing my cheek, throws her arms around Dozer, and squeezes. He clings on to her like she's leaving right this second, and it damn near breaks my heart that this is going to be a reality soon.

"What the hell is wrong?" We haven't even heard the car pull up as Beauty gets out of it.

"These twats have been 'thinking' apparently!" Ray huffs out at both of us, using the air quotes around thinking, causing us to at least smile a little.

"I'd bought you dinner as you forgot yours!" Beauty states, holding up a bag from the diner and a shake.

"Oooh, what we got?" Ray lets go of Dozer, heading over to Beauty and grabbing the bag before hugging her and opening it.

"Seen as you've been 'thinking' and it's taken it out of you, why don't I take this, and you take the afternoon off and take Beauty somewhere nice?"

"You've literally just had a burger, fries, a shake and probably onion rings, knowing Barbie!" Dozer laughs at her.

"That was ages ago!"

"We've literally only been back thirty minutes, Ray!" I shake my head at her. That girl really loves food. I'm not sure why she isn't the size of a house.

"Exactly, it was ages ago. Beauty, you're a legend! Dozer, see you tomorrow, and Dice, later, gator!"

She stalks into the garage, happy dancing at the burger and shake as I scrub a hand down my face. "What the fuck are we gonna do?" Dozer asks, concern written all over his face.

"I honestly don't know, man, but I'll look into it and see if I can come up with a way for her to stay. If she wants to, that is."

"You don't honestly think she'd leave, do you?"

"I hope not, but what's she got to stay for here?" Waving at Beauty, I head to my room to get a shower and see what the fuck's going on in my head as I can't let her leave, or if it goes tits up with the club and my brothers, I need an exit strategy so I can go with her. I can't be on my own again, and even though I love my brothers to death, I feel this girl is my ride-or-die. She gets me, and I'm allowed to just be myself with her.

Tank

I'm on the track behind the clubhouse, not quite as far up as the barn, but a little way past the gym. I can hear a rustling in the undergrowth by the trees. I stand silently, listening to where the sound is coming from. It's invaded by a *thump, thump, thump,* getting closer. Spinning around, I can see Ray running along the track towards me. It's early, maybe sixish.

She looks at me, confused. "Hey, big guy! What you up to?"

I glare at her, and putting my fingers to my lips, I turn my back on her and crouch down, looking through the trees.

She creeps up beside me. "What are we looking for?" she whispers.

Turning to look at her, I hear the noise again. It's slightly to my right, so I take a step forward and listen again, moving toward the rustle, gently accessing where I was stepping before taking the step. I hold my hand up to Ray to stay where she is.

Crouching down again, I reach slowly towards the raven that's struggling on the ground. It looks like it has a broken wing. I gently scoop it up, rising from the ground as I turn. Ray's frozen, staring at me.

"Shit, it's injured," she whispers.

"Yeah," I grunt at her, shuffling out of the undergrowth and back to the track. We slowly walk back in the direction of the clubhouse.

"You need a hand?" she asks curiously.

I shrug a shoulder at her heading back down the track. "You got a box?"

"I've got a shoe box! Any good?"

"Sure."

She runs off towards the van, and by the time I'm at the side of the clubhouse, she's just locking up.

This little guy needs some TLC. Walking into my room, Ray's right behind me. She puts the box on my bed and goes into the bathroom, grabbing a load of toilet roll and shredding it for the bottom of the box.

I frown at her, and she just shrugs. "Little guy needs to be comfy." She smiles at me.

"Here." I pass the raven towards her. "Like this!" I show her how to hold it, then head to medical for some bandage tape, a pipette and scissors, stopping at the kitchen for some fruit and finding some burger meat in the fridge. I grab some of that too.

As I walk back into my room, Ray is walking around, taking in all my framed pictures on the walls. I love birds and drawing. My walls are full of framed drawings I've done of local birds, but I love ravens, so there are more than a few of them.

"Tank, these are beautiful! Did you draw these?" I nod at her. I turn my back and head over to the bed where the box still sits.

I cut the bandage into long thin strips. It's sticky, so it will stick to itself while Ray holds the raven's body. I pull out its wing gently and feel along the bones, feeling the break. I check the bones are aligned as best as I can, then tape the wing in a cross, holding it together, and tape the wing to itself to stop the bird from opening it. Once that's secure, I tape the wing around the bird, under the other wing and back to itself, holding it firm against its own body.

Laying it in the box, I head to the bathroom to fill a cup with water and go back to sit beside Ray.

"How do you know what to do?" she asks, cocking her head to the side and watching me drop a few drops of water onto the raven's beak before it opens up and swallows some. I also grab a tiny piece of the meat and place it in front of the bird. It snatches it, gulps it down, and I grin. I love birds. They're my happy place.

I shrug at her as I continue to feed and water the raven.

"My mom showed me how." I didn't talk much about my life before this one, I just don't see any point, but my passion for birds has followed me into this life.

Once I've fed the bird and got some more fluids in it, I settle the box in the far corner of the room. The break isn't too nasty. It hasn't come through the skin, but it will still take six to eight weeks to heal.

"You can teach them to talk." I smile at her.

"Really?" Her face lights up, and it makes me smile even more. She actually seems to have a gentle side, too, like me. She's an enigma. She seems to be what we all need when we need it.

I know she has helped Priest find that thief at the club and dealt with it for him, and Blade was a little quite a bit ago, and she made up this stupid drinking knife-throwing game which he loves and pulled him out of his funk.

She's spending a lot of time with Dice, and people think they're fucking, but I'm not so sure. Something is going on, but I don't think it's what everyone's thinking. The way he looks at her like she's the answer to everything, it's something more than fucking, something more unique.

Ray has slid up the bed and is leaning back against the headboard. She taps the bed at the side of her, and I eye her with suspicion. What's she after?

"I won't bite!" She grins at me, but I'm not so sure.

I know dangerous people, I can sense it in them, and Ray, she's one of the most dangerous people I know, more dangerous than most of the guys in this place, and there are some seriously fucking dangerous people here. The way she looks makes her even more dangerous. She's unnervingly beautiful, so clever, looks unimposing, and is easily underestimated due to her gender and size, and that's what makes her deadly.

Tapping the bed beside her again, I sit down. "Tell me about them," she asks. "The ravens, I mean! They make me feel at home. The woods near where I grew up had them all over, and I used to crack my bedroom window to hear them. I'd just lay on my bed and listen to their chatter."

Resting my head back against the headboard, she shuffles over a bit to give me some more room. "They're very intelligent… They can figure out ways to get food and hide it and try and trick other ravens into thinking they've hidden it somewhere else. They can also mimic human speech, so in theory, you can teach them to talk, and they can also recognise people. They're smarter than crows and much bigger, too. A group of them is called an unkindness, and some people believe that they symbolise death and bad luck. And some believe them to be the ghosts of murder victims. They can live to be twenty to forty-five." I smile thinking about that.

"Wow, you really know a lot about them, huh?" She leans her head on my shoulder, and I rest my head on hers, don't ask me why. It just feels… sweet.

"What was it like where you grew up?" I ask her. She seems quite vulnerable sitting here beside me.

She sighs. "It was amazing, my dad and my pas bought a forest!" She huffs out a laugh

"Pas…?" I question

"Yeah, I had my biological dad and four of his best friends. When my mum died, they all raised me, so I have… had… four pas. They're all my dads, really, and my brothers too. And with the forest came farmland, well, a massive plot of land which was mainly forest with a massive lake in it. There were some old, almost farm-like buildings and a farmhouse which they renovated. They built an adventure centre around the lake, and we grew up in the forest, my brothers and me."

"How many brothers do you have?"

"Two… well, three… well, I suppose two now."

Ignoring the fact that she can't seem to decide between two or three, I ask, "Are you close?"

"Complicated."

"How so?"

"Well, I suppose it's not, not really. I had three brothers. I'm close with two of them and have always been, and the other one, not so much. He pretty much hated me till he died when we were nineteen."

"Where are they now?"

"My Pa Bernie moved back to the States with my Ma and their sons, my brothers, a while ago when his mum became ill. They all live in Heighton."

"So that's who you've been seeing while you were there. When Dice tracked you, he kept losing you in Heighton for days!"

Ray lets out a small laugh. "Stalkers, much?" She nudges my shoulder. "Yeah I've been staying with them on and off. I've missed them a lot since they've been back here."

"What are they like?"

"My pas or my brothers?"

"Both."

I scooch down on the bed and roll onto my side to look at her, and she looks down at me, wrinkling her nose and grinning.

"I wasn't comfy." I shrug at her, so she comes to join me rolling to face me.

"My twin, Bas—Sebastian—he's the one that died. He looked a little more like my dad with brown hair and blue eyes, but he hated me and my brothers. We used to stay together and stay away from him. My other brothers, Bran, two months younger than me, and Dane, eighteen months younger, all look very similar. I look more like them." She grabs her phone and scrolls through, finding a pic of all three of them together, handing me the phone.

"Shit, you could pass for triplets! But they're not your real brothers…. I mean, like blood. Not if one's two months younger, even I know that doesn't work."

"No, we're closer. They're the family I chose, the family that chose me. My blood brother turned his back on all of us. They are my brothers. I would die for both of them. We've always been close, same with my dad and my pas. They all treated us the same growing up. They are my brothers and my dads. I was just… lucky, I guess.

"I had their mum, my ma, four pas, a dad and two brothers that loved me, and one that couldn't bear the sight of any of us." She shrugs at that. "I even look like three of my pas. I'm a mix of all of them!" She scrolls and shows me another picture of five men standing in front of the forest.

"Shit," I breathe out, chuckling as I hold the phone up to her face and glance back and forth between the pic and her. "So, who's who?" I roll onto my back, and she shoves closer to me. I lay my arm out, and she lifts her head to rest it on my chest and shuffles into my side.

She points between them. There were two shorter, two taller and one in the middle. "That's my biological dad, Daniel, with brown hair and blue eyes. That's JJ. He's got chocolate brown hair and hazel eyes, not unlike yours." I feel her smile against my chest. "That's Cade and Bernie. I'm most like them two, attitude, sense of humour, well, I suppose I'm Cade's mini-me, with a bit of everyone else thrown in, and that's Steven."

I hug her tighter as she scrolls again while I hold the phone up.

"That's my ma. She's Bran and Dane's biological mum."

"Fuck, you look like her too!"

She breathes out a laugh. "Yeah, it's always confusing the hell out of people… It's just my family. To me, it's normal … I mean, we're not normal, we're fucking bonkers, but you'll see when you meet them."

"You'd like me to meet them?" I smile. I don't think anyone has ever wanted me to meet their family. I mean the guys here, my brothers, none of us really have family, well, not the inner circle. Most of us don't, there are a few siblings out there somewhere, but none of us have parents left.

"Definitely!" She grins back at me as she starts scrolling again, showing me pictures of the Adventure Centre and her family. She shows me a picture of her twin, you can see the resemblance, but you wouldn't believe they were twins, just that they were maybe related. She talks me through where they were taken and all about the Adventure Centre, which sounds like an amazing place to visit, let alone grow up.

The phone rings in my hand, and we both jump a mile. "Shit, it's Dozer. What time is it?" She grabs the phone off the bed where I dropped it.

"Where the fuck are you?" he bellows out the phone.

"Shit, Dozer, sorry, lost track of time, be there in five, old-timer, don't blow a gasket, K?" Then she hangs up and swings her legs off the bed. "Can I come back later and check on Odin?"

"Odin?" I laugh as she cocks her head to the raven in the shoebox in the corner of the room.

"Yeah, Odin, he was known as the raven god, right?" She winks at me as she heads for the door. "Catch ya later, big guy!"

Clicking the door shut behind her, I can't wait to spend more time with her. She makes me feel shit I haven't felt before. I feel content when she's around, happy. She even makes me feel seen. I don't think I've ever talked that much to anyone but her... I could talk to her all day.

Viking

I'm sitting at the bar waiting for Savage. It's our turn to head into town for our Community Outreach Programme. It's something the club does once a month. Many of us have come from shitty backgrounds, and although we aren't the best role models, we like to hang out with the kids at the community centre, talk to them, teach them a few things, and try and steer them towards a better life.

A lot of them are bringing themselves up or are in foster care, and the centre offers them a warm meal and company. We donate our time for free and also donate money to help them reach as many kids as they can, we definitely aren't saints, but we know what it's like, and if we can help one kid stay off the streets, then it's worth a couple of hours a month to give them something different to focus on.

"Hey, little 'un, what you doing here at this time of day? Shouldn't you be at work?"

Ray slides into the seat beside me, nudging my shoulder with hers. "You stalking me too? What is it with you lot and knowing where I am and what I'm doing? You got a tracker on me?"

I bark out a laugh at her. "Dice is right about you. You are fucking ridiculous!"

"For your information, I've had a cracking day and got all my shit sorted early, and everything went right for a change, so I actually got away early, even Dozer's left for the day."

"Well, fuck me, that never happens. Well, it didn't till you arrived anyway!"

"Is Tank in his room? I'm gonna go see Odin."

"Who the fuck's Odin?"

"The raven we rescued the other day." She cocks a brow at me like I'm the fucking stupid one.

I shake my head at her. "Not a fucking clue! Haven't seen him. I'm waiting on Savage, then heading out myself."

Jumping down from the stool, she punches me in the arm. "Catch ya later then, knobhead!"

"Rude!"

She just laughs as she heads towards Tank's room. She's really starting to get under our skin, that one. I know Priest said he felt she belonged, but it feels like she's been here all along. Scrubbing my hand down my face, I sit dicking around on my phone. Savage should be here any minute, and then we can head off. I check my watch. He's cutting it close, so I decide to give him a call.

"What's up, Viking?"

"Where are you?"

"I'm at the shop. Where else would I be?"

"Fucking hell, you're supposed to be coming to the C.O.P. with me!"

"Fuck's sake, that's tonight? Shit, man, I totally forgot. Can you get someone else to go? I'm here for another two hours!"

"Jesus, Savage, way to fuck up!"

"Sorry, man, okay, hope you get sorted!"

Motherfucker. Well, this sucks. Ray hasn't come back yet, so Tank must be in. Shoving my stool back, I head to ask him to fill in.

I knock on the door. "Tank, man, it's Viking. I need a favour."

The door swings open, Tank's wearing a pair of grey sweats, and Ray's laid on his bed looking at home.

"What?" Tank says, then just stands there. Sometimes he's a right Chatty Cathy, and others, it's like getting blood out of a fucking stone. Looks like tonight is the latter.

"It's Savage's turn to go to C.O.P. with me, and he's let me down. I need a second!"

"Can't."

"Why not? Come on, man, I need to get going, and there's no one else around. I'll owe ya!"

"What's C.O.P.?" Ray asks, rolling over on the bed to lay on her stomach facing me.

"It's a community thing where we hang out with the kids at the community centre. We do it once a month in pairs, and Savage bailed."

"I'll come!" Ray starts to roll off the bed.

"Sorted," Tank says as he heads to lie down on the bed where Ray had just got up from.

"Fine, come on, little 'un. Thanks."

"Catch ya later, big man!" She winks at Tank. "Bye, Odin." She shoots over her shoulder as she walks out the door. "So what's this involve? I'm armed, so we should be good," She taps the side of her boot.

"Jesus, Ray, they're kids, not convicts."

"Exactly, kids are fucking horrible things. At least you know what convicts are in for. Kids, on the other hand? It pays to be prepared."

I shake my head. "Maybe I should go on my own. It might be safer!"

"Nah, sounds like you might need backup. Come on, Vike. It could be fun!"

I huff out a breath. "Just don't get stabby, okay? These kids have been through it, so we just go have a laugh, play a few games, chat, nothing heavy. Just light entertainment, okay?"

"What about punchy? Will I need to get punchy?"

"Fucking hell. Thanks, Ray. I'm just gonna head out on my own!"

She throws her arm around me. "Chill, Vike, I'm pulling ya pisser!"

"You're doing what to my pisser?"

She just laughs as we get to the bike. She jogs over to the garage to get the spare helmet, and then we're on our way.

We pull up at the community centre in Ravenswood. It's in one of the poorer areas. We're like a big brother scheme, if you like, mentoring kids, so fuck knows what they're gonna make of Ray.

The girls love to flirt even though they are only kids, and the lads just think they're too cool, but Ray will throw a whole other dynamic in. This might be an epic fuckup on my part. "Shit!" I scrub a hand down my face before hanging my helmet on the bars.

"Let's do this!" She grins as we walk up to the doors, fuck is it too late to cancel. I mean, surely they can manage without us!

As we walk into the large reception room, it smells like stale sweat and pine disinfectant. Martha's checking the kids in at the door as we stroll over. "Well, hi, Viking, my dear. How are you?"

"I'm good, Martha. Thanks, this is Ray. She's gonna help me out today. Savage can't make it!"

Martha's in her early thirties but acts like a fifty-something. She's asked me out a couple of times, but she isn't my cup of tea. She's slim, well skinny, and isn't bad to look at, she has a short blonde bob with brown eyes. I think her hair's dyed as it doesn't look like Ray's or Scar's. It's kind of orangey-blonde, like a bad dye job. She has red lipstick on, smeared across her teeth and makes me cringe when she grins, and too much perfume, giving a sweet sickly smell to the air around her. She has on skintight jeans and a tight top, but she isn't womanly at all, not like Ray or Scar. She's all skin and bones.

"Hmm." She eyes Ray. "Well, not sure how that's gonna go. You know what the kids are like. They might eat princess here alive!" She grins at Ray, clearly jealous, and spits the word "princess" as an insult. Fuck, Martha's normally sweet and a little flirt, but she clearly isn't a fan of Ray.

Doubling over with her hands on her knees and gasping for breath, Ray bursts out laughing, glaring back at Martha. "Ah, don't worry yourself about little old me. I can take care of myself. Maybe you should worry more about getting your lipstick on your lips instead of your teeth, and the next time you fall in that

God-awful granny perfume, I hope someone pulls you out quicker. You fucking reek." She leans in and sniffs, screwing up her face. "Or maybe it's desperation I smell!" Then, leaning in right against her ear, she whispers," I can see your green-eyed monster from here, sweetheart, might wanna tuck that fucker away before it gets your throat punched!" She pulls back, winks at her, and then links her arm through mine. "Shall we get started, gorgeous?"

I grin at her like a dickhead because Martha's face is a fucking picture. Ray's really not the best person to try and intimidate or try and make look small, but I think Martha got away lightly, and for some reason, I just love the fire in Ray. Maybe Priest's right about her.

Walking into the hall, I clap my hands, and it booms around, echoing back to me. All the kids spin around and smile, heading over to me. There's a gang of four girls who never really take part. They're too cool for that, and definitely the bitchy girls. Oh shit, maybe Ray wasn't the best person to bring here.

Before I can say anything, Charlotte kicks off. "Who the hell's that?" she snarls, popping her gum, twisting her hair around her finger and popping her hip out.

Fucking hell. Ray has only just walked in. She hasn't even said anything yet.

"Shut up, Charlotte!" Travis says to her. "You're only jealous because she's fit, and you're a hag!"

"Hey, hey, kids!" Ray shouts out over the whole room, her voice demanding authority.

Charlotte winces away slightly, still trying to be top dog.

"Firstly," Ray spits out, "I don't have to be here, so I can leave if you want, but then you guys will miss out on all the cool shit I can show you. Secondly, you missy!" She points straight at Charlotte. "Need to learn to read the room better than that. You've no idea who I am and what I'm capable of!" Taking a step closer to Charlotte, she leans over, "You know that saying my bark is worse than my bite?"

"Yeah, and?" Charlotte tosses her hair over her shoulder, crossing her arms over her chest. Ray takes another step closer, making Charlotte's head bob back slightly, then takes another step, causing Charlotte to back up a couple of steps. Ray's a good six inches taller than her, and she glares down at Charlotte with her lip peeled back at her. "Well, try me motherfucker!" She licks down her canine tooth, grinning that feral grin of hers. "I'll let you be the judge of that one!"

Then she claps her hands, and Charlotte about shits herself. "So let's get this motherfucking show on the road, shall we? What are we doing first?" She swings around and grins at me.

"Well, what about a little demonstration, Ray, of your… talents." I raise my eyebrows at her. I know she can fight, but I wonder what else she has.

Laughing a maniacal laugh, she looks around the room. "Fine," she says. "What equipment have we got? Any mats? Apples? A staff or pool cue will do!"

"There's a bag of apples in the kitchen," Chase says. "Shall I grab them for you, Ray?"

"That would be great, sweetheart. Thank you." She tosses him a genuine smile.

After that, the lads are like putty in her hands, and a few of the girls start to come around once their

Queen Bee has been stomped on a little. I'm not sure what Ray is going to do, but I can't wait! She's wearing a black long sleeve T-shirt, black jeans, and combat boots. She takes her boots and socks off, handing me the knife she had slid in there. I just shake my head at her tucking it in mine. Two of the boys have gone to get four mats from the store cupboard, and one has gone to grab a broom.

"Right, everyone, take a seat in the bleachers. I don't want anyone getting injured," I say, chuckling.

As the boys lay the mats out, Ray starts stretching, and I can hear Charlotte bitching to one of the girls. "Who the fuck does she think she is? I bet whatever she thinks she's gonna do is so boring!"

Ray just grins while carrying on stretching once the mats are laid down. She unscrews the broom head and tosses it to the side, handing me the apples. "Hang on to those, will ya? I don't need them yet!"

Standing in the middle of the mats, she points the broom handle at Charlotte. "Don't get too comfy there, missy. You can be my volunteer for the next bit, but first let me warm up a little. So do any of you know any martial arts or self-defence?"

One boy raises his hand. "I did a little karate before I ended up in foster care." He flushes a little, shame, maybe embarrassment.

"Brilliant. What's your name?" Ray asks.

"Derek." He flushes again.

"Once I'm done here, you can be my second, Derek." She winks at him, and he flushes a little more. Ah, so cute. I grin, crossing my arms over my chest.

"So, I know lots of martial arts. I'll give you a little demonstration first. Then, if you like, I can teach you all a few basic self-defence moves after and see how we get on! Sound good?" The majority of the kids perk up at that.

Ray does a couple more stretches, then bows to the kids before stepping into a fighting stance and shouting, "Ki ai!" as she swings the broom handle around her body and neck.

She looks like she would have stricken a blow on an opponent. She shouts, "Ki ai!" then she starts flipping and landing on one knee, swinging the staff around in a mesmerisingly fast blur of motion. Fuck, she's graceful but also deadly.

The kids are fascinated and are all oohing and ahhing. I just can't keep the smile off my face as she does a backflip spinning the staff around and landing facing the kids, she bows, and they all stand up, cheering. Well, all except Charlotte, but fuck her. She's a bitch anyway.

"Wanna step up then, Charlotte?" Ray challenges, tossing the broom handle to the side while she catches her breath. Charlotte heads over to the mat and stands in what only can be described as a bitch pose, arms crossed, hip popped. "Brilliant," Ray says. "You stand just like that for me." She turns and nods at me, and I throw her an apple. She turns, placing it on Charlotte's head.

"What the fuck are you doing?" Charlotte snarls at Ray.

Ray grins. "You're gonna wanna stay so still for this. If I miss, I might just knock your head off. Derek, you any good at catching?"

Derek nods. "Yep, Ray, I can catch."

"Brilliant. I want you to stand over there on the edge of the court."

He goes to stand on the line a good ten to fifteen metres away at least. The mats are in the centre of the room, and Ray places Charlotte at the back, facing the kids. Ray walks to the edge of the mat. "Okay, everyone ready? Charlotte, you need to hold extremely still, or Derek"—she winks at him—"will be catching your head rather than the apple, okay?"

Charlotte grimaces, and Ray winks at her, stepping up to the side of her and bowing. Ray takes a fighting stance but puts her hand on Charlotte's arm and whispers, "Just stand still, okay, and trust me, this will be cool."

Back in the fighting stance, Ray nods to Derek, and he nods back. She makes eye contact with Charlotte, and then she leaps into the air roundhouse kicking the apple off the top of Charlotte's head and sending it soaring down the court to Derek, where he has to jump up to catch it, whooping when he does.

All the kids clap again, and Ray steps up beside Charlotte. "Take a bow, kid!" she says, and Charlotte does, smiling a little as if she thought the applause was for her.

"Okay, who wants to learn some shit?" Everyone raises their hands. "Okay, form four lines, one at the side of each mat. Leave your shoes and socks on the bleachers." Ray steps up to the middle. "Okay, so firstly, this row is one, this one, two, then three, and finally four. When I call your number, I want that person to run and attack me any way you like. Once you've got up off the mat, go to the back of the line.

Once we've gone through that, I will show you a few moves, and you can have a go."

For the next two hours, Ray throws those kids around that court like her life depends on it, teaching them blocks and techniques to get out of trouble but instilling in them that the best way is to run and run fast.

The kids have a blast. When it's time to go, there are still nine kids who haven't done the last bit, so Ray makes Martha wait till she's got through them all, which pisses Martha off no end, but the kids fucking love it, and I've spent the last nearly four hours doing fuck all!

As we leave Martha to lock up, half a dozen kids are waiting outside for us. Charlotte's one of them. Ray goes straight up to her. "You have fun tonight?"

"Kind of," she says, still trying to be cool. Ray winks at her. "I'll take it!" She grins back at her.

"Will you be coming back sometime, Ray?" one of the kids asks over their shoulder as she's walking away.

"Maybe, depending on if I'm still here or not. I'll have to go back home to England in a few months. I'll try and make sure I come again before that, though. I can if you want me to."

There is a chorus of approval. "Stay safe, kiddos!" Ray yells after them.

"You're leaving?" I screw my face up at her.

"Yeah, I'm only on a tourist visa. I shouldn't really even be working. We're supposed to be travelling." Grabbing the helmet off the bike, she slams it onto her head, and I can't help the pit that falls into the bottom of my stomach. She's gonna leave?

What the actual fuck? I knew she was going to leave, but hearing it from her... I can't let that happen. I barely know her, but I feel like she's been in my life forever. She feels like gravity holding me here, as if it's somehow easier to breathe with her around. If she goes... nope, can't even think about it. Fuck, this is not gonna end well. I need to speak to the boys.

Ray

I'm not even mad that I've barely seen Scar all week, and with the weekend coming up, we have plans with Demi. I need to grab the bike I'm gonna borrow from Pa Bernie's at some point this week. Then, the boys and I are heading out on the camping trip next weekend.

The weekend flies by, and after meeting up with Demi for the weekend, she fills us in on the fact that she and Bran are now a couple. Shocker. I'm so happy for them. They are great together.

Scar's getting on great with Boyband. I'm helping Roach with his training and getting on great at work, but I feel a little restless or maybe a little... settled.

I want to explore a bit, and travel around, so we decide that Scar and I will stay this week. I will go on the camping trip with the boys at the weekend, and Scar will talk to Boyband about leaving the following week and heading further afield. We aren't saying we're leaving and not returning; we are going to see how it goes. How do we know we have found our place if we don't try somewhere else to give us a chance to miss it?

The guys have really grown on me, and I don't want to push my luck and get stuck somewhere when we've barely seen anywhere, and I'm falling for them all. Dice has fast become one of my closest brothers here, they're starting to feel like family, and that freaks me out a little, if I'm honest. We barely know each other, but this feeling that I hold for them all is clouding my judgement, making me want to stay to make a life here. But then I feel guilty for missing home, and I think some time away would solidify my feelings either way. I know Pa, Ma, Bran, and Dane want me to stay here, especially so I can help out where needed with the little problem we're having with the family business. Nothing major, just a Chihuahua nipping at the back legs of the bullmastiff, barely a gnat of a problem, but still irritating all the same. And we need to deal with it sooner rather than later.

Demi doesn't seem happy but understands and has decided to work extra shifts so she can save up. When we go back to the UK, she wants to come with us for a while.

Scar's adamant about ending things with Boyband, even though it doesn't have to be like that. She feels it's better to make a clean break if we don't come back this way, but she thinks even if I've found my place here, she will still be heading home. She never intended to stay. Maybe she only thought that as she thought I didn't intend to stay, but what if I do want to stay? I'd never make her choose, that's for sure.

Walking into the garage, I see Dozer in the office outback and head over with the coffee and bacon cobs. Sitting down for breakfast, I explain our plan but ask him to keep it to himself. I'm gonna tell the guys while we're on our camping trip. Scar will tell Boyband while I'm away, and then we will stay the following week and head out Saturday. While Dozer understands he has me for the next two weeks, he also lets me know he isn't happy.

I think he's kind of liked having me here, and he's getting to spend more time with Beauty. He's made good headway on the lodge he's doing up. He clearly doesn't want me to go and offers me a full-time job, which I tell him I will have to decline for now. He also tells me I can pick any of the guys I want to fuck, and he can make that happen if I stay. I mean, what the fuck, Dozer? But who knows about the future? The job, I mean, not a guy.

We just feel it's time to move on, and by that, I mean I'm freaking the fuck out at how close I'm becoming to these people and this life, and I need to take a step back to figure this shit out.

Seriously, all the hugging and touching and not losing my shit is weird in itself, but I seriously love these guys, and secretly, I think Scar's in love with Boyband too, and that's why she's pushing to leave. She thinks she should jump ship before getting hurt when he gets bored, but in reality, he's as in love with her as she is with him.

Dozer

It's after lunch, and I've had my head down working since Ray delivered her bombshell this morning, which shouldn't have been a bombshell at all, but fuck that bitch, it really was. I've been ignoring her all morning, avoiding eye contact, and only speaking if she speaks to me.

I mean, I understand, I really do, but fuck her and her swooping in, upending the whole club with her fucking shining personality and all that shit just to plan on swooping away like some fucking holiday romance never to be seen again. To say I'm pissed is an understatement.

All the guys seem to "understand," but fuck that. I've finally managed to spend some quality time with my wife, for fuck's sake. I'm finally making headway with the lodge. I've done more these last few weeks than I have in the last year. We can almost see the end in sight, but now it will be back to twelve to thirteen-hour days at the garage. I'll get home, eat, sleep, rinse and fucking repeat.

I don't know if my marriage can take going back to that again. I mean, I love my wife more than anything, but I'm a grumpy fucker at the best of times, but if I have to go back to that life again, I know I will be unbearable. My wife's a saint, but even she has her limits. I could lose everything now we've had a taste of a better work-home balance, and fuck me if I'm selfish. I don't want to lose that!

"You good?" she asks.

"Yup!"

"Wanna talk about it?"

"No. What the fuck Ray?" I'm smacked in the back of the head by a wet fucking towel. I turn around to glare at her. I get a bucket of water in the face for my trouble. "What the fuck is wrong with you?" I snarl at her.

"Me? Nothing!" She turns back to the bike she's working on and starts it up.

"Are you fucking shitting me right now?"

She revs the engine, cupping her ear, mouthing, "Sorry I can't hear you!"

As I open my mouth to reply, she revs the engine again, closing my mouth then opening it again once she stops, only she revs it again and smirks at me like the fucking motherfucking fuck she fucking is. "Fucker!" I snarl at her, turning on my heels and storming out of the garage, stomping straight into Dice.

"Whoa, watch it, man! What's crawled up your butt?"

"Ask your fucking girlfriend!" I storm off to kill someone, preferably not Ray, as I need her. I'll never find another mechanic like her, so I can't murder her yet. Well, not until she's leaving, then all bets are off.

I stomp my way to the bar, but as I walk in, it's empty, so I walk straight out the back door and head up towards the lodge. I might as well put my time to good use, seeing as I can't face being in the garage with her right now.

I want to hug her tight and beg her not to leave. I want to punch her in the face, as I know she's gonna leave anyway.

Storming through the door of the lodge, I let out an almighty yell. "Fuck!" I pick up a paintbrush and throw it across the room. I slide down the wall and sit with my head in my hands. Fuck knows how long I sit like that before getting to my feet and walking over to the kitchen cabinets, which are all still flat-packed. I slump down on the floor and start building them.

The lodge is large, with an open-plan living kitchen diner to the left, patio doors out onto the deck, and a master bedroom at the back with patio doors out to the same deck. A smaller bedroom at the front and a bathroom in the middle. The main part of the lodge is exposed wooden beams and walls, while the wall where the bedrooms and bathroom are is plastered and needs painting. I've also got the kitchen to finish fitting, all the tiling to do around the bathroom and kitchen and then decorate the bedrooms. And that main wall… fuck, there is so much to do. There are wooden floors throughout leading to a patio door out onto the back, which leads out to the deck that wraps across the back of the property, but then it's just open land. There are no fences enclosing gardens or anything like that, and out the front, there's a porch where I'm gonna build a swing seat for Beauty that looks out across the lake and the fishing dock.

I must have been here a few hours as I've finished building all the cabinets and roughly positioning them ready to fit when the door flings open, and she walks in like I'm still not going to rip her head off and kick it out into the lake.

"Oh, don't mind me, just come the fuck in!"

"Thanks, I will!" She grins at me.

"What the fuck you doing here, Ray? I wanna be on my own."

"Firstly, I'm here because you're behaving like a motherfucking raging bitch, and secondly, I don't give a fuck."

"I'm not in the mood, Ray. Just fuck off... please?"

"Come on, Dozer, talk to me, scream at me, punch me if you like, but don't fucking ignore me like a little bitch."

I shoot to my feet and get straight in her face. "Do you have any fucking idea what you're doing? Huh? To me, to the guys? You've waltzed in here without a care in the world, got all the big badass biker scum to care and give a shit, then you're just gonna fuck off like we mean fuck all. I mean, that's seriously fucked up, Ray!"

I didn't see it coming, I mean, I should have, but I just saw red when she started, and while I was having my rant, I didn't notice the shift, and by the time I'm sat on my ass, a good four foot away from her with a sore fucking face, I hadn't realised what was happening.

"Did you just fucking punch me?"

"Well, clearly it was too subtle if you're having to fucking ask. Shall I do the fucker again? Maybe I'll knock your teeth out this time?" She glares at me, bouncing on the balls of her feet and curling her finger at me as if to say, "Come on then, motherfucker." She grins at me.

"Argh!" I run at her, lifting her off her feet around her waist while she elbows and punches me in the top of the head, shoulders and back of the neck as I barrel through the open doorway.

I vaguely hear Viking shouting, "What the fuck's wrong with you two?" as she's still punching and now kneeing me, although they aren't half as hard as the punch that knocked me on my ass. I kinda feel like she's going easy on me, but fuck her. I run to the dock and go to throw her in the lake, screaming, "Motherfucker!"

Unfortunately for me, she's a slippery little fucker, and as I let go of her, she has hold of me, yanking. The momentum drags us both over the edge with an almighty splash as we both crash through the water's surface. As I come up, gasping for air, she's already being pulled out of the water by Priest. Viking's standing with his arm crossed over his chest.

Great. Motherfuckers are gonna take her side because she's a fucking girl! A girl that punched me that hard, she knocked me on my ass a good four fucking feet away from her, then managed to drag me into the motherfucking lake too.

Making my way to the dock, I reach up, and Viking pulls me out. He and Priest are both standing between us, glancing back and forward. Ray's stare is enough to make a weaker man piss himself. She's panting and has her fists and teeth clenched.

"What the fuck's going on?" Viking spits in both our directions.

"Fucking her, that's what. Ask her what's going on?" I spit back.

"Fuck you, Dozer!" she snarls, turning and storming away. Viking steps after her, but Priest steps in front of him. "You don't wanna go after her when she's like that, man. She won't take too kindly, and I don't want her to do something she'll regret."

"So, start talking. What the fuck was that all about?" Viking crosses his arms across his massive chest, and they block the dock, so I can't get past.

"Just a difference of opinion!" I shrug. Fuck knows why I'm not telling them what I know, but the minute I speak those words, I know they'll come true, so I'm keeping my lips sealed for as long as I can. I step forward to go.

Priest put his hand on my chest. "That was more than a difference of opinion, Dozer. Do we need to be worried?" Yes, yes, they fucking do, but I know what they mean. They mean do they need to be worried for Ray's safety. Am I gonna pull something and hurt her?

Shaking my head, I stride past them both and head into the lodge slamming the door behind me and punching it for good measure. Yep, I really handled that well!

I wait in the lodge till Viking and Priest leave the dock, and then I head home. Fuck her, fuck them and fuck everything. I need to see Beauty. She'll know what to do.

I stomp through the door and slam it behind me.

"What the fuck's wrong with your grumpy ass?"

"Don't fucking start, Beauty. I'm not in the mood. Fucking Ray, that's what's up, she's fucking leaving in two fucking weeks, and we got into a fight, and she punched me, knocking me on my ass and threw me into the lake outside the lodge! Fucking bitch!"

She actually smirks at me. "Ray? As in Ray? One-hundred-and-twenty-pounds at most Ray hit you, and knocked you on your ass, and threw you in the lake? That Ray?" Then she bursts out laughing, clutching at her chest. "Seriously, Ray?"

"You're supposed to be on my side!" I cross my arms over my chest and sulk. Yep, I'm a dude in my thirties who got his ass handed to him by a girl in her twenties who's half my size, at least. And I'm totally fucking butthurt about it, motherfucker! "She's leaving?"

She finally realises what my problem is, and fuck, she sits down on the couch. "She's leaving?" She's having the same thoughts as me. This could be the end of us, and there isn't a damn thing we can do to stop it.

"Yep! She's fucking leaving!"

Ray

Well, the week goes by in the blink of an eye. I've been working flat out at the garage but sneaking up to the lodge and breaking in to fix it. I know Dozer won't have the time once I've gone, and he's making the most of spending time with Beauty while I'm still here.

He hasn't been to the lodge since our fight, so it's perfect, and everything's up there already. I've fitted the kitchen, tiled the splashback, and painted the two bedrooms. I'm a walking zombie living on caffeine and bad decisions. I don't know if I'm gonna get the bathroom tiled and the big wall in the main living area finished, and I need to grout the splashback, but there are only so many hours in a day. I have two weeks, and I think I can manage as long as he stays away. The bathroom's gonna be a long job, so I'm doing everything else first, but I might need some help.

Dozer had brought Beauty around to spend more time with me, but after what happened between us, I think she's more of a buffer. I know what he's trying to do. He wants there to be another reason for me to stay, and she's great, she really is. I can see us both being great friends if we return this way. Her real name's Shirley, but she truly is beautiful, almost like a beauty queen with her fiery red hair and bright blue eyes with a sexy edge. It turns out she owns the party planning shop in Ravenswood and explains to me that it's a big business round these parts and that she does all the event planning for the club too.

She isn't tall at all, maybe five foot five. She's a natural redhead, more auburn than anything, her hair's in waves showcasing the oranges, reds and golds shimmering down to just past her shoulders, and she has beautiful blue eyes, a similar colour to Scar's like a tropical ocean. They are super rare on a redhead, apparently. She's petite with creamy white skin and freckles along her cheeks and shoulders. She's glamorous and too classy to be with Dozer. I mean, I really see the *Beauty and the Beast* thing. They are total opposites, but they are high school sweethearts and have only ever been with each other. It's kind of sweet, really.

They really shouldn't work, but clearly, they do. Dozer and I are acting like nothing has happened, but every now and then, we catch each other eyeing the other cautiously. He really is a stubborn fucker!

Roach is doing great, and he's really taking it all in. I have spoken to Bran about stepping in to help with Roach's training, and he has agreed, so I have that in place. Roach doesn't seem thrilled about me leaving, almost put out, even though his training won't be affected at all. He's acting weird.

Dozer's trimming down on the amount of work he's taking in for when we leave. I'm gonna be sorry to see the back of this place, but I just need to see what else is out there, something that fits like a glove.

This place is great, and the guys are all brilliant, and I'm starting to get attached. I think that's why I decided we need to get out while we still can.

I'm not sure I'll find anything that fits as well as here, but I still need to try.

Before things get complicated, we need to branch out, and Scar agrees she's fallen for Boyband and doesn't think this life will be for her. I think it's because she's bumming around with nothing to do but be with him, but I may be wrong.

I've managed to do everything at the lodge apart from tiling the bathroom; that's my job for next week. Everything else is done apart from the furniture to go in. I've even cleaned the place, so it's ready, well, almost. It's kind of my sorry and thank you to Dozer. He has been a great friend, and I'm gonna miss him.

Come the weekend, we pack up and head towards the diner, then up the coast road towards Gosport Harbour, before heading back down towards the campsite. Apparently, it's only about twelve miles away from the MC, but we take the scenic route, pulling along a one-track road surrounded by woodland and then coming to a massive clearing. This place is breathtaking.

We come to a small bridge going over a river. As we cross it, you can see the waterfall at the end, and as we wind around, the lake comes into view. A slope down to a grass area turns into a small beach at the side of the lake. The whole side's a hill with a waterfall cascading into the pool below. It's stunning.

We set up camp near the beach and sit down to eat and drink. My stomach churns at the thought of telling them, and I know I'm gonna have to bite the bullet and do it soon.

I take a deep breath. "Guys, I need to talk to you all!" Once I have their attention, I start filling them in with what we have planned. We're gonna stay till next weekend, and then we are heading out. I explain it might not be forever. I just need to see what else is out there. They're silent for a while, but let's just say they are not happy, and they're blatantly obvious about it too.

The night just turns into a bit of a shit storm. After thinking about it for a little while, most of the guys take turns shouting at me while I have to bite my tongue and not deck any of them, but seriously, what's their fucking problem?

"You all knew I was only visiting, you knew I lived in the UK, and I'm here on a trip. So what are you acting like Neanderthals for? It's almost like I've cheated on you. None of us are even together. If you have something to say, I suggest you shut the fuck up as I'm done! I'm gonna head back!" I stand. The guys all dive up from where they were sitting.

The next thing I know, Viking is grabbing me and shaking me. "No, little 'un, you are not going anywhere. How the fuck can you even think of leaving us, and what about Dice? You're one of us now. You can't just leave. It's not happening. We won't accept it, nope!"

Shrugging him off, I turn as Tank grabs me. Tank's a little shorter than me, maybe five foot nine, but he's that wide, too. He doesn't speak much normally. His biceps are as big as my face. He's literally built like a tank.

He's solid but steady, normally calm, but the rage that's vibrating through him is immense. He looks at me with those usually warm hazel eyes with flecks of gold in them. They normally sparkle with humour at my antics, but now there's something else. Hurt, maybe. His golden brown hair and tanned skin are so full of scars and tattoos. The only thing he says is, "No. Don't go!" He holds me in a bear hug, looking into those eyes which gloss over as I struggle in his arms. "Ray, Don't go!" Then a strangled "Please?" whispers out of his lips as his eyes close, resting my palm on his cheek.

"Tank, look at me."

He breathes out a steady breath to calm himself, looking across at the boys standing behind me, keeping my hand on his face. I turn to look at them all. "Guys, what's going on? I know you wouldn't be throwing me a leaving party, but I didn't think you would feel quite so… " I trail off, trying to find the right words.

"Angry?" comes from Viking.

Priest looks at me. "Livid?"

"Abandoned?" Jesus, Blade knows how to hit where it hurts.

"Disposable?" Fuck, Dice. They are killing me here, yet he's supposed to be coming with me if things don't go as planned.

With a sorrowful breath, Tank looks into my eyes. "Betrayed?"

"Fuck, I was thinking melodramatic, but holy shit, guys!" I scream at no one in particular, and I start pacing. "Why did you all have to make this so hard? So fucking difficult? Fuck you!" I point at Viking. "And fuck you, and especially you!" I point at Dice, swinging around to point at Blade, "And fuck you too!" I aim at Priest. "And fuck you as well!" I glare at Tank. "Fuck you, fuck you all and... Fuck your kids and your kids' kids, and their fucking kids too!"

I pant and stomp backwards and forwards along the small beach, kicking at pebbles and sending sand flying everywhere.

"Way to overreact," mutters Viking,

"Yeah, Ray, a bit harsh on the kids, and the kids' kids. That hurts!" Dice groans as I spin and scowl at the motherfucker. He's playing me right now, playing into their hands, and I can see through him. Bastard!

"Yeah, Ray, what will they ever do to you!" Priest snarls under his breath.

Tank lets out a shaky breath and then loses it. He just starts laughing, and then everyone looks at him, and all the boys start chuckling one by one. The laughter is roaring out of them.

I'm stunned, mouth open, glancing between them like they have gone insane. I think they have. I think they have finally lost the plot. I definitely think their cheese had slid off their cracker. They are a few sandwiches short of a picnic. The lights are on, but nobody's home. You get the gist? There's definitely some kind of mental breakdown happening in front of me. As they clap each other on the shoulders, bending over to steady themselves on their knees and gasping for breath, only one thing comes to mind.

"Fucking facepalm emoji!" And just like that, Tank runs at me, picks me up, and throws me into the lake.

I come up, gasping for air, "What the fuck, Tank? Arsehole!"

"That's for making me love you and then trying to leave like we mean nothing."

My head's just out of the water, and I shake it. My fucking phone's in my pocket. The only saving grace is the keys are still in the bike.

Viking shouts over, "I fucking love you too, so if you dare come out, I'm throwing you back in myself!"

"Fuck, guys, come on! Be reasonable!" I bellow back.

"Come back out if you dare, and you'll see how much we all love you, as we'll throw you off the waterfall for good measure!"

"Fuck, Priest, that's a bit dark!" I don't know what the fuck to do or say. I mean, what can you say to that? Blade and Dice approach, giving me a hand, or so I thought, till they lean down, grab an arm and a leg each, and launch me further into the lake.

"You fucking bellends, you absolute cockwombling dickwads! You motherfucking, skanking, bollocking, dick-twatting cuntboxes! I fucking love every single one of you twat waffles!" Sighing, I rise to my feet. I'm now chest deep in the fucking water, absolutely dripping wet. Shrugging and wading back to shore as I'm still thigh-deep, I stop.

"Don't suppose anyone brought a towel, did you?" I try to tip the water out of my ear and squeeze out my hair. I look like a drowned rat as I stalk out of the lake. "Let's hug it out, guys."

I run towards Tank dripping, with my arms opening wide, throwing myself around him and wetting him while peppering kisses across his face. He just laughs and hugs me harder.

I feel the guys close in and try and wring me out during the hug. At least, that's what I think they're doing. I can hardly breathe. "Well, that sucked!"

Tank kisses my cheek. "I'm not sorry. You belong with us!"

I huff. "Fine!"

"Fine?" Viking barks out.

"Yeah, fine." They all squeeze tighter. "Fuck, guys. I can't breathe!"

Smiling at me, Priest replies, "Tough. Suck it up. We need this!"

"Jesus, how did you ever get the name Priest? You're fucking dark, man, seriously dark!"

Blade punches me in the arm.

"We need a new name. If you're staying now, you're one of us!" Dice points between us all.

"New name?"

"Yeah, can't be The Fucked Up Five now there are six of us!" Tank acknowledges.

"Guys, I think we're running before we can walk here. I might still need to head off at some point, and I need to talk to Scar. What if she still wants to go? And—"

Viking thrusts his finger against my lips. "Shush, little 'un, you're spoiling it!"

So I just shut up and hug them. When I start shivering, I decide we need to make a fire to dry out.

Setting everything up we need on the beach, we light the fire and huddle around it. The guys start stripping off, laying their clothes over the bikes to dry until they all stand around the fire in their boxers.

"Ray, you need to get out of those wet clothes; otherwise, you'll catch your death," Viking points out.

"It's okay, I'll be fine. I'm starting to warm up now anyway!"

"Ray, don't be daft. Come on, you're gonna end up sick," Blade chastises me, but I shift uncomfortably.

"Hey!" Tank says. "You know we don't look at you like that, right?" While he says that, he eyes Dice, unsure still if we are fucking or not.

I just reply, "Yeah, I know, it's not that… It's just, well… I've kind of kept a lot hidden. Fuck, I kinda want to keep it all hidden, but I suppose if I'm gonna be part of this, I'm gonna have to fill you in!"

Looking around at all their blank faces, I take a deep breath. I remove my blade from my boot, slide my boots and socks off, and grab my jeans. "Motherfucker!" I pull my phone out of my pocket, "Shit, that's fucked!" There's just a blank screen fucking brilliant.

I slide my jeans down my legs, revealing the black, white and grey skulls and roses tattoo, which encases my left hip, butt cheek, whole thigh, over my knee and down my calf, covering the whole of my leg to just above my ankle.

I mean, this in itself isn't weird by any means. I look around at the guys' faces, they don't say anything, and they don't even look shocked that I have tattoos. Dice's scanning their faces, too. He has seen these tattoos already, but none of the others I've got.

I have a tonne of piercings, so it isn't a far stretch to believe I would have some tattoos. It's more the content of the tattoos that I'm hiding than the fact that I have them.

Taking in another deep breath, I lift the hem of my black long sleeve T-shirt and slowly drag it over my head, again with no real issue, the same skulls and roses encasing my right shoulder and engulfing my whole arm to my wrist. I let out a really long shaky breath as I stand there in my bra and pants. The guys still don't seem fazed by that at all, either.

"I don't get the issue," Viking shrugs.

"So you have tats, hardly surprising," says Priest.

Reaching behind me to unclasp my bra, I cross my arms and hold my breasts, shimmying out of the bra and placing it near my boots. Then, taking another deep breath, I slowly turn, showing the guys my back.

There are definitely a couple of gasps. I hear him step forward, and then I feel a hand running ever so gently down my back over my tattoo. I glance over my shoulder. It's Tank. I already knew it was him. I'm attuned to each of them now, their energy and smell, almost like a set of different energy vibrations for each.

Breathlessly he says. "This is you, isn't it?" I nod, "You really do belong with us!"

I smile over my shoulder as the others come to check it out in the light of the fire. At the bottom of my tattoo are three graves. The only way to describe it is a pinup Grim Reaper, all monochrome.

It's actually me, the Grim Reaper, in a black hooded robe, holding my finger to my lips to silence the person seeing it. It's our secret. I don't let just anyone see this tattoo, asking them to keep my secret, my eyes, the only bit of colour in any of my tattoos, and they are blue-grey, the hood's up, and my long hair is plaited over my shoulder and hanging down the front of the robe.

I'm holding a scythe over my shoulder, the blade curling across my actual shoulders but below the neckline of my clothing, where the skulls and roses have turned into smoke clouds. My left leg is sticking out of the hooded cloak, there are no tattoos on it, though, and I'm wearing my New Rock boots, knee bent, resting on the top of a gravestone.

There's a raven on one of the other graves, and the moon's low in the sky behind me. Feeling another hand run down my spine, it makes me shudder.

"You cold, little 'un?" Viking asks me, shaking my head. I look around at the awe on all their faces.

"Just not used to people seeing me like this." I gesture down my back.

"Who did it? They're very talented, Ray, it's so detailed," Priest quizzes.

I sigh. "A guy called Jer did it all."

"Sounds like there's a story there, too," Blade points out.

"Yeah, well, that's a story for when I've got at least two bottles of tequila in me," I huff out.

"It's beautiful." Tank breathes so close to me that I can feel his breath on my shoulder. "How long ago did you have this all done?"

"I had it done after my brother was murdered. I was nineteen when we started it. It took months and months. I promised myself that I would kill the three guys who murdered him and tried to murder me." Turning around, I show them the stab wounds between my ribs and in my gut.

"Let me grab a top out of my bag, and I'll start at the beginning."

After changing, we all huddle around the fire, taking the tequila in one hand and scrubbing the other down my face.

"So my family is a little... Unconventional. My dad and his friends were SAS and Navy SEALs. They all retired before my mum had me and built the Adventure Centre together. Anyway, fast forward to when my brother and I were four. Mum died, and one of my dad's friends had two sons, one four and one two.

"My dad really struggled with two kids aged four, and Ma Marie had two of her own, so the guys stepped in. I call them my pas. Really, I grew up with five dads. I still have four dads. My biological dad died before I came here.

"They tried to keep us away from my brother Bas. He was... horrible even then. He was the one that started the nickname Reaper. He used to bully us and tease me the worst, saying I was like some Grim Reaper skulking in the shadows, just not on anyone's radar. No one cared about me. I was the weird one, the Reaper.

"He used it as an insult, but I kind of liked it, and it also gave me a name for the other part of me, the one that was not so easy to ignore, the one that fights and murders and is terrifyingly badass, the one I'd never fully embraced. Having a name for her helped me compartmentalise.

"I can shift into *her* when I need that calm resolve, the stealthy, psychotic, dangerous defender, the protector, the fierce warrior that never backs down.

"To keep us occupied as kids, my dad and my pas taught us to ride bikes and repair them, to shoot and hunt and fish, to defend and protect, to be badass little motherfuckers. In reality, the three of us are lethal.

"We're all trained in mixed martial arts, knife-throwing, archery, axe throwing. I also do parkour and gymnastics, among other things. We had the best childhood ever.

"Anyway, My brother was an arsehole, so Bran, Dane and I were brought up as siblings. We're still so close now, always have been.

"Bas, my biological brother, got mixed up in a load of shit with a drug dealer and ended up owing them a shit tonne of money. They sent some goons after him, but the car they forced off the road, the one they thought Bas was driving, was mine. They had followed me to one of the back lanes, then ran me off the road. They then dragged me out of the car. I was injured and concussed with minor lacerations, bumps and bruises, so they video-called Bas to get him to help me.

"Needless to say, he was a dick and refused, said he didn't give a shit and they could do what they liked with me, to which they decided to pin me down in the ditch at the side of the road to stab me twice, not just stab, but slowly force the knife in then slowly taking it out before slowly stabbing it back in. When I tried to get up, they pushed me back down, sat, and watched me bleeding out with my brother on a video call.

"They left me in the ditch, bleeding and shouting after them. When I'd lost enough blood to be woozy, one of my pas heard Bas laughing and shouting back that he didn't give a shit, kill me for all he cared. They could fuck me for the money."

Taking a deep breath. "What I'm about to say, no one else knows, not even Scar, so this goes no further, you hear me? I fucking mean it. I'm trusting you, Don't make me regret it!"

I make them all swear that this goes no further, and I believe them. I honestly just want to share the burden. I'm not angry about how my brother died, he deserved it, and I say I killed the guys who murdered him, but really, it was the guys who tried to kill me. It was my vengeance I sought, not his.

"Anyway, my Pa heard and traded my brother for me. Pa told them he would bring Bas if they gave him my location. He knocked Bas out and loaded him in the car. They told him where I was, and he drove out to get me. Once he arrived, he threw Bas at them in the ditch, grabbed me and stuffed me in the car, drove me to the hospital, and never looked back. They killed him, the police came by the next day to say they found the car and Bas was dead in the ditch beside it, they'd burnt his body, and I ended up in hospital for a few days.

"When I got home, my Pa hadn't told them he'd handed my brother over for my life, and I didn't say anything either. He never asked me to lie for him, but I would die for him, and if he hadn't traded my brother's life for mine, then I would have been dead in that ditch. I lost so much blood I wouldn't have made it much longer.

"Eventually, before coming here, I sought vengeance in his name. That's what my dad thought anyway, but it was a cover. For me, it was my vengeance for them trying to kill me. That's the story behind the tattoo.

"I was going to kill three men who tried to kill me, and it was mine and my pa's secret that we'd traded Bas's life for mine. The guys got off on some bullshit technicalities, apparently. They all had alibis, so I must have been wrong; too delirious from the blood loss to make a correct ID. It didn't matter anyway. I'd already had the tattoo done and was just biding my time, ready to take them down. My dad ended up with lung cancer and asked me to end his life by euthanasia." I shrug. "So we used his death as an alibi, and I snuck out and killed the three guys before coming back and killing my dad." It was silent for what felt like an eternity.

"Fucking hell," Tank whispers out.

"Yup," I say before taking the biggest drink of tequila and emptying a third of the bottle.

"Holy fuck, Ray, that's fucked up!" Blade states.

"Your own brother…?" Priest asks.

"Yep, he was a right wanker."

Contemplating everything, Viking cocks a brow at me. "How old were you when you learnt to shoot?

"First time with a gun? Six. Totally proficient, cleaning guns stripping and reassembling them? Eight."

"How did you kill them?" Tank asks.

"Knife to the carotid. One, I climbed through the window while he was taking a dump and stabbed him, the other was asleep on the sofa, and the last, I jumped him and then burnt the house down around them."

"Nice… Have you shot someone before?" Priest asks.

"Yup." I take another swig. "I shot my Pa Bernie when I was seven."

"Holy fuck," Viking mutters almost to himself. "Bet you shit yourself."

"Nah, we'd had training that day, and I asked him what it was like to shoot someone, and he said I would never find out as I didn't have what it took to be ruthless. I argued that I did, and he laughed at me so hard, so I shot him in the arse!"

"Oh," was Tank's reply to that little gem. "How about when you stabbed someone? How old were you then?"

"I was around eight. Pa Steven, same thing. He told me I was too precious to stab anyone. I didn't have it in me. So I stabbed the fucker in the thigh with a steak knife while we were sitting having dinner. He soon stopped laughing at the thought of me stabbing anyone when the knife was jammed in his leg."

"Jesus, Ray!" Priest shakes his head.

"Turns out Pa Bernie hadn't told any of them about the shooting, so it all came out then. None of them underestimated me after that unless they wanted to push my buttons and reverse psychology me, which the bastards sometimes did.

"That's when they all started using the name for that side of me, normally, I was Ray, but when I flipped the switch, I was Reaper." I shrug. "It kind of seemed right, and it fit *her* personality. *She's* ruthless, can think clearly in heightened situations, *she* only has one default mode, and that's fighting no flight at all. *She's* quick thinking and has got me out of my fair share of jams over the years!"

"You're ruthless, Ray. You are Reaper. She's you. You're the same person!" Dice says under his breath.

"What about Jer?" Blade cocks a brow at me, flicking his switchblade between his fingers.

I slide my lip ring through my teeth before answering. "Great tattooist, older guy, fucked for two years while he added extra detail to the tattoos, my Pa found out and beat the shit out of him, didn't see him again. Let's leave that one there, yeah?" I nod at them all, taking another gulp of tequila.

"Any other talents that might come in handy?" Dice asks. He's been rather quiet until now, he knew a lot more than the others, and I'm sure now I'm spilling secrets, he's wondering if I'm gonna spill his, but it's not mine to spill. I know I spilt the trading Bas secret, but that's mine to tell, and I didn't name my Pa.

I shrug. "Besides knife-throwing, axe throwing, archery, fixing bikes, parkour, gymnastics, martial arts, that's not enough? There's also my magnetic personality, callisthenics and shibari!"

"Shifuckingwhatnow?" Tank barks out.

"Another top secret, okay? Shit, I've definitely drunk too much if I'm giving all my secrets to you bunch of twat waffles! Okay, so shibari originated from Hojo-jutsu. It was a type of rope binding to restrain captives and a form of torture before morphing again into the erotic bondage Kinbaku translates as 'the beauty of tight binding.' You're looking at me like I've got three fucking heads."

Tank shakes his head. "I didn't understand a word of that shit!"

"Fuck's sake, it's Japanese bondage, tying people up, but it looks fancy as fuck, okay? Jesus!"

"Well, why didn't you just say that?" Dice asks.

I finish the bottle and shake my head. "My brain is fried, and before I start sharing any more secrets, I'm going to fucking sleep. Night, knobheads!"

I stalk to my bike and grab the sleeping bag. I throw it out on the grass at the end of the beach and tuck myself in. Fuck, that was exhausting.

Scar

Ray has headed off with the guys, and I'm left with Ares. We have a couple of drinks, and I ask if we can go to his room because I need to talk to him. Things have been so great between us, but I know we have to move on.

We are both getting a little too attached to the guys here. Neither of us knows what kind of future we can expect, so we need to make a move. At least that way, we will know if we're meant to come back.

As we get to Ares' room, he pushes me up against the inside of the door. "Fuck, princess, you're goddamn beautiful. I love it when you need to talk." He drives his tongue between my lips, and I melt into him.

"Ares, Babe! I really do need to talk to you. I need a clear head. Back up a sec, would you?" I push him back slightly.

"What the fuck, princess? What's going on?"

"Me and Ray have been talking." I take a deep breath and mutter out a "fuck" as I slam my head back into the door and bang it again and again. "Fuck, fuck!"

"Hey, princess, don't do that. What the fuck's wrong?"

Looking at the floor, I mumble, "We're leaving."

He huffs out a laugh. "For a minute there, I thought you said you were leaving."

Without looking at him and turning my head away, I say it again, just as quietly as before. "We're leaving."

"No… if you're leaving, you have the fucking guts to tell me to my face!" He grabs me by the chin and forces my face to meet his, our breaths are both coming in heavy now, but I can feel the anger radiating off him. "Say it!" he grits out.

I try to drop my head, but he won't let me. "We're leaving, Ares!" It's barely a whisper.

An almighty roar comes from him, and he punches the door right at the side of my head. I flinch as he yanks the door open and me with it and stalks back to the bar, leaving me there in shock, petrified of what he's gonna do. For a few moments, I just breathe, trying to clear my head. I haven't even had the chance to explain.

After taking a few minutes to get myself together, I spin after him. As I get to the bar, he's sitting there with a drink in front of him, head in his hands, my breaths are coming in ragged, and I just stare at him from the corridor.

A few seconds later, the door flies open, slamming into the wall. I glance around and see a beautiful girl. She's model thin, her hair's dyed silver with dark shadow roots, and she's wearing a black leather bra with a full sleeve tattoo down her right arm. She has thick black eyeliner on and bright red lips, a short leather mini skirt with a tattoo on her left thigh and thigh-high heeled boots. She's stunning, strutting in like she owns the place.

Ares looks to the door catching eyes with me before moving on to see who's walking in. I just freeze there. I can't take my eyes off her. I stare at her as she struts towards Ares.

"Hey honey, you miss me?" Leaning over him, she kisses along his neck, and he closes his eyes and necks his drink. She slides her hand around him and down towards his dick.

I flinch, more at the fact that he lets her. He opens his eyes, staring straight at me while she rubs his dick through his jeans. I'm frozen, my hands over my mouth, eyes filled with unshed tears.

He closes his eyes and tilts his head back, then blinks a couple of times while she rubs him some more through his jeans and kisses and nips along his jaw. He looks straight at me again, still letting her fucking touch him and kiss him, and then he grabs her wrist and turns on the stool to face her.

"What the fuck you doing here, Shay?" He rises to meet her eye to eye. She leans in one hand runs over his chest while the other rubs up the back of his neck. She pulls him in, and he kisses her back for a split second before grabbing her wrists in both hands.

"Come on, honey. You're not still mad about our little disagreement, are you? I gave you time to cool off. Now I'm back, so you can apologise to me."

"Me? Apologise? You're off your fucking head!"

"Honey?" She leans in for another kiss, but he shoves her back and looks over towards me as I step out of the corridor.

She follows his line of sight. "Ah, there she is, the slut who thinks she can replace me! Well, I've got news for you, bitch, you've kept him warm for me, and now I'm here to claim back what's mine!" She takes a few steps towards me, and before I know what's happening, she has my hair in her hand and slaps me around the face. I think my head would have flung off if she wasn't holding my hair.

I scream and grab my face as she's ripped away from me. One of the guys has her in a bear hug.

I open my eyes, and Ares has my wrists in his hand, and he's trying to move my hands from my face to see it.

"Fuck, princess, I'm sorry. Are you okay?" He pulls me to his chest. He spins towards her. "You can fuck off out of here, Shay. You're not fucking welcome here anymore. You're no longer part of this club. Now just fuck off before I make you!"

She laughs a sadistic laugh that makes her sound deranged. "You gonna pick that that fucking kindergarten teacher over me? Are you fucking kidding me right now, Ares? I mean fucking, look at her. She's like something out of *The Sound of Music*, she doesn't even compare to me, honey, and you know it! Don't make this mistake, Ares. I will fucking ruin you!" Pulling me behind him, he looks at the guy holding her talking calmly and quietly.

"Put her out. Put the word out that if she sets foot back around here, she's to be shot on sight, no questions asked. You're fucking dead to this club,

Shay. Now leave, because I won't tell you again!" Turning, he drags me back to the bar and grabs us both a drink while Shay is being manhandled out of the club. Fifteen minutes later, the guy comes back.

"She's gone!"

Ares nods and cups my face. "You okay?"

"I'm shaken, but I'm okay. I think I need to go back to the van and sort myself out. I'm sure I look a right state. I should get some ice on my face. Will you come to talk to me tomorrow? I need to explain."

"Yeah." He nods, and he grabs my hand to walk me out. When he gets to the veranda, he kisses my cheek and lets me go. He gets his fags out and blows out a deep breath before lighting up, so I carry on walking.

I get round the side of the building, and I break down, tears streaming down my face, and I just sob. I sob at losing this man I was falling for. I sob at the embarrassment of being slapped in front of him and doing nothing. I'm also heartbroken that he let her touch him like she did while he looked at me like he did. If it had been Ray, she would have smacked that grin off her face, but me? I just gasped and stood there in shock.

What the fuck am I doing? I don't belong here. I don't fit here. I'm totally out of my depth. It was fun while it lasted, but we have to move on. As I round the back of the garage, I feel my head snap back, and I try to let out the mightiest of screams as I'm dragged down to the floor, but I'm punched in the gut simultaneously and lose my breath.

I'm kicked in the ribs multiple times, then what feels like a kick to the face as I breathe and scream.

I hear a shout from the clubhouse and a thundering of boots across the parking lot, but Shay jumps on me, gets a few more punches to my face, then climbs off and kicks me again before running off.

I'm dazed, and I can't open my eye, and when I try to breathe, my ribs fucking sting. Shit, this is bad. The next thing I know, I'm being scooped up as I gasp.

"Fuck! Get Doc! Search the area for that bitch and bring her to me! She's fucking dead!" Ares bellows the orders at the dark figures around him, but I can't make out who they are.

My eyes are rolling back in my head, and I think I'm having a panic attack.

"Princess, you're gonna be okay. I've got you!" I pass the fuck out, and everything stays black but goes silent.

Pain radiates through my ribs as I gasp awake and try to sit up, causing a slight scream to come from my lips and black spots to form over my eyes.

"Woah! Woah, princess! Don't move. You have at least badly bruised ribs. You need to stay still, okay?"

I try to open my eyes, but only one will open. "Water!" I croak, tilting my head. Ares brings a cup to my lips.

"Doc's gonna give you something to help you sleep. I'm here, though, okay?"

"I wanna go home!" I rasp

I feel the needle go into my arm, and I start to feel sleepy. "Ray?" I rasp out. "Need Ray!"

"She's camping, princess. I'm trying to find them, but their cells aren't working, but I'm looking, okay?"

Ares

Doc has just given her an injection to knock her out, and her eyes roll back into her head. Well, the one eye. The other is swollen and barely open. Fuck, she's a mess. What the fuck have I done?

There's a slight knock at the door. I head over to it and ask, "What do you want, Roach?"

"Just wondered if you need anything, Pres?"

"Nah, I'm good, kid. Thanks, though, yeah?"

He nods. "She gonna be okay?"

"Yeah, she's gonna be out of it for a while and black and blue for longer, but we don't think there's anything broken."

"Ray's gonna have a fucking fit when she gets back."

I scrub a hand through my hair. "Don't fucking remind me. She's gonna blame me for this, and fuck knows what she's capable of. Anyway, kid, head off now, yeah? See ya tomorrow, okay?"

"Okay, Pres. Text me if you need anything other than going against Ray. She scares the shit out of me. I mean, holy shit, she's hot, but fuck…"

"Will do."

I close the door, chuckle under my breath, and lock it for good measure. She's definitely one person I don't want as an enemy. Let's hope this doesn't end as badly as I feel it's gonna. I've upped security tonight and messaged everyone to shoot on sight if anyone of them sees Shay. She's a snake, and I'm not willing to risk her hurting Scar again. There's no way on earth that fucking slut's gonna wreck this for me!

I set the ball rolling, messaging Dice to tell him to search traffic cams and all that when he gets back. I know my way around a computer, but that guy's skill level is crazy scary. I've left a million and one voicemails for Ray but nothing. They're all together, so it stands to reason if I can't get one, I can't get the rest. Fuck, I can't believe they want to leave.

I sit there staring at her almost shallow breathing, gasping for breath in her sleep. It clearly hurts to take each breath. Her brow creases on every inhale, and a small wince with every exhale. Her eye is black and swollen and almost completely closed. What part of her eye I can see is bright red and bloodshot. It looks like she's been kicked in the face at least a few times and definitely in the ribs more than a few times. Her ribs were black and blue and angry red and swollen, some bits purple. She's a fucking mess. She was covered in blood when I got to her.

After seeing her like that, I know I can't let her go. I'm totally in love with her. I need to come up with a way to get them to stay. I have found my reason for breathing, and I will skin Shay alive if I ever see her again.

Checking on Scar, I kiss her forehead. It's the only part of her face not bruised. I grab a blanket and settle into the chair for the night. Fuck knows if I'm gonna sleep, but I'm emotionally exhausted. I'd seen the look on Scar's face when I let Shay kiss me and then touch me like she did. What the fuck was I thinking?

I know what I was thinking. I wanted to hurt Scar like I was hurt to make her think I didn't give a shit about her, but this? Not this. Fuck, this is all my fault. I should have listened to what Scar was trying to tell me about leaving instead of throwing an epic tantrum and storming out.

I knew they were travelling. I knew they lived in England, so it stands to reason they would be going back at some point, but honestly, I'd just assumed she would feel the same way about me that I did her and just never leave, I suppose.

I jolt up off the chair. There is a small rap at the door. I take a breath and try to slow my racing heart, calming myself. I click the lock open.

"Roach?"

"Hi, Pres. Got you some breakfast."

"What time is it?"

"It's eight."

"Shit, Roach. Can you grab me my laptop from the office? Here are the keys. Can you try and get a hold of Ray and the guys? Let me know if you manage it."

"Sure, Boss."

Grabbing my phone, I dial the only person in the world other than Scar I want to talk to, my best friend. "Fuck, man, it's good to hear your voice!"

"You okay, Brother? You don't sound good."

"Shay came back!"

"Fucking stupid bitch, what did she do?"

"She's fucked Scar up, man. She's a mess, bro. I don't know what to do. This is all my fault, Steel. What the fuck am I supposed to do?"

Steel's my best friend. I need him back here. We've been through so much together, we met in juvie in our teens, and when we left, we got better at stealing cars, made a shit load of money and brought this place together. I don't know what the fuck to do.

"Hey, Brother, listen, that's not true... Listen here. You look after her, don't let her out of your sight, okay? I'm coming back!"

I take a deep breath to calm my nerves. "Nah, man, I'm good. I just needed to hear your voice. Thanks, man!"

"You sure?"

"Yeah, she's out of it anyway. There's nothing we can do until Dice returns Monday morning. How long you gonna be there for?"

"About another week, Brother, but I will get cracking. If I can get back sooner, I will, okay? Call me if you need me! Love you, Brother!"

"Love you too, bro!"

"Fuck!" I spit out as I hang up, taking a deep breath.

There's another soft rap on the door as Roach brings what I've asked for. Dozer stops by with Beauty, her fiery red hair and sharp blue eyes fuller than normal. They haven't spent much time together, but Beauty's such a caring person she's struggling to see Scar like this. She helps me clean Scar up a bit. She's still out of it. For that much, I'm grateful. I don't know if I'll ever forgive myself for this. I've sent a patrol out with a few guys riding around looking for Shay. I'm gonna string that bitch up!

The days are the longest. She's still knocked out. Doc came by this morning and hooked her up to an IV to get fluids and pain meds into her, but she hasn't even flinched.

"I added another sedative to the IV. I'll come back later and take it out. It should last till morning and then wear off naturally; she won't be as groggy then when she finally wakes up but will be in some discomfort and pain for a good few days, if not longer. We just need to keep an eye on her. Call me if you need anything!" Doc smiles before leaving the room.

I haven't left myself. I've stayed with her the whole time. The guys have bought me food and drinks, and I sit for hours beside her bed, taking in every bit of damage I have caused, every bruise, every cut, every frown and crease of her brow, every wince letting me know how much pain she's actually in.

Fuck, if I were any kind of a man, I would let her go and just be like, "Yeah, cool, it was fun, cheers!" and let her be on her way, but I'm a selfish, selfish man, and I know something extraordinary when I find it, and I know there will be no way I can let her go now. I will burn the world to ash for her. I need her to stay so I can prove it to her.

I'm starting to get tired. I've tried every technique I can to track Shay and find her, but she's like a fucking snake. You don't see her till she's striking. Fuck, I wish Ray had been here. She would have destroyed that bitch, and my biggest problem would have been how deep to dig the hole and where!

I must have managed an hour of sleep at most when there was a knock at the door. Fuck, there is always someone checking in. These two girls have turned this club on its head without us even noticing. Fuck, they can't leave. I doubt The Fucked Up Five is gonna take the news any better than I have. Hopefully, she will have told them while they're away rather than just before she leaves. That's gonna be an epic shitstorm of vast proportions if ever there was one, almost like a natural disaster! Answering the door, I'm dead on my feet.

"Doc," I rasp out.

"Fuck, Pres, you look like shit! I'm here to take the IV and that out. How's she doing?"

I scrub a hand down my face and seriously think about my answer. "Fuck, Doc, she's fucked up. I'm not sure. I suppose only time will tell."

Nodding, he steps around me, does what he needs to do, and then goes to leave, gripping my shoulder. "She might wake up in the next few hours now I've taken the IV out. Any problems, let me know but try and convince her to try and sleep till at least the morning. The better she sleeps, the quicker she'll heal."

The door closes behind him. I settled back into the chair, pulling the blanket up around my neck. I've barely slept, no more than an hour at a time, then a wince or a stutter of breath would shock me awake, lurching out of the chair to check on her before dozing back off again once I've seen she isn't any worse.

I've settled back to sleep, drifting off into a dreamless deep sleep.

"Fuck."

I'm startled awake. "Hey, hey, don't move. I'm coming!"

Scar

Waking up, I feel groggy. Looking around, Ares is asleep in the chair. It's dark. Is it Saturday night already? I try to get up. "Fuck."

"Hey, hey, don't move. I'm coming!" Ares replies sleepily from the chair in the corner.

"I'm fine. I just need the bathroom!" Picking me up, Ares carries me to the bathroom and takes me inside. He helps me to the toilet, but I make him leave.

After peeing, I wince and drag myself over to the mirror. "Jesus!" I huff out. My eye is black, and although it's nearly fully shut, it's puffy as hell. I feel like my face is puffy, and my lip is split. I'm wearing one of Ares's T-shirts, so I lift it up to take in the damage.

I take in the bruises all the way across my abdomen, pressing them. I wince as Ares charges in the door. "What the fuck are you doing? Stop pressing them. You need to leave them. Sit down and let me put some Tiger Balm on you!" He puts the toilet seat down and I sit.

"I need a shower. What time is it?"

"It's 8.30 p.m."

"Fuck, I've slept the whole day?"

He softens his voice. "Princess, it's 8.30 p.m. Sunday night. You've been asleep for most of the last two days."

I tear up. "Ray?"

"I can't find her, but she'll be back tomorrow morning. She's at work at nine. They went off-grid, so I've not been able to track their phones and don't have the manpower to send guys looking for them. Princess, don't worry, okay? I got you!" He pulls me into his chest. "Let's get you showered and back to bed, okay, princess? You should feel a little less out of it tomorrow once the drugs Doc gave you wear off."

I nod and let him pull me into the shower. He dries me off with a big fluffy towel and pulls me back towards the bed. He comes back with a clean T-shirt, and I pass back out again.

I wake up at 5.30 a.m. feeling sore but not groggy, so that's something. I'm awake, but Ares is asleep on the chair. Fuck, I don't want to leave him.

I need to talk to Ray. I need her to listen to me and let me stay, but I also know if she wants to leave, I will follow her to the ends of the earth. That's if he wants me to stay, that is. He might be looking after me out of guilt. He might really want her. She's stunning, and look at me. I mean, for fuck's sake, I'm a state. If he wants her, I will go. I won't fight. I will leave. I just need to know.

"Ares," I croak out, my voice scratchy from lack of use. He shoots up off the chair.

"Shit, princess, you gave me a scare." He comes and sits at the side of me on the bed and cups my face. Lifting the water bottle to my lips, I gulp it down, soothing my scratchy throat. "Are you up for talking?" He asks in an almost whisper. I nod.

"I need to explain things to you, but I need you to listen, okay? You don't understand what it's like, me and Ray. Sighing, I take a deep breath. "Fuck!"

"Shallow breaths, princess, it's gonna be sore for a while."

I nod. "I can't leave her. If she wants to go, I can't stay. I owe her my life, Ares. She saved my life and then put me back together again. I owe her everything."

"Princess, that's not fair. She can't hold it over your head. Whatever it is, that's not fair!"

"You don't understand, she doesn't, she's not like that, but I can't live without her. I'm nothing without her; if she wants to leave, I must choose her. I will always choose her!" I sob out, my one open eye while my other eye just aches.

"What are you trying to say, princess?"

"She's my everything, Ares. If she left me, it would kill me. If she goes, I will choose her. I can't leave her. She owns my soul!"

Gasping, he pushes me back slightly. "You're in love with her, aren't you? You're fucking in love with her!" He stands and starts pacing across the bottom of the bed, shaking his head. "Why didn't I see it? How the fuck can I compete with her? She's fucking stunning, funny, hard as fucking nails, amazing with bikes, she's a fucking wet dream for fuck's sake, and what do I have to fucking offer you? How can I compete with her? With fucking her!" he spits, grabbing his hair, tugging it, and hitting his hands against his head.

"Ares, please, you don't understand. It's not like that. Babe, please listen, okay? just sit down and listen!" I take a slow breath and release it shakily. "I'm not in love with Ray. Not anymore, anyway. Not like that!"

Standing again, he glares at me. "You and Ray? You and fucking Ray? I fucking knew it. I knew you were too good to be true, too good to be mine, to like me for me!" He's spiralling, pacing back and forwards, and he stops at the door. "Fuck!" he bellows, punching the door, then shaking his hand out.

"Ares!" I yell and wince.

"Princess, shit, babe, I'm sorry, fuck, let's do this later, okay? You're not up to it!"

I release another shaking breath. "Ares!" I say firmly. "Sit the fuck down! Now!"

Glaring at me but not saying a word, he slides onto the bed as I force myself into a better position sitting next to him.

"I need you to shut the fuck up and listen. I don't have the energy for tantrums and shouting, so shut the fuck up till I'm done, okay? Then you can throw your tantrums all in one fucking go!"

I think he senses a shift in my tolerance and attitude as he settles beside me and nods.

"Everyone knows Ray's side of the story, but this is my side of the story. No one outside the family knows so this goes no further. Whether I stay or I go, I just want you to understand why, okay?"

He nods again, reaching up to hold my hand. "Just tell me the truth. That's all I ask, okay?"

I nod, closing my eye and taking yet another fucking breath. This is gonna suck fucking balls!

"I was fifteen-ish. I'd been to school and was in town heading for the train. I checked my watch, and I was gonna be late. I'd been dicking around in town, so I needed to hustle. There was a dodgy cut-through behind some shops, it was an alleyway into what would have been a loading area, and a couple of fence boards had been removed so you could squeeze through, saving about a fifteen-minute walk around.

"As I got into the loading area, there was a dumpster against the wall, and as I walked past it, I was grabbed."

I'm starting to breathe heavily. I squeeze my eyes tight. I can feel the sweat on my brow. I can feel my skin burning up, Ares squeezes my hand, and it grounds me. I open my eyes and meet his gaze.

"One grabbed me round my chest and mouth to stop me screaming, and the other grabbed my legs. I'd been distracted looking at my phone. I was thrown on the ground on the other side of the dumpster. One held my hands above my head by kneeling on them and had his hand over my mouth, shoving the side of my face into the floor. The other guy was— "

"You don't have to say it."

"I'm okay. I just need a minute. The other guy was cutting off my underwear with a knife. I was thrashing and kicking, so he pushed the knife to my throat." I point to the faint scar on my neck under my jaw. You can only see it if you know where to look.

"He told me what he was gonna do to me, gloating while leaning over me, then that his friend was gonna do the same while he held me, and I was gonna be a good girl and not fight back and not make a noise, and if I was good, they would let me live.

"I was a virgin, but they didn't give a shit as he shoved himself inside me. I tried to scream, but the sting and the burn ripped through me, and he dug the knife in further. He started slamming into me over and over again, and I just cried. The pain was immense, like nothing I'd felt before. My head was shoved to the side, forcing his weight onto my cheek and pushing me into the floor.

"I was at the side of the dumpster, so I just stared underneath, hoping it would be over. There was a snail shell I could see glinting in the sun towards the opposite side of the dumpster, and I just focused on that. After what felt like a lifetime, I saw a pair of shoes, and my eyes widened. I tried to scream, but nothing came out. He was still slamming into me. My back was bleeding and raw from the thrusting up and down across the concrete, all I could smell was stale sweat and rotting rubbish, but those shoes were shiny, they were clean, and they stopped. She bent down, looking under the bin. My eyes went wide when they locked, mine with hers, and she lifted a finger to her lips, shushing me. I scrunched my eyes closed, but the grunting and pounding carried on.

"I thought she had left me. I thought I was gonna die. The guy who was holding my face and my hands had ripped my shirt open and was pawing at me, groping one breast, and the guy who was thrusting into me was groping the other, and his hand had dropped the blade, and he now had his hand round my throat, squeezing.

"I tried to breathe, but I was struggling. Short, shallow breaths were all I could manage. My vision was starting to blacken around the edges, but the thrusting had slowed.

"Apparently, he wanted to drag it out longer. I opened my eyes and stared straight into his, the guy pounding into me. He had this look, this animalistic, feral, almost deranged look, as he licked his lips and panted, pounding and pounding over and over. He was relentless.

"That's when it all went red and warm. It happened so fast that the guy holding me fell to the side, eyes wide, clutching his neck. My eyes were fixed on him before I realised he was no longer holding me down. A dark shadow passed over me as my gaze shot to the guy who was raping me. She had jumped on him, straddling him, throwing him off me. She pinned him down and stabbed him in the neck over and over, then in the chest. Once he stopped thrashing, she stood and turned, her gaze fell on mine, and we just stared. She was in a school uniform, a school I didn't recognise, and her white blouse was covered in red. It was dripping from her face. She was panting for breath.

"I looked back at both guys' eyes wide open, covered in blood. She had killed them both. She'd saved me.

"She crouched down and scooped me into her arms against the wall. She took her phone out and called the police and an ambulance. She sat with me the whole time. We were both covered in blood. It wasn't until she was arrested that I realised what had happened. It pulled me out of my shock. I told her my dad was a lawyer and not to say a word till he got there. She nodded and was taken away. Honestly, that moment gave me something else to focus on. I couldn't let her go down for saving me. I needed to save her.

"I was taken to hospital, and my dad met me there. I told him everything, and then I forced him to go see her. I didn't even know her name. My dad found her and helped her make her statement, leaving out the bit where she used her own knife. We both said they had a knife each, and she grabbed and used one, and then she was held in a detention centre while they processed her waiting for a hearing.

"I wasn't allowed to see her. I talked Dad into taking her on as a client pro bono, and he told me she was fourteen but wouldn't tell me anything else. After all the tests and recovering in the hospital, I was sent home. I stopped eating. I stopped going to school. My friends gave up on me. I barely left the house. I couldn't remember the last time I showered. I stopped caring, and I wanted to die.

"Dad was working on her case all hours God sent. I was depressed and had tried to take an overdose and ended up having my stomach pumped, and in the hospital, I had to have a mental health check.

"It was months later that my dad told me he had managed to get her off, and she received a conditional discharge. So for years since, the police have always hounded her for the slightest little thing, but they never made anything stick. Even before we came out here, they had her down at the station for questioning about three suspicious deaths. She's been hounded for nearly nine years because she saved me.

"Anyway, Dad told her everything after she got off, and she turned up at the house. She walked into my room, and I broke down, just fell in her arms and sobbed. She stayed for hours. She just held me. And once I'd stopped sobbing, and it was more of a whimper, She said, 'You're done!' When I looked at her, she kissed my forehead, wiped away my tears and said, 'You're done now. You will not allow them to take another second of your time. You're alive! You make it count!' She pulled me up and told me I fucking stunk like a polecat. That I needed to shower. We were going out.

"When I looked at her to tell her I didn't think I could, she just glared at me and said, 'Go shower. I promise I won't ever let anything happen to you.'

"I got ready, and we went out for food. My dad was so happy he transferred me to Ray's school, and she's had my back ever since. She sorted me out, brought me into her family, never left my heart, and made me whole again. She saved me that day. She forced me to go to uni to study law like my dad, I nearly lost everything because of them, and she gave it me all back and more.

"She's been saving me ever since. She would never ask me to choose her over anyone, and she would never do anything to hurt me, but I can't ever leave her. I owe her everything. I don't know how to not love her with everything that I am and not be indebted to her. She's never told me what she went through for me. She just said it was me or them, and she chose me, and she would do it again over and over again. She chose me before she knew me, so I choose her. I will always choose her!

"We did have a relationship shortly after. We were young, and all these feelings were so big we mistook them for romantic love, lust and infatuation, but in the end, it was a sisterhood love. She's my ride-or-die. She's the other half of my soul. She's been my sister ever since that day. I can't leave her if she wants to go. Regardless of what I feel for you, I will have to go, Ares. I'm sorry."

"So you do feel something for me?"

"What?"

"You said regardless of how you feel about me. That means you feel something, yes?"

"Yes, of course. I'm not sure what, but there's definitely something there."

"Then that I can work with. Just stay even just a little longer for me, a few more weeks, just give me that, a few more weeks, and then we can see! You need to listen to me, okay? Listen to what I need to say. I've thought of nothing else for the last two days, so I need you to hear me, okay?"

"Okay," I rasp out.

"Don't go! Please don't go! I can't bear it. I don't know what's happening between us. I just know that when I saw you like that on the floor near the van, I knew I couldn't lose you. Just stay. We'll figure it out, okay? Just stay at least for a few weeks. I'll talk to Ray. I'll beg her to stay. I'll offer her anything she wants!"

"Okay!" I breathe out, barely a whisper.

"Okay? Just like that?"

"Yeah, okay, just like that!"

"Fuck, thank God!" He sweeps me up into his arms. I grimace but hold on tight. Maybe I can have them both. Maybe I can be happy with Ares and convince Ray to stay, but deep down, I know if I tell her how I feel about him and ask her to stay, she would, for me. Ray would burn the world to the ground with every fucker in it and wouldn't give a shit. I just don't know if I want to hand her the matches.

"I need to go to the van to wait for Ray. I need to speak to her before she goes to work." Ares helps me get ready and walks me over to the van. It's a little after 7.30, so I don't think she will be long. I make myself some breakfast, and Ray comes through the door just before eight.

"Fucking hell, Scar! You shit me up! Jesus, what the hell happened to you? Did fucking Boyband do that? I will fucking kill him. I swear to Hades himself I will rip his bollocks off and smother him with the soggy fucking end!" She spins around as if she's about to leave again and carry that threat out.

"Ray, don't... it wasn't... it wasn't him, okay? Please just take a shower, and then we can talk. You look fucking filthy!"

She walks up and cups my face gently, glancing over all the damage and searching my eyes in case

I'm lying to her, but she knows I would never lie to her. "Scar you, okay? Seriously?"

"Yeah, I'm okay. I'll make you breakfast. Just grab a shower quick, okay? There's a lot we need to talk about!"

"Scar, talk to me now. A shower can fucking wait, babe. Tell me, who did this to you?"

"It's a long story, and I would sooner you have had a shower, Ray; you honk like wet dog and pond water!"

Grabbing her T-shirt and pulling it up to her nose, she grimaces. "Give me a name first, and then I'll shower!"

Nodding, I take a mildly deep breath. "Shay!"

"Shay? Fucking Ares's ex, the fucking psycho who took the knife to his bike?"

"Yep, now shower, then I'll fill you in!"

"Fine, but you spill fucking everything you hear me!"

I just nod, and she heads for a shower. She's out in record time.

After getting out of the shower, Ray enters the kitchen, tying her hair into a high ponytail and pulling on her boots. She stuffs a knife in her boot and covers it with her jeans.

"Do you really need to go to work armed?" I chuckle at her, wincing as my eyes crease.

"From the look of you!" she gestures wildly in my direction. "It's not the stupidest idea I've ever had. Come on then, spill. When the fuck am I killing her for this?" Pointing at my face again.

I let out a shaky breath. "Okay, so—"

Before we can get a chance to talk, there's a knock at the door.

From where I'm sitting, I can just see the side of her face. She looks confused as fuck, and then I hear two guys with what sounds like Mexican accents. Ray has her hand on the wall at the side of the door. She lifts her finger to me to keep silent. I shrink back against the wall just back from the window, half hidden by the curtain.

"¡Ah, pequeña perra!" a deep, Mexican-accented voice spits out. Did he just say, "Ah, little bitch?"

The other voice laughs. "Just where Shay said she'd be!" His voice isn't as gruff, with almost a feminine softness, but it's another man.

The next thing I know, Ray's holding her hands up as if they're pointing a gun at her.

"Now hurry up, *perra*. We need to get out of here before anyone notices you're gone!"

She turns her back, raises her hands, and backs down the steps. She mouths, "K.F.D, Call Pa B." she backs out of the van and shuts the door.

I look out the window as she's being forced into a brown van at gunpoint, and then they speed off, screeching out of the gates, taking my fucking heart and soul with them. Will I ever see her again?

To be continued…

Acknowledgements

For those of you who have made it this far, thank you for taking a chance on an unknown author releasing this, my debut book. I've poured my swinging brick and little black soul into this series, and my swinging brick thanks you from the bottom of it for your support. I couldn't have done it without you all,

My mum and son.

My boozy book club bestie,

My besties,

My queen.

The girls at United.

And anyone who's read my book, liked a post, or shared a video, no matter how small you think the gesture, I appreciate you all!

There are four books in this series, so if you loved this as much as I loved writing it and can't wait to see what trouble Ray can find, stand by and get ready to ride this rollercoaster with me. I promise it won't be dull! This is only the beginning!

Buckle up, buttercup. It's about to get bumpy!

Books by Harley Raige

The Reapers MC, Ravenswood Series

Reaper Restrained 1 Aug 23
Reaper Released TBA
Reaper Razed TBA
Reaper's Revenge TBA

Printed in Great Britain
by Amazon